He had desired Thea Beldaniel as he had desired no other woman since his first youth; he had adored the undefined Elder Race as he had adored no gods in his life; he had donned a cool surface and a clear logical mind at need, and afterward returned to his dim warm abyss. Yet somehow it was not he who did these things but others. They used him, entered and wore him... How could he find revenge for so inward a rape?

SATAN'S WORLD

by POUL ANDERSON

A BERKLEY MEDALLION BOOK
published by
BERKLEY PUBLISHING CORPORATION

to Dana and Grace Warren

Library of Congress Catalog Card Number 79-89786

SBN 425-03361-9

BERKLEY MEDALLION BOOKS are published by
Berkley Publishing Corporation
200 Madison Avenue
New York, N.Y. 10016

BERKLEY MEDALLION BOOK ® TM 757,375

Printed in the United States of America

Berkley Medallion Edition, April, 1977

This novel has been published, in a somewhat different form, in
Analog Science Fact-Science Fiction for May through August,
1968.

I

ELFLAND is the new section of Lunograd. So it is written, and therefore believed by the computers of administrative authority. Living beings know better. They see marvels, beauties, gaieties, a place for pleasure and heartbreak. They experience a magic that is unique.

But in the old town underground, the machines are always working.

Near a post on the frontier between these two universes, David Falkayn halted. "Well, my love," he said, "here's a pleasant spot for an adios."

The girl who called herself Veronica lifted one hand to her lips. "Do you mean that?" she asked in a stricken voice.

A little taken aback, Falkayn regarded her closely. She made enjoyable looking anyhow: piquant features, flowing dark hair in which synthetic diamonds twinkled like stars, spectacular figure in a few wisps of iridescent cloth. "Oh, not permanently, I hope." He smiled. "I simply had better get to work. Shall I see you again this evenwatch?"

Her mouth quivered upward. "That's a relief. You startled me. I thought we were strolling, and then with no warning you—I didn't know what to imagine. Were you getting rid of me or what?"

"Why in the galaxy should I do any such ridiculous thing? I've known you, let's see, just three standard days, isn't it, since Theriault's party?"

She flushed and did not meet his gaze. "But you might want a lot of variety in women, as well as everything else you've missed in space," she said low. "You must realize you can take your pick. You're the glamour man, the cosmopolitan in the real sense of the word. We may follow the latest gossip and the newest fashion here, but none of us girls has traveled past Jupiter. Hardly any of the men we know have, either. Not a one of them compares to you. I've been so happy, so envied, and so afraid it will come to a sudden end."

Falkayn's own blood beat momentarily high. Smugness tempted him. Few indeed had won their Master Merchant's certificates as young as he, let along become confidential associates of an uncrowned prince like Nicholas van Rijn, or served as fate's instrument for entire planets. He reckoned himself fairly good-looking, too: face rather snub-nosed, but high in the cheekbones and hard in the jaw, eyes a startling blue against tanned skin, curly yellow hair bleached by foreign suns. He stood an athletic 190 centimeters tall; and he might be newly arrived from the outermost bourn of known space, but Luna's best clothier had designed his pearl-gray tunic and gold culottes.

Whoa, there, son. An animal alertness, developed in countries for which man was never meant, stirred to life within him. *She isn't performing for free, remember. The reason I didn't tell her in advance that today I return to the job still holds good: I'd prefer not to have to worry about prearranged shadowings.*

"You flatter me outrageously," he said, "especially by giving me your company." His grin turned impudent. "In exchange, I'd love to continue outraging you. Dinner first, though. Maybe we'll have time for the ballet too. But dinner for certain. After my long while outside the Solar System, exploring wild new planets, I'm most anxious to continue exploring wild new restaurants"—he bowed—"with such a delightful guide."

Veronica fluttered her lashes. "Native scout glad-glad servem big captain from Polesotechnic League."

"I'll join you soon's I can manage after 1800 hours."

"Please do." She tucked an arm beneath his. "But why part at once? If I've declared myself on holiday—for you—I can keep on with you to wherever you're bound."

His animal showed teeth. He must remind himself to stay relaxed. "Sorry, not possible. Secrecy."

2

"Why?" She arched her brows. "Do you actually need theatricals?" Her tone half bantered, half challenged his manhood. "I'm told you stand high in the Solar Spice & Liquors Company, which stands high in the Polesotechnic League, which stands above planetary law—even the Commonwealth's. What are you afraid of?"

If she's trying to provoke me, flashed through Falkayn's mind, *might be worth provoking right back at her.* "The League isn't a unity," he said as if to a child. "It's an association of interstellar merchants. If it's more powerful than any single government, that's simply because of the scale on which star traders necessarily operate. Doesn't mean the League is a government too. It organizes cooperative, mutual-benefit activities, and it mediates competition that might otherwise become literally cut-throat. Believe me, however, rival members don't use outright violence on each other's agents, but chicanery is taken for granted."

"So?" Though a lecture on the obvious was perhaps insulting, he thought the resentment that flickered in her expression came too fast to be uncalculated.

He shrugged. "So, with all proper immodesty, I'm a target figure. Right-hand man and roving troubletwister for Old Nick. Any hint as to what I'll be doing next could be worth megacredits to somebody. I have to watch out for, shall we say, commercial intelligence collectors."

Veronica released him and stepped back. Her fists clenched. "Are you implying I'm a spy?" she exclaimed.

As a matter of fact, Falkayn thought, *yes.*

He wasn't enjoying this. In search of inner peace, he let his gaze travel past her for a second. The setting was as lovely and not altogether real as she was.

Elfland was not the first unwalled community built on the Lunar surface. But on that account, its designers could take advantage of previous engineering experience. The basic idea was simple. Spaceships employ electromagnetic screens to ward off particle radiation. They employ artificially generated positive and negative fields not only for propulsion, not only for constant weight inside the hull at every acceleration, but also for tractor and pressor beams. Let us scale up these systems until they maintain a giant bubble of air on an otherwise empty surface.

In practice, the task was monumental. Consider problems like leakage, temperature regulation, and ozone layer control. But they were solved; and their solution gave to the Solar System one of its most beloved resorts.

Falkayn saw a park around the girl and himself, greensward, arbors, flowerbeds that were a riot of rainbows. In Lunar gravity, trees soared through heights and arcs no less fantastic than the splashing fountains; and people walked with that same marvelous bounding lightness. Behind the crowds, towers and colonnades lifted in fanciful filigree multitudinously hued. Birds and elevated streets flew between them. Perfumes, laughter, a drift of music, a pervasive murmur of engines wove through the warm air.

But beyond and above stood Luna. Clocks ran on GMT; a thousand small suns hanging from bronze vines created morning. Yet the true hour neared midnight. Splendid and terrible, darkness struck through. At zenith, the sky was black, stars icily visible. South swelled the cloudy-bright-blue shield of Earth. The close observer could see twinkles on its unlit quarter, the megalopolises, dwarfed to sparks by that least astronomical distance. The Avenue of Sphinxes gave a clear westward view to the edge of air, an ashen crater floor, Plato's ringwall bulking brutally over the near horizon.

Falkayn's attention went back to Veronica. "I'm sorry," he said. "Of course I don't intend anything personal."

Of course I do. I may range in the galactic outback, but that doesn't mean I'm an especially simple or trusting soul. Contrariwise. When a lady this desirable and sophisticated locks onto me, within hours of my making planetfall . . . and obliges me in every possible way except telling me about herself—a little quiet checking up by Chee Lan proves that what vague things she does say are not in precise one-one correspondence with truth—what am I supposed to think?

"I should hope not!" Veronica snapped.

"I've sworn fealty to Freeman van Rijn," Falkayn said, "and his orders are to keep everything belowdecks. He doesn't want the competition to get in phase with him." He took both her hands. "It's for your own sake too, heartlet," he added gently.

She let her wrath fade. Tears came forth and trembled on her lids with what he considered admirable precision. "I did want to . . . to share with you . . . more than a few days' casual pleasure, David," she whispered. "And now you call me a spy at worst, a blabbermouth at"—she gulped—"at best. It hurts."

"I did nothing of the sort. But what you don't know can't get you in trouble. Which is the last place I'd want you to be in."

"But you said th-there wasn't any—violence—"

"No, no, absolutely not. Murder, kidnapping, brain-scrub . . . Polesotechnic League members don't indulge in such antics. They know better. But that doesn't mean they're tin saints. They, or certain of their hirelings, have been known to use fairly nasty ways of getting what's wanted. Bribery you could laugh at, Veronica." *Ha!* Falkayn thought. *"Jump at" is the correct phrase, I suspect. What retainer were you paid, and what're you offered for solid information about me?* "But worse approaches are possible. They're frowned on, but sometimes used. Every kind of snooping, for instance; don't you value your privacy? A hundred ways of pressure, direct and indirect, subtle and unsubtle. Blackmail—which often catches the innocent. You do a favor for somebody, and one thing leads to another, and suddenly the somebody has fastened the screws on you and begun tightening them."

As you probably figure to do with me, his mind added. Wryly: *Why shouldn't I let you try? You're the devil I know. You'll keep off the devils I don't know, and meanwhile provide me some gorgeous fun. A dirty trick, perhaps, for a cunning unscrupulous yokel like me to play on a naïve city operator like you. But I believe you get honest enjoyment out of my company. And when I leave, I'll give you an inscribed firestone bracelet or something.*

She pulled loose from his grasp. Her tone stiffened again. "I never asked you to violate your oath," she said. "I do ask not to be treated like a spineless, brainless toy."

Ah, so. We put frost back in the voice, eh? Hoarfrost, to

be exact. Well, I can't argue for the rest of this week. If she won't reverse vectors, forget her, son.

Falkayn snapped to virtual attention. His heels clicked. A machine might have used his throat. "Freelady, my apologies for inflicting my society upon you under conditions you appear to find intolerable. I shall not trouble you further. Good day." He bowed, wheeled, and strode off.

For a minute he thought it hadn't worked. Then she uttered almost a wail, and ran after him, and spent a tearful time explaining how she had misunderstood, and was sorry, and would never, never get off orbit again, if only he—

She might even be partly sincere. Twenty-five percent, maybe?

It helped, being a scion of a baronial house in the Grand Duchy of Hermes, Falkayn reflected. To be sure, he was a younger son; and he'd left at an early age, after kicking too hard against the traces that aristocrats were supposed to carry; and he hadn't visited his home planet since. But some of that harsh training had alloyed with the metal of him. He knew how to deal with insolence.

Or how to stick with a job when he'd really rather prolong his vacation. He got rid of Veronica as fast as was consistent with a reconciliation scene, and proceeded on his way.

II

First he passed through a large sporting goods store on the other side of the park. He should be able to shake off any followers among the wares on exhibition. The vac suits and vehicles were less bulky than he had counted on. But then, a jaunt into the Lunar mountains, rescue flitters available within minutes of a radio call, was not like hiking off on an unmapped world where you were the sole human being for several light-years. The collapsible boats with their gaudy sails were more helpful. He wondered how popular they were. Lake Leshy was small, and low-weight sailing tricky until you got the hang of it—as he had learned beyond the Solar System.

Emerging from a rear door, he found a kiosk and entered the dropshaft. The few people floating down the gee-beam with him seemed like ordinary citizens.

Maybe I'm being overcautious, he thought. *Does it matter if our competitors know I've paid a visit to Serendipity, Incorporated? Shouldn't I try to remember this isn't some nest of nonhuman barbarians? This is Terra's own moon, at the heart of the Commonwealth! The agents of the companies don't fight for naked survival, no holds barred; essentially, they play a game for money, and the losers don't lose anything vital. Relax and enjoy it.* But habit was too strong, reminding him of the context in which that last bit of advice had originally been given.

He got off at the eighth sublevel and made his way along the corridors. Wide and high, they were nonetheless crowded with traffic: freightways, robotic machines, pedestrians in workaday coveralls. Their facings were in plain pastel tones, overlaid by an inevitable thin film of grime and oil. The doors opened on factories, warehouses, shipping depots, offices. Rumble and rattle filled the air, odors of crowded humanity, chemicals, electrical discharges. Hot gusts struck out of fenced-off grilles. A deep, nearly subliminal vibration quivered through rock and floor and shinbones, the toil of the great engines. Elfland was a pretty mask; here, in the industrial part of old Lunograd, were the guts.

Gagarin Corridor ended, like many others, at Titov Circus. The hollow cylinder of space, reaching from a skylighting dome where Earth and stars gleamed, down to the depths of excavation, was not as big as Falkayn's impression had been from its fame. But it was built in early days, he reflected. And certainly the balconies which encircled it on every level were thronged enough. He must weave his way through the crowds. They were local people mostly, workers, businessmen, officials, monitors, technicians, housewives, showing more in their gait and mannerisms than in their bodies the effects of generations on Luna. But there were plenty of outsiders, merchants, spacemen, students, tourists, including a wild variety of nonhumans.

He noted that the prestigious stores, like Ivarsen Gems, occupied cubbyholes compared to newer establishments. Really big money has no need to advertise itself. Boisterous noises from the Martian Chop House tempted him to stop in for a mug of its ale, which he'd heard about as far away as Betelgeuse. But no... maybe later... duty was calling, "in a shrill unpleasant voice," as van Rijn often said. Falkayn proceeded around the balcony.

The door he reached at length was broad, of massive bronze, decorated with an intricate bas-relief circuit diagram. Stereoprojection spelled SERENDIPITY, INC. a few centimeters in front. But the effect remained discreet. You might have supposed this outfit to have been in operation these past two centuries. And instead, in—fifteen years, was that the figure?—it had rocketed from nowhere to the very firmament of the Polesotechnic League.

Well, Falkayn thought, *in a free-market economy, if you see a widespread need and can fill it, you get rich fast.*

8

Actually, when Old Nick organized his trade pioneer teams, like mine, he set them to doing in a physical way what Serendipity was already doing in its computers.

A certain irony here. Adzel, Chee Lan, and I are supposed to follow up whatever interesting reports our robot probes bring back from hitherto unvisited planets. If we see potentially valuable resources or markets, we report back to van Rijn, very much on the q.t., so he can exploit them before the rest of the League learns they exist. And yet I, the professional serendipitist, have come to Serendipity, Inc. like any hopeful Earthlubber businessman.

He shrugged. His team had been overdue for a visit to the Solar System. Having arrived, they might as well see if the data-processing machines could free-associate them with an item that pointed in some profitable direction. Van Rijn had agreed to pay the fees, without bellowing very much.

The door opened. Instead of a lobby, Falkayn entered a room, luxuriously draped but miniature, from which several other doors led. A vocolyre sang, "Good day, sir. Please take Number Four." That led down a short, narrow passage to still another door, and thus finally to an office. Unlike most chambers in Lunograd, this one did not compensate for lack of windows with some landscape film played on a wall screen. In fact, though the carpeting was deep and rich blue, walls azure, ceiling mother-of-pearl, air flower-scented, furniture comfortable, the total effect was somewhat stark. At one end, a woman sat behind a large desk. The battery of secretarial gadgets around her suggested a barricade.

"Welcome," she said.

"Thanks," he replied with an attempted grin. "I felt as if I were invading a fortress."

"In a way, sir, that was correct." Her voice could have been pleasantly husky, the more so when she spoke Anglic with a guttural accent that not even his widely traveled ear could identify. But it was too crisp, too sexless; and her smile gave the same impression of having been learned. "Protection of privacy is a major element of our service. Many do not wish it known they have consulted us on a specific occasion. We partners receive each client in person, and usually need not call on our staff to help."

That better be the case, Falkayn thought, *seeing what a whopping sum you charge just for an appointment.*

She offered her hand without rising. "I am Thea Beldaniel." The clasp was perfunctory on both sides. "Please be seated, Freeman Kubichek."

He lowered his frame into a lounger. It extended an arm, offering excellent cigars. He took one. "Thanks," he repeated. "Uh, now that I'm here, I can drop the *nom du phone.* Most visitors do, I'm sure."

"Actually, no. There is seldom any reason, until they are alone with the machines. Of course, we are bound to recognize many because they are prominent." Thea Beldaniel paused before adding, with a tactfulness that appeared equally studied, "Prominent in this galactic neighborhood, that is. No matter how important some beings may be, no living brain can recognize them all, when civilization extends across scores of light-years. You, sir, for example, are obviously from a colonized planet. Your bearing suggests that its social structure is aristocratic, yourself born into the nobility. The Commonwealth does not have hereditary distinctions. Therefore your home world must be autonomous. But that leaves quite a few possibilities."

Since he had long been curious about this organization, he tried to strike up a genuine conversation. "Right, Freelady. I'm not on political business, though. I work for an Earth-based company, Solar Spice & Liquors. My real name's David Falkayn. From Hermes, to be exact."

"Everyone knows of Nicholas van Rijn." She nodded. "I have met him personally a few times."

I must confess to myself he's the main reason I've been lionized, Falkayn thought. *Reflected glory. By now, high society is abuzz about me. Invitations are pouring in, from the emperors of industry, their wives, daughters, hangers-on, to the bold space ranger and his partners, in honor of our (largely unspecified) exploits among the far stars. But that's because we aren't just any bold space rangers, we're Old Nick's bold space rangers.*

A paradox remains. The Beldaniel sisters, Kim Yoon-

*Kun, Anastasia Herrera, Freeman and Freelady Latimer—
the founders and owners of Serendipity, Inc., which aims to
correlate all the information in known space—they haven't
heard about us. They don't go out in society. They keep to
themselves, in these offices and in that castle where outsiders
never visit.... I truly would like to get a rise out of this
woman.*

She wasn't bad-looking, he realized piecemeal. Indeed,
she could be called handsome: tall, lithe, well formed, no
matter how the severe white slacksuit tried to conceal that
fact. Her hair was cut short, but this only emphasized a good
shape of head; her face was practically classic, except that
you thought of Athene as showing a bit more warmth. Her
age was hard to guess. She must be at least in her forties. But
having taken care of her body and, doubtless, advantage of
the best antisenescence treatments, she might be older by a
decade, and yet show merely the same gray streak in brown
tresses, slight dryness in the clear pale skin, crow's-feet about
the eyes. Those eyes were her best feature, Falkayn decided,
wide-spaced, large, luminous green.

He started his cigar and rolled the smoke about his
tongue. "We may find ourselves bargaining," he said. "Don't
you buy information, either for cash or for remittance of
fees?"

"Certainly. The more the better. I must warn you that we
set our own prices, and sometimes refuse to pay anything,
even after the item has been given us. You see, its value
depends on what is already stored in the memory banks. And
we can't let others see this. That would risk betrayal of
secrets entrusted to us. If you wish to sell, Freeman Falkayn,
you must rely on our reputation for fair dealing."

"Well, I've visited a lot of planets, species, cultures—"

"Anecdotal material is acceptable, but not highly paid
for. What we most desire is thorough, accurate, document-
ed, quantitative facts. Not necessarily about new discoveries
in space. What is going on on the major civilized worlds is
often of greater interest."

"Look," he said bluntly, "no offense meant, but I've been
wondering. I work for Freeman van Rijn, and in an

11

important capacity. Suppose I offered you details about his operations that he didn't want released. Would you buy them?"

"Probably. But we would not then release them to others. Our whole position in the Polesotechnic League depends on our trustworthiness. This is one reason why we have so few employees: a minimal staff of experts and technicians—all nonhuman—and otherwise our machines. In part, it is a good reason for us to be notoriously asocial. If Freeman van Rijn knows we have not been partying with Freeman Harleman of Venusian Tea & Coffee, he has the fewer grounds for suspecting us of collusion with the latter."

"Coffee grounds?" Falkayn murmured.

Thea Beldaniel folded her hands in her lap, sat back, and said, "Perhaps, coming from the frontier as you do, Freeman, you don't quite understand the principle on which Serendipity, Inc., works. Let me put it in oversimplified language.

"The problem of information retrieval was solved long ago, through electronic data storage, scanning, coding, and replication. But the problem of information usage continues acute. The perceptual universe of man and other space-traveling species is expanding still more rapidly than the universe of their exploration. Suppose you were a scientist or an artist, with what you believed was a new idea. To what extent has the thought of countless billions of other sophonts, on thousands of known worlds, duplicated your own? What might you learn from them? What might you contribute that is genuinely new? Well, you could ransack libraries and data centers, and get more information on any subject than is generally realized. Too much more! Not only could you not read it all in your lifetime, you could not pick out what was relevant. Still worse is the dilemma of a company planning a mercantile venture. What developments elsewhere in space will collide, compete, conceivably nullify their efforts? Or what positive opportunities are being overlooked, simply because no one can comprehend the total picture?"

"I've heard those questions asked," Falkayn said. He spoke dryly, with puzzlement rather than resentment at being patronized. Was this woman so insensitive to human feelings—hell, to ordinary human common sense—that she must lecture a client as if he were some six-legged innocent newly hauled out of his planet's Stone Age?

"Obvious, of course," she said imperturbably. "And in principle, the answer is likewise obvious. Computers should not merely scan, but sift data. They should identify possible correlations, and test them, with electronic speed and parallel-channel capacity. You might say they should make suggestions. In practice, this was difficult. Technologically, it required a major advance in cybernetics. Besides . . . the members of the League guarded their hard-won knowledge jealously. Why tell anything you knew to your rival? Or to public data centers, and thus indirectly to your rival? Or to a third party who was not your competitor but might well make a deal with your rival—or might decide to diversify his interests and himself become your rival?

"Whether or not you could use a datum, it had cost you something to acquire. You would soon go bankrupt if you made a free gift of every item. And while secrets were traded, negotations about this were slow and awkward.

"Serendipity, Inc., solved the problem with improved systems—not only better robotics, but a better idea for exchanging knowledge."

Falkayn sat back with his cigar. He felt baffled, fascinated, the least bit frightened. This female was even weirder than he had been told the partners were. Giving a basic sales pitch to a man who'd already bought an appointment . . . in God's name, *why?* Stories were rife about the origin of these people. But what story might account for the behavior he was observing?

Beneath her quick, level words, intensity gathered: "The larger the information pool, the greater the probability of making a correlation that is useful to a given individual. Thus the creation of such a pool was to the general benefit, provided that no one gained a special advantage. This is the service that we have offered. We draw on ordinary sources, of course. And that in itself is valuable, there being so many libraries and memory banks scattered on so many planets. But in addition, we buy whatever anyone cares to tell, if it is worthwhile. And we sell back whatever other data may be of interest to him. The important point is, this is done anonymously. We founders of the business do not know or wish to know what questions you ask, what answers you get, what you relate, how the computers appraise it, what additional conclusions their logic circuits draw. Such things stay in the machines. We only concern ourselves or our staff with a specific problem if we are requested to. Otherwise our sole attention is on the statistics, the input-output average. Our firm has grown as trust in us has grown. Innumerable private investigations have show that we favor no one, do not blurt anything out, and cannot be corrupted. So has the accumulated experience of doing business with us."

She leaned forward. Her gaze was unblinking on him. "For example," she said, "imagine that you did wish to sell us confidential information about your company. Mere word-of-mouth assertions would be filed, since a rumor or a falsehood is also a datum, but would probably not be believed. The usual precautions against commercial espionage should safeguard documentary evidences. But if this fails—yes, we will buy it. Crosschecks will quickly show that we have bought thief's goods, which fact is noted. If your employer was the only one who possessed the information, it will not be given out until somebody else has registered the same thing with us. But it will be taken into account by the logic circuits in preparing their recommendations—which they do impersonally for any client. That is to say, they might advise your employer's rival against a certain course of action, because they know from the stolen information that this will be futile. But they will not tell him why they offer such counsel."

Falkayn got a word in fast while she caught up on her breathing. "That makes it to everybody's advantage to consult you on a regular basis. And the more your machines are told during consultations, the better the advice they can give. Uh-huh. That's how you grow."

"It is one mechanism of growth for us," Thea Beldaniel said. "Actually, however, information theft is very minor. Why should Freeman van Rijn not sell us the fact that, say, one of his trading ships happened upon a planet where there is a civilization that creates marvelous sculptures? He is not in the art business to any significant extent. In exchange, he pays a much reduced fee to learn that a crew of hydrogen-breathing explorers have come upon an oxygen-atmosphere planet that produces a new type of wine."

"I'm not clear about one thing," Falkayn said. "My impression is he'd have to come in person to be told any important fact. Is this true?"

"Not in that particular case," she answered. "His needs would be obvious. But we must safeguard privacy. You, for example—" She paused. The strangeness left her eyes; she said shrewdly, "I would guess that you plan to sit down before the machine and say, 'My name is David Falkayn. Tell me whatever might be of special interest to me.' No doubt you have good reason to expect that the memory banks include something about you. Now don't you realize, sir, for your own protection, we can't let anyone do this? We must ask for positive identification."

Falkayn reached into his pocket. She raised a palm. "No, no," she said, "not to me. I don't have to know whether you really are who you claim to be. But to the machine—retinal scan, fingerprints, the usual procedures if you are registered in the Commonwealth. If not, it will suggest other ways to establish yourself to its satisfaction." She rose. "Come, I'll take you there and demonstrate its operation."

Following her and watching, Falkayn could not decide whether she walked like a frigid woman.

No matter. A more interesting thought had struck him. He believed he could tell why she behaved the way she did, dwelt on elementary details through she must realize he knew most of them already. He'd encountered that pattern elsewhere. It was usually called fanaticism.

III

SEATED alone—and yet not alone, for the great quasi-brain was there and had already spoken to him—Falkayn took a moment to consider his surroundings. Though he had spent his life with robots, including his beloved Muddlehead, this one felt eerie. He tried to understand why.

He sat in an ordinary self-adjusting chair before an ordinary desk with the standard secretarial apparatus. Around him were bare gray walls, white fluorolight, odorless recycled air, a faint humming through stillness. Confronting him was a basic control panel and a large 3D screen, blank at the moment. What was strange?

It must be subjective, he decided, his own reaction to the mystery about this organization. The detectives of a wary League had verified that the founder-owners of Serendipity, Inc., had no special ties to any other group—or, for that matter, to anyone or anything, human or nonhuman, throughout known space. But their origin remained obscure. Their chilly, graceless personalities (Thea Beldaniel was evidently typical of the whole half-dozen) and aloofness from society only emphasized that basic isolation.

Their secret could not be ferreted out. Quite apart from the regard for privacy inherent in today's individualism, it wasn't feasible. The universe is too big. This tiny segment of the fringe of one spiral arm of a single galaxy which we have somewhat explored and exploited . . . is too big. In going to thousands of suns that intrigue us, we have passed by literally millions of others. It will take centuries even to visit them, let alone begin to understand them a little. And meanwhile, and forever, beyond the outermost radius of our faring will lie nearly all the suns that exist.

The partners had entered the Solar System in a cargo vessel loaded with heavy metals. Selling that for a good price, they established their information enterprise. Though they ordered many parts on Earth, the basic logic and memory units were brought from Elsewhere. Once, out of curiosity, Nicholas van Rijn had bribed a Commonwealth customs inspector; but that man merely said, "Look, sir, I verify that imports aren't dangerous. I make sure they don't carry disease, and aren't going to blow up, that sort of thing. What else can we stop, under a free trade law? What Serendipity got was just a shipment of computer-type stuff. Not human-made, I'm sure. You get an eye for, uh, style, after a few years in my job. And if, like you tell me, nobody can quite duplicate the kind of work it's been doing since it was installed . . . well, jingles, sir, isn't the answer plain to see? These people found a planet that can do tricks we aren't up to yet, nobody we know about. They made a deal. They kept quiet. Wouldn't you? *Don't* you, sir?"

Falkayn started from his reverie. The machine had spoken again. "Pardon?" he said. Instantly: *What the devil am I doing, apologizing to a gadget?* He picked his cigar from the rack above the disposer and took a nervous puff.

"David Falkayn of Hermes and the Solar Spice & Liquors Company, your identity has been verified." The voice was not the flat baritone of most human-built robots; it was high, with a curious whistling quality, and varied both pitch and speed in a way hard to describe. "Your name is associated with a number of accounts in these data banks, most notably the episodes involving Beta Centauri, Ikrananka, and Merseia." *Judas priest!* Falkayn thought. *How did it learn about Ikrananka?* "Many items are logically connected with each of these, and in turn connected with other facts. You will understand that the total ramifications are virtually infinite. Thus it is necessary to select a point and search the association chains radiating from it in a limited number of directions. If none of them are productive, other lines are tried, and eventually other starting points, until a satisfactory result is obtained." *Or until I run out of money.* "What type of search do you wish conducted?"

"Well—I—" Falkayn rallied his shaken wits. "How about new markets on extrasolar planets?"

"Since confidential information is not released here, you are asking no service which ordinary data centers cannot provide."

"Now, wait. I want you to do what you're uniquely built to do. Take the points Me and Cash, and see what association chains exist between 'em."

"Commenced."

Did the humming louden, or did the silence deepen? Falkayn leaned back and struggled to relax. Behind that panel, these walls, electrons and quanta hurtled through vacuum; charges and the absence of charges moved through crystal lattices; distorted molecules interacted with magnetic, electric, gravitational, nuclear fields; the machine thought.

The machine dreamed.

He wondered if its functioning was continuous, building immense webs of correlation and inference whether or not a client sat here. Quite probably; and in this manner, it came closer than any other entity to comprehending our corner of the universe. And yet the facts must be too many, the possible interconnections between them uncountable. The fruitful few were buried in that sheer mass. Every major discovery has involved a recognition of such rare meaningful associations. (Between the water level in a bath and the weight of gold; between the pessimism of a small-town parson and the mechanism of organic evolution; between the Worm Ouroboros, that biteth its own tail, and the benzene molecule—) Living creatures like Falkayn, coming from the living cosmos to the cave where this engine dwelt, must be what triggered its real action, made it perceive the significance of what had hitherto looked like another isolated fact.

"David Falkayn of Hermes!"

"Yes?" He sat bolt upright and tensed.

"A possibility. You will recall that, a number of years ago, you showed that the star Beta Centauri has planets in attendance."

Falkayn couldn't help crowing, uselessly save that it asserted his importance in contrast to the huge blind brain. "I should forget? That was what really attracted the notice of the higher-ups and started me to where I am. Blue giant suns aren't supposed to have planets. But this one does."

"That is recorded, like most news," said the machine, unimpressed. "Your tentative explanation of the phenomenon was later verified. While the star was condensing, a nucleus still surrounded by an extensive nebular envelope, a swarm of rogue planets chanced by. Losing energy to friction with the nebula, they were captured.

"Sunless planets are common. They are estimated to number a thousand or more times the stars. That is, nonluminous bodies, ranging in size from superjovian to asteroidal, are believed to occupy interstellar space in an amount greater by three orders of magnitude than the nuclear-reacting self-luminous bodies called stars. Nevertheless, astronomical distances are such that the probability of an object like this passing near a star is vanishingly small. Indeed, explorers have not come upon many rogues even in mid-space. An actual capture must be so rare that the case you found may well be unique in the galaxy.

"However, your discovery excited sufficient interest that an expedition set forth not long afterward, from the Collectivity of Wisdom in the country of Kothgar upon the planet Lemminkainen. Those are the Anglic names, of course. Herewith a transcript of the full report." A slot extruded a spooled microreel which Falkayn automatically pocketed.

"I know of them," he said. "Nonhuman civilization, but they do have occasional relations with us. And I followed the story. I had somewhat of a personal interest, remember. They checked out every giant within several hundred light-years that hadn't been visited before. Results negative, as expected—which is why no one else bothered to try."

"At that time you were on Earth to get your Master's certificate," the machine said. "Otherwise you might never have heard. And, while Earth's data-processing and news facilities are unsurpassed in known space, they are nonetheless so overloaded that details which seem of scant importance are not sent in. Among those filtered-out items was the one presently under consideration.

"It was by chance that Serendipity, Inc., obtained a full account several years later. A Lemminkainenite captain who had been on that voyage tendered the data in exchange for a reduction of fee for his own inquiries. Actually, he brought information and records pertaining to numerous explorations he had made. This one happened to be among them. No significance was noticed until the present moment, when your appearance stimulated a detailed study of the fact in question."

The man's pulse quickened. His hands clenched on the chair arms.

"Preliminary to your perusal of the transcript, a verbal summary is herewith offered," whistled the oracle. "A rogue planet was found to be approaching Beta Crucis. It will not be captured, but the hyperbola of its orbit is narrow and it will come within an astronomical unit."

The screen darkened. Space and the stars leaped forth. One among them burned a steady steel blue. It waxed as the ship that had taken the pictures ran closer.

"Beta Crucis lies approximately south of Sol at an approximate distance of two hundred and four light-years." The dry recital, in that windful tone, seemed to make cold strike out of the moving view. "It is of type B_1, with a mass of approximately six, radius four, luminosity eight hundred and fifty times Sol's. It is quite young, and its total residence time on the main sequence will be on the order of a hundred million standard years."

The scene shifted. A streak of light crossed the wintry stellar background. Falkayn recognized the technique. If you cruise rapidly along two or three orthogonal axes, recording photomultipliers will pick up comparatively nearby objects like planets, by their apparent motion, and their location can be triangulated.

"In this instance, only a single object was detected, and that at a considerable distance out," said the machine. "Since it represented the lone case of passage that the expedition found, closer observation was made."

The picture jumped to a strip taken from orbit. Against the stars hung a globe. On one side it was dark, constellations lifting over its airless horizon as the ship moved. On the other side it shimmered wan bluish white. Irregular markings were visible, where the steeper uplands reared naked. But most of the surface was altogether featureless.

Falkayn shivered. *Cryosphere,* he thought.

This world had condensed, sunless, from a minor knot in some primordial nebula. Dust, gravel, stones, meteoroids rained together during multiple megayears; and in the end, a solitary planet moved off between the stars. Infall had released energy; now radioactivity did, and the gravitational compression of matter into denser allotropes. Earthquakes shook the newborn sphere; volcanoes spouted forth gas, water vapor, carbon dioxide, methane, ammonia, cyanide, hydrogen sulfide . . . the same which had finally evolved into Earth's air and oceans.

But here was no sun to warm, irradiate, start the chemical cookery that might at last yield life. Here were darkness and the deep, and a cold near absolute zero.

As the planet lost heat, its oceans froze. Later, one by one, the gases of the air fell out solid upon those immense glaciers, a Fimbul blizzard that may have gone for centuries. In a sheath of ice—ice perhaps older than Earth herself—the planet drifted barren, empty, nameless, meaningless, through time to no harbor except time's end.

Until—

"The mass and diameter are slightly greater than terrestrial, the gross density somewhat less," said the brain that thought without being aware. "Details may be found in the transcript, to the extent that they were ascertained. They indicate that the body is quite ancient. No unstable atoms remain in appreciable quantity, apart from a few of the longest half-life.

"A landing party made a brief visit."

The view jumped again. Through the camera port of a gig, Falkayn saw bleakness rush toward him. Beta Crucis rose. Even in the picture, it was too savagely brilliant to look near.

But it was nonetheless a mere point—distant, distant; for all its unholy radiance, it threw less light than Sol does on Earth.

That was ample, however, reflected off stiffened air and rigid seas. Falkayn must squint against dazzle to study a ground-level scene.

That ground was a plain, flat to the horizon save where the spaceboat and crew had troubled it. A mountain range thrust above the world's rim, dark raw stone streaked with white. The gig cast a blue shadow across diamond snow-glitter, under the star-crowded black sky. Some Lemmin-kainenites moved about, testing and taking samples. Their otter shapes were less graceful than ordinarily, hampered by the thick insulating soles that protected them and the materials of their spacesuits from the heat sink that such an environment is. Falkayn could imagine what hush enclosed them, scarcely touched by radio voices or the seething of cosmic interference.

"They discovered nothing they considered to be of value," said the computer. "While the planet undoubtedly has mineral wealth, this lay too far under the cryosphere to be worth extracting. Approaching Beta Crucis, solidified material would begin to sublime, melt, or vaporize. But years must pass until the planet came sufficiently near for this effect to be noticeable."

Unconsciously, Falkayn nodded. Consider the air and oceans of an entire world, chilled to equilibrium with interstellar space. What a Dante's hell of energy you'd need to pour in before you observed so much as a little steam off the crust!

The machine continued. "While periastron passage would be accompanied by major geological transformations, there was no reason to suppose that any new order of natural phenomena would be disclosed. The course of events was predictable on the basis of the known properties of matter. The cryosphere would become atmosphere and hydrosphere. Though this must cause violent readjustments, the process would be spectacular rather than fundamentally enlightening—or profitable; and members of the dominant culture on Lemminkainen do not enjoy watching catastrophes. Afterward the planet would recede. In time, the cryosphere would re-form. Nothing basic would have happened.

"Accordingly, the expedition reported what it had found, as a mildly interesting discovery on an otherwise disappointing cruise. Given little emphasis, the data were filed and forgotten. The negative report that reached Earth did not include what appeared to be an incidental."

Falkayn smote the desk. It thrummed within him. *By God,* he thought, *the Lemminkainenites for sure don't understand us humans. We won't let the thawing of an ice world go unwatched!*

Briefly, fantasies danced in his mind. Suppose you had a globe like that, suddenly brought to a livable temperature. The air would be poisonous, the land raw rock . . . but that could be changed. You could make your own kingdom—

No. Quite aside from economics (a lot cheaper to find uninhabited planets with life already on them), there were the dull truths of physical reality. Men can alter a world, or ruin one; but they cannot move it one centimeter off its ordained course. That requires energies of literally cosmic magnitude.

So you couldn't ease this planet into a suitable orbit around Beta Crucis. It must continue its endless wanderings. It would not freeze again at once. Passage close to a blue giant would pour in unbelievable quantities of heat, which radiation alone is slow to shed. But the twilight would fall within years; the dark within decades; the Cold and the Doom within centuries.

The screen showed a last glimpse of the unnamed sphere, dwindling as the spaceship departed. It blanked. Falkayn sat shaken by awe.

He heard himself say, like a stranger, with a flippancy that was self-defensive, "Are you proposing I organize excursions to watch this object swing by the star? A pyrotechnic sight, I'm sure. But how do I get an exclusive franchise?"

The machine said, "Further study will be required. For example, it will be needful to know whether the entire cryosphere is going to become fluid. Indeed, the very orbit must be ascertained with more precision than now exists.

Nevertheless, it does appear that this planet may afford a site of unprecedented value to industry. That did not occur to the Lemminkainenites, whose culture lacks a dynamic expansionism. But a correlation has just been made here with the fact that, while heavy isotopes are much in demand, their production has been severely limited because of the heat energy and lethal waste entailed. Presumably this is a good place on which to build such facilities."

The idea hit Falkayn in the belly, then soared to his head like champagne bubbles. The money involved wasn't what brought him to his feet shouting. Money was always pleasant to have; but he could get enough for his needs and greeds with less effort. Sheer instinct roused him. He was abruptly a Pleistocene hunter again, on the track of a mammoth.

"Judas!" he yelled. *"Yes!"*

"Because of the commercial potentialities, discretion would be advantageous at the present stage," said the voice which knew no glories. "It is suggested that your employer pay the fee required to place this matter under temporary seal of secrecy. You may discuss that with Freelady Beldaniel upon leaving today, after which you are urged to contact Freeman van Rijn." It paused, for a billion nanoseconds; what new datum, suddenly noticed, was it weaving in? "For reasons that may not be given, you are strongly advised to refrain from letting out the truth to anyone whatsoever before you have left Luna. At present, since you are here, it is suggested that the matter be explored further, verbally, in the hope that lines of association will open to more data that are relevant."

—Emerging, two hours later, in the office, Falkayn stopped before the woman's desk. "Whew!" he said, triumphant and weary.

She smiled back, with something akin to pleasure. "I trust you had a successful time?"

"And then some. Uh, I've got a thing or two to take up with you."

"Please sit down." Thea Beldaniel leaned forward. Her gaze grew very bright and level. "While you were in there, Captain Falkayn, I used another outlet to get from the bank what data it has about you. Only what is on public record, of course, and only in hope of serving you better. It is quite astonishing what you have accomplished."

So it is, Falkayn agreed. "Thank you," he said.

"The computers do not do all the computing in this place." By heaven, she did have a little humor! "The idea occurred to me that you and we might cooperate in certain ways, to great mutual advantage. I wonder if we could talk about that, too?"

IV

FROM Lunograd, the Hotel Universe challenges a galaxy: "No oxygen-breathing sophont exists for whom we cannot provide suitable accommodation. Unless every room is already occupied, we will furnish any such visitor with what is necessary for health, safety, and satisfaction. If equipment and supplies on hand are insufficient, we will obtain them upon reasonable advance notice and payment of a reasonable extra charge. If we fail to meet the terms of this guarantee, we will present the disappointed guest with the sum of one million credits of the Solar Commonwealth."

Many attempts are made to collect, by spacemen in collusion with the most outlandish beings they can find. Twice the cost of fulfilling the promise has exceeded the megacredit. (In one case, research and development were needed for the molecular synthesis of certain dietary materials; in the other case, the management had to fetch a symbiotic organism from the visitor's home planet.) But the publicity is well worth it. Human tourists especially will pay ten prices in order to stay here and feel cosmopolitan.

Chee Lan afforded no problems. The most advanced trade routes on her world—"trade route" comes nearer to translating the concept than does "nation"—have been in close contact with man since the first expedition to O_2 Eridani A II discovered them. Increasing numbers of Cynthians arrive at the Solar System as travelers, merchants, delegates, specialists, students. Some go on to roam space professionally. Chee was given a standardized suite.

"No, I am not comfortable," she had snapped when

Falkayn called to ask if she was. "But I shouldn't have expected them to produce a decent environment for me, when they can't even get the name of my planet right."

"Well, true, you call it Lifehome-under-Sky," Falkayn answered blandly; "but over on the next continent they—"

"I know, I know! That's exactly the trouble. Those klongs forget Tah-chih-chien-pi is a complete world, with geography and seasons. They've booked me into the next continent, and it's bloody cold!"

"So ring up and bitch," Falkayn said. "You're good at that."

Chee sputtered but later followed his advice.

An Earthling would probably not have noticed the adjustments that were made. He would have continued to be aware simply of a gravity 0.8 standard; a reddish-orange illumination that varied through a fifty-five-hour diurnal-nocturnal period; hot wet air, full of musky odors; pots of giant flowers scattered about the floor, a vine-draped tree, a crisscrossing set of bars used not merely for exercise but for getting from place to place within the rooms. (The popular impression is wrong, that Cynthians are arboreal in the sense that monkeys are. But they have adapted and adjusted to the interwoven branches of their endless forests, and often prefer these to the ground.) The Earthling would have observed that the animated picture which gave the illusion of a window showed jungle, opening on a savanna where stood the delicate buildings of a caravanserai. He would have paid attention to the scattered books and the half-finished clay sculpture with which Chee has been amusing herself while she waited for Falkayn to carry out the business that brought the team here.

At this moment, he would have seen her turn from the phone, where the man's image had just faded, and squat in arch-backed tension.

Tai Tu, with whom she had also been amusing herself, tried to break the thickening silence. "I take it that was one of your partners?" He knew Espanish, not Anglic.

"Yes, do take it," Chee clipped. "Take it far away."

"I beg your gracious elucidation?"

"Get out," Chee said. "I've got thinking to do."

Tai Tu gasped and goggled at her.

The hypothetical observer from Earth would probably have called her cute, or actually beautiful; many of his species did. To Tai Tu, she was desirable, fascinating, and more than a little terrifying.

When erect, she stood some ninety centimeters tall, and her bushy tail curled upward a full half that length. Lustrous white angora fur covered her otherwise naked form. A long-legged biped, she nonetheless had five prehensile toes on either foot, and walked digitigrade. The arms, scarcely less long and muscular, ended in hands that each possessed five four-jointed rosy-nailed fingers and a thumb. The round, pointed-eared head carried a short-muzzled face whose flat nose and dainty mouth were fringed with whiskers like a cat's. Above, the enormous emerald eyes were emphasized by a mask of the same blue-gray hue as feet, hands, and ears. Though hirsute, viviparous, and homeothermic, she was not a mammal. The young of her race eat flesh from birth, using their lips to suck out the blood.

Tai Tu was smaller and a less aggressive carnivore. During their evolution, male Cynthians were never required to carry the cubs through the trees and fight for them. He had been flattered when Chee Lan told him—a humble visiting professor at Lomonosov University, whereas she was a xenologist in the service of Nicholas van Rijn—to move in with her.

Still, he had his pride. "I cannot accept this treatment," he said.

Chee bared her fangs. They were white and very sharp. She jerked her tail at the door. "Out," she said. "And stay."

Tai Tu sighed, packed his belongings, and returned to his former quarters.

Chee sat for a while alone, scowling even more blackly. At last she punched a number on the phone. There was no response. "Damnation, I know you're in!" she yelled. The screen remained blank. Presently she was hopping up and down with rage. "You and your stupid Buddhist meditations!" After a hundred or so rings, she snapped the switch and went out the airlock.

The corridors beyond were Earth-conditioned. She

adjusted to the change without effort. Of necessity, members of the same space team have much the same biological requirements. The slideways were too slow for her. She bounded along them. En route, she bowled over His Excellency, the Ambassador of the Epopoian Empire. He cawed his indignation. She flung such a word back over her shoulder that His Excellency's beak hung open and he lay voiceless where he had fallen for three minutes by the clock.

Meanwhile Chee reached the entrance to Adzel's single room. She leaned on the doorchime button. It produced no results. He must really be out of this continuum. She punched dots and dashes, emergency code signals, *SOS. Help. Engine failure. Collision. Shipwreck. Mutiny. Radiation. Famine. Plague. War. Supernova.* That untranced him. He activated the valves and she cycled through the lock. The quick change of pressure made her eardrums hurt.

"Dear me," rumbled his mild basso profundo. "What language. I am afraid that you are further from attaining enlightenment than I had estimated."

Chee looked up toward Adzel's countenance, and up, and up. A weight of two and a half Terran gees, the hellish white blaze of a simulated F-type sun, the loudness of every sound in this dense, parched, thunder-smelling atmosphere, struck her and quelled her. She crawled under a table for shelter. The chamber's austerity was unrelieved by a film view of illimitable windy plains on that planet which men called Woden, or by the mandala that Adzel had hung from the ceiling or the scroll of Mahayana text he had posted on a wall.

"I trust your news is of sufficient importance to justify interrupting me at my exercises," he went on, as severely as possible for him.

Chee paused, subdued. "I don't know," she confessed. "But it concerns us."

Adzel composed himself to listen.

She studied him for a moment, trying to anticipate his response to what she had to say. No doubt he would feel she was overreacting. And maybe that was right. But she'd be flensed and gutted if she'd admit it to him!

He bulked above her. With the powerful tail, his centauroid body had a length of four and a half meters and mass exceeding a ton. A barndoor-broad torso, carrying a pair of arms and quadridigital hands in proportion, lifted the head more than two meters above the four cloven hoofs, at the end of a longish neck. That head was almost crocodilian, the snout bearing flared nostrils and an alarming array of teeth. The external ears were solid bony material, like the row of triangular dorsal plates which made a serration from the top of his pate to the end of his tail. Yet the skull bulged far backward to hold a considerable brain, and beneath overhanging brow ridges, his eyes were large and brown and rather wistful. Scutes armored his throat and belly, scales the rest of him. Yet they were a lovely, shimmering dark-green on top, shading to gold underneath. He was respected in his field of planetology, or had been before he quit academe to take sordid commercial employment. And in some ways, he was biologically closer to human than Chee. Besides being warm-blooded and omnivorous, he came of a species whose females give live birth and suckle their infants.

"Dave phoned me," Chee said. Feeling a bit more her usual self, she added with a snort, "He finally dragged himself away for a few hours from that hussy he's been wasting our time on."

"And went to Serendipity, Inc., as per plan? Excellent, excellent. I hope material of interest was revealed to him." Adzel's rubbery lips formed League Latin rather than the Anglic Chee was using, in order to stay in practice.

"He was certainly skyhooting excited about it," the Cynthian replied. "But he wouldn't mention details."

"I should think not, over an unsealed circuit." Adzel's tone grew disapproving. "In this town, I understand, every tenth being is somebody's spy."

"I mean he wouldn't come here either, or have us come to his hotel, and talk," Chee said. "The computer warned him against it, without giving a reason."

The Wodenite rubbed his jaw. "Now that is curious. Are not these quarters proof against snooping devices?"

"They ought to be, at the rates we pay. But maybe a new kind of bug has come along, and the machine's learned about it confidentially. You know SI's policy on that, don't you? Dave wants us to radio the home office for more money and buy a 'restricted' tag for whatever he was told today. He says once we're back on Earth, he can safely chatter."

"Why not beforehand? If he cannot leave Luna immediately at least we could take a jaunt in our ship with him. That won't be gimmicked, not while Muddlehead is active."

"Listen, you glorified bulligator, I can see the obvious quicker than you, including the obvious fact that of course I'd suggest the ship. But he said no, not right away, at least. You see, one of the partners in SI invited him to spend a while at that castle of theirs."

"Strange. I had heard they never entertain guests."

"For once you heard right. But he said this anthro wants to discuss business with him, wouldn't tell him what but hinted at large profits. The chance looked too good to miss. Only, the invitation was for immediately. He'd just time to duck back to his place for a clean shirt and a toothbrush."

"Will Freeman van Rijn's affair wait?" Adzel said.

"Presumably," Chee said. "At any rate, Dave wasn't sure the socializing mood of the partners would last if he stalled them. By every account, their souls consist of printed circuits. If nothing else comes of visiting them at home, he felt this was a unique chance for an inside view of their outfit."

"Indeed." Adzel nodded. "Indeed. David acted quite correctly, when the opportunity concerns an organization so powerful and enigmatic. I do not see what makes you feel any urgency. We two simply have to spend a few more days here."

Chee bristled. "I don't have your stone-brained calm. The computer put Dave onto something big. I mean astronomical—money by the planetful. I could tell that by his manner. Suppose his hosts aim to do him in, for the sake of getting at that thing themselves?"

"Now, now, my little friend," Adzel chided. "Serendipity, Inc., does not meddle in the business of its clients. It does not reveal their secrets. As a rule, the partners do not even know what those secrets are. They have no ties to other organizations. Not only repeated private investigations, but the experience of years has confirmed this. If ever they had violated their own announced ethic, ever shown special favor or prejudice, the repercussions would soon have laid the deed bare. No other member of the Polesotechnic League—no group thoughout the whole of known space—has proven itself more trustworthy."

"Always a first time, sonny."

"Well, but think. If the strain is not excessive," Adzel said with rare tartness. "For the sake of argument, let us make the ridiculous assumption that Serendipity did in fact eavesdrop on David's conference with the computer, and has in fact decided to break its word never to seize private advantage.

"It remains bound by the covenant of the League, a covenant which was established and is enforced for good pragmatic reasons. Imprisonment, murder, torture, drugs, brainscrub, every kind of direct attack upon the psychobiological integrity of the individual, is banned. The consequences of transgression are atavistically severe. As the saying goes on Earth, the game is not worth the lantern. Hence the resources of espionage, temptation, and coercion are limited. David is immune to bribery and blackmail. He will reveal nothing to hypothetical surveillance, nor will he fall into conversational traps. If female bait is dangled before him, he will delightedly accept it without touching the fishhook. Has he not already—"

At that point, in a coincidence too outrageous for anything other than real life, the phone buzzed. Adzel pressed the Accept button. The image of Falkayn's latest girl friend appeared. His partners recognized her; they had both met her, briefly, and were too experienced to believe the old cliché that all humans look alike.

"Good evenwatch, Freelady," Adzel said. "May I be of assistance?"

Her expression was unhappy, her tone unsteady. "I apologize for disturbing you," she said. "But I'm trying to get hold of Da—Captain Falkayn. He's not come back. Do you know—?"

"He isn't here either, I am sorry to say."

"He promised he'd meet me . . . before now . . . and he hasn't, and—" Veronica swallowed. "I'm worried."

"A rather urgent matter arose. He lacked time in which to contact you," Adzel lied gallantly. "I was asked to convey his sincere regrets."

Her smile was forlorn. "Was the urgent matter blond or brunette?"

"Neither, Freelady. I assure you it involves *his* profession. He may be gone for a few standard days. Shall I remind him to phone you upon his return?"

"I'd be grateful if you would, sir." She twisted her fingers together. "Th-thank you."

Adzel blanked the screen. "I am reluctant to state this of a friend," he murmured, "but occasionally David impresses me as being rather heartless in certain respects."

"Huh!" Chee said. "That creature's only afraid he'll get away without spilling information to her."

"I doubt it. Oh, I grant you such a motive has been present, and probably continues in some degree. But her distress looks genuine, insofar as I can read human behavior. She appears to have conceived a personal affection for him." Adzel made a commiserating noise. "How much more conducive to serenity is a fixed rutting season like mine."

Chee had been calmed by the interruption. Also, her wish to get out of this lead-weighting bake oven that Adzel called home grew stronger each minute. "That is a good-looking specimen, by Dave's standards," she said. "No wonder he delayed getting down to work. And I don't suppose he'll be overly slow about returning to her, until he's ready to haul gravs off Luna altogether. Maybe we needn't really fret on his account."

"I trust not," Adzel said.

V

BY flitter, the castle in the Alps was not many minutes from Lunograd. But those were terrible kilometers that lay between; mountaineering parties never ventured so far. And a wide reach of land and sky around the site was forbidden—patrolled by armed men, guarded by robot gun emplacements—with that baronial absoluteness the great may claim in a civilization which exalts the rights of privacy and property.

A nonhuman labor force had built it, imported for the purpose from a dozen remote planets and afterward returned, totally dispersed. For a while, local resentment combined with curiosity to yield fantastic rumors. Telescopic pictures were taken from orbit, and published, until half the Commonwealth knew about gaunt black towers, sheer walls, comings and goings of ships at a special spaceport, in the Lunar mountains.

But gossip faded with interest. Large estates were common enough among the lords of the Polesotechnic League—most of whom carried on in a far more colorful fashion than these recluses. Furtiveness and concealment were a frequent part of normal business practice. For years, now, Serendipity, Inc., had been taken for granted.

To be sure, Falkayn thought, *if the society news learns I've been chauffeured out here, actually gotten inside*—A sour grin tugged at his mouth. *Wouldn't it be cruel to tell the poor dears the truth?*

The scenery was spectacular, from this upper-level room where he stood. A wide viewport showed the downward sweep of rock, crags, cliffs, talus slopes, to a gash of blackness. Opposite that valley, and on either side of the castle plateau, peaks lifted raw into the constellations. Earth hung low in the south, nearly full, nearly blinding in its brilliance; interminable shadows surrounded the bluish spotlight that it cast.

But you could watch the same, or better, from a number of lodges: where there would be merriment, music, decoration, decent food and decent talk. The meal he had just finished, shortly after his arrival, had been as grimly functional as what he saw of the many big chambers. Conversation, with the four partners who were present, had consisted of banalities punctuated by silences. He excused himself as soon as he could. That was obviously sooner than they wished, but he knew the glib phrases and they didn't.

Only in the office had he been offered a cigar. He decided that was because the gesture was programmed into the kind of lounger they had bought. He reached inside his tunic for pipe and tobacco. Kim Yoon-Kun, a small neat expression-less man in a pajama suit that managed to resemble a uniform, had followed him. "We don't mind if you smoke at the table, Captain Falkayn," he said, "though none of us practice the . . . amusement."

"Ah, but I mind," Falkayn answered. "I was strictly raised to believe that pipes are not allowed in dining areas. At the same time, I crave a puff. Please bear with me."

"Of course," said the accented voice. "You are our guest. Our sole regret is that Freeman Latimer and Freelady Beldaniel cannot be present."

Odd, Falkayn thought, not for the first time. *Hugh Latimer leaves his wife here, and goes off with Thea's sister.* Mentally, he shrugged. Their pairing arrangements were their own affair. If they had any. By every account, Latimer was as dry a stick as Kim, despite being an accomplished space pilot. The wife, like Anastasia Herrera and no doubt the sister of Thea, succeeded in being more old-maidish than the latter. Their attempt to make small talk with the visitor would have been pathetic had it been less dogged.

What matters, Falkayn thought, *is getting out of here, back to town and some honest fun. E.g., with Veronica.*

"This is not an ideal room for you, though," Kim said with a starched smile. "You observe how sparsely furnished it is. We are six people and a few nonhuman servants. We built this place large with a view to eventual expansion, bringing in more associates, perhaps spouses and children in time, if that proves feasible. But as yet we, ah, rattle around. I believe you and we should converse in a more amenable place. The others are already going there. We can serve coffee and brandy if you wish. May I conduct you?"

"Thanks," Falkayn said. The doubtless rehearsed speech did not quench his hope of soon being able to leave what had proven to be a citadel of boredom. "We can start talking business?"

"Why—" Startled, Kim searched for words. "It was not planned for this evenwatch. Is not the custom that social activity precede . . . that one get acquainted? We assume you will stay with us for several days, at least. Some interesting local excursions are possible from here, for example. And we will enjoy hearing you relate your adventures in distant parts of space."

"You're very kind," Falkayn said, "but I'm afraid I haven't time."

"Did you not tell the younger Freelady Beldaniel—"

"I was mistaken. I checked with my partners, and they told me my boss has started to sweat rivets. Why don't you sketch out your proposition right away, to help me decide how long he might let me stay in connection with it?"

"Proper discussion requires material we do not keep in our dwelling." Impatience, a touch of outright nervousness, cracked slightly the mask that was Kim Yoon-Kun. "But come, we can lay your suggestion before the others."

The knowledge hit Falkayn: *He's almighty anxious to get me out of this particular room, isn't he?* "Do you mean we'll discuss the commencement of discussions?" he hedged. "That's a funny one. I didn't ask for documentation. Can't you simply explain in a general way what you're after?"

"Follow me." Kim's tone jittered. "We have problems of security, the preservation of confidences, that must be dealt with in advance."

Falkayn began enjoying himself. He was ordinarily a genial, obliging young man; but those who push a merchant adventurer, son of a military aristocrat, must expect to be pushed back, hard. He donned hauteur. "If you do not trust me, sir, your invitation was a mistake," he said. "I don't wish to squander your valuable time with negotiations fore-doomed to fruitlessness."

"Nothing of the sort." Kim took Falkayn's arm. "Come along, if you please, and all shall be made clear."

Falkayn stayed put. He was stronger and heavier; and the gravity field was set at about Earth standard, the usual practice in residences on dwarf worlds where muscles would otherwise atrophy. His resistance to the tug did not show through his tunic. "In a while, Freeman," he said. "Not at once, I beg of your indulgence. I came here to meditate."

Kim let go and stepped back. The black eyes grew still narrower. "Your dossier does not indicate any religious affiliation," he said slowly.

"Dossier?" Falkayn raised his brows with ostentation.

"The integrated file of material our computer has about you—nothing except what is on public record," Kim said in haste. "Only in order that our company may serve you better."

"I see. Well, you're right, except that one of my shipmates is a Buddhist—converted years ago, while studying on Earth—and he's gotten me interested. Besides," Falkayn said, warming up, "it's quite a semantic quibble whether the purer sects of Buddhism are religious, in the ordinary sense. Certainly they are agnostic with respect to gods or other hypothetical animistic elements in the reality-complex; their doctrine of karma does not require reincarnation as that term is generally used; and in fact, nirvana is not annihilation, but rather is a state that may be achieved in this life and consists of—"

And then it was too late for Kim.

The spaceship slanted across the view, a lean cylinder that glowed under Earthlight and shimmered within the driving gravfields. She swung into vertical ascent and dwindled from sight until lost in the cold of the Milky way.

"Well," Falkayn murmured. "Well, well."

He glanced at Kim. "I suppose Latimer and Beldaniel are crewing her?" he said.

"A routine trip," Kim answered, fists knotted at sides.

"Frankly, sir, I doubt that." Falkayn remembered the pipe he held and began to stuff it. "I know hyperdrive craft when I see them. They are not used for interplanetary shuttling; why tie up that much capital when a cheaper vessel will do? For the same reason, common carriers are employed interstellar wherever practical. And full partners in a big company don't make long voyages as a matter of routine. Clear to see, this job is on the urgent side."

And you didn't want me to know, he added unspoken. His muscles grew taut. *Why not?*

Wrath glittered at him. He measured out a chuckle. "You needn't have worried about me, if you did," he said. "I wouldn't pry into your secrets."

Kim eased a trifle. "Their mission is important, but irrelevant to our business with you," he said.

Is it? Falkayn thought. *Why didn't you tell me at the beginning, then, instead of letting me grow suspicious?—I believe I know why. You're so isolated from the human mainstream, so untrained in the nuances of how people think and act, that you doubted your own ability to convince me this takeoff is harmless as far as I'm concerned . . . when it probably isn't!*

Again Kim attempted a smile. "But pardon me, Captain Falkayn. We have no desire to intrude upon your religious practices. Please remain, undisturbed, as long as you wish. When you desire company, you may employ the intercom yonder, and one of us will come to guide you to the other room." He bowed. "May you have a pleasant spirtual experience."

Touché! Falkayn thought, staring after the man's back. *Since the damage has been done, he turns my yarn right around on me—his aim being to keep me here for some time, and my navel-watching act presenting him with an extra hour—but what's the purpose of it all?*

He lit his pipe and made volcano clouds, strode to and fro, looked blindly out the viewport, flung himself into chairs and bounced up again. Was he nursing an empty, automatic distrust of the merely alien, or did he feel a real wrongness in his bones?

The idea was not new with him, that information given the computers at Serendipity did not remain there. The partners had never let those circuits be traced by an independent investigator. They could easily have installed means for playing back an item or listening in on a conversation. They could instruct a machine to slant its advice as they desired. And—cosmos—once faith in them had developed, once the masters of the League started making full use of their service, what a spy they had! What a saboteur!

Nevertheless the fact stood: not one of those wary, wily enterprisers had ever found the least grounds for believing that Serendipity was in unfair collaboration with any of his rivals, or attempting to sneak in on anyone's operations, not even to the extent of basing investments on advance knowledge.

Could be they've decided to change their policy. That planet of mine could tempt the most virtuous into claim-jumping. . . . But sunder it, that doesn't feel right either. Six personalities as rigid as these don't switch from information broker to pirate on an hour's notice. They don't.

Falkayn checked his watch. Thirty minutes had passed, sufficient time for his pretense. (Which probably wasn't believed anyway.) He strode to the intercom, found it set for its station number 14, flipped the switch and said, "I'm done now."

Scarcely had he turned when Thea Beldaniel was in the doorway. "That was quick!" he exclaimed.

"I happened to be near. The message was relayed to me." *Or were you waiting this whole while?*

She approached, halting when they both reached the viewport. Her walk was more graceful, in a high-necked long-sleeved gown, and her smile more convincingly warm, than before. A gawkiness remained, and she poised stiffly after she had entered his arm's length. But he felt himself attracted for some odd reason. Maybe she was a challenge, or maybe she was just a well-formed animal.

He knocked out his pipe. "I hope I didn't give offense," he said.

"Not in the least. I quite sympathize. The outlook inspires you, does it not?" She gestured at a control panel. Lights dimmed; the eldritch moonscape stood forth before their vision.

No pressure on me now, Falkayn thought cynically. *Contrariwise. The longer I dawdle before reporting to Old Nick, the happier they'll be. Well, no objections from my side for the nonce. This has suddenly gotten interesting. I have a lot of discreet curiosity to satisfy.*

"Glory out there," she whispered.

He regarded her. Earthlight lifted her profile from shadow and poured softly downward. Stars glimmered in her eyes. She looked into their wintry myriads with a kind of hunger.

He blurted, caught by an abrupt compassion that surprised him, "You feel at home in space, don't you?"

"I can't be sure." Still she gazed skyward. "Not here, I confess. Never here. You must forgive us if we are poor company. It comes from shyness, ignorance ... fear, I suppose. We live alone and work with data—abstract symbols—because we are fit to do nothing else."

Falkayn didn't know why she should reveal herself to him. But wine had been served at dinner. The etiquette book could have told them this was expected, and the drink could have gone to her inexperienced head.

"I'd say you've done fine, beginning as complete strangers," he told her. "You did, am I right? Strangers to your whole species?"

"Yes." She sighed. "You may as well know. We declined to state our background originally because, oh, we couldn't foresee what the reaction might be. Later, when we were more familiar with this culture, we had no reason to tell; people had stopped asking, and we were set in our asocial ways. Besides, we didn't want personal publicity. Nor do we now." She glanced at him. In this blue elflight, the crisp middle-aged businesswoman had become a young girl again, who asked for his mercy. "You won't speak ... to the news ... will you?"

"On my honor," he said, and meant it.

"The story is simple, really," said her muted voice. "A ship, bound from one of the colonized planets in search of her own world. I understand those aboard left because of a political dispute; and yet I don't understand. The whole thing seems utterly meaningless. Why should rational beings quarrel about—No matter. Families sold everything they had, pooled the money, bought and outfitted a large ship with the most complete and modern robotic gear available. And they departed."

"Into the complete unknown?" Falkayn asked, incredulous. "Not one preliminary scouting expedition?"

"The planets are many where men can live. They were sure they would find one. They wanted to leave no hint to their enemies where it was."

"But—I mean, they must have known how tricky a new world can be—tricks of biochemistry, disease, weather, a million unpredictable tricks and half of them lethal if you aren't on your guard—"

"I said this was a large, fully stocked, fully equipped vessel," she retorted. The sharpness left her as she went on. "They were prepared to wait in orbit while tests proceeded. That was well for us. You see, en route the radiation screens broke down in a bad sector. Apart from the nursery, where we infants were, which had an auxiliary generator, every part of the ship got a fatal dose. The people might have been saved in a hospital, but they could never reach one in time, especially since the autopilot systems were damaged too. Supportive treatment kept them functional barely long enough to fix the screens and program some robots. Then they died. The machines cared for us children; raised us, in a loveless mechanical fashion. They educated those who survived—willy-nilly, a hodgepodge of mainly technical information crammed into our brains. We didn't mind that too much, however. The ship was such a barren environment that any distractions were welcome. We had nothing else except each other.

"Our ages ranged from twelve to seventeen when we were found. The vessel had kept going under low hyperdrive, in the hope she would finally pass within detection range of somebody. The somebodies proved to be nonhuman. But they were kindly, did what they were able for us. They were too late, of course, for the shaping of normal personalities. We stayed with our rescuers, on their planet, for several years.

"Never mind where," she added quickly. "They know about the League—there have been occasional brief encounters—but their leaders don't want an ancient civilization corrupted by exposure to your cannibal capitalism. They mind their own lives and avoid drawing attention to themselves.

"But the physical environment was not good for us. Besides, the feeling grew that we should attempt to rejoin our race. What they learned from our ship had advanced our hosts technologically in several fields. As a fair exchange— they have an unbendable moral code—they helped us get a start, first with a valuable cargo of metal and later with the computer units we decided we could use. Also, they are glad to have friends who are influential in the League; sooner or later, increased contact is unavoidable. And that," Thea Beldaniel finished, "is the story behind Serendipity, Inc."

Her smile went no deeper than her teeth. Her voice held a tinge of the fanaticism he had met in her office.

Only a tinge? But what she'd been relating here was not operational procedure; it was her life!

Or was it? Parts of the account rang false to him. At a minimum, he'd want more details before he agreed it could be the absolute truth. No doubt some fact was interwoven. But how much, and how significant to his purposes?

"Unique," was all he could think to say.

"I don't ask for pity," she said with a firmness he admired. "Obviously, our existence could have been far worse. I wondered, though, if—perhaps"—voice and eyes dropped, fluttered in confusion—"you, who've seen so much, done so much beyond these bounds—if you might understand."

"I'd like to try," Falkayn said gently.

"Would you? Can you? I mean . . . suppose you stayed a while . . . and we could talk like this, and do, oh, the little things—the big things—whatever is human—you might be able to teach me how to be human...."

"Is that what you wanted me for? I'm afraid I—"

"No. No. I realize you . . . you must put your work first. I think—taking what we know, we partners—exchange ideas with you—we might develop, something really attractive. No harm in exploring each other's notions for a while, is there? What can you lose? And at the same time—you and I—" She half turned. One hand brushed against his.

For an instant, Falkayn almost said yes. Among the greatest temptations that beset mankind is Pygmalion's. Potentially, she was quite a woman. The rogue could wait.

The rogue! Awareness crashed into him. *They do want to keep me here. It's their whole purpose. They have no definite proposals to make, only vague things they hope will delay me. I must not let them.*

Thea Beldaniel flinched back. "What's wrong?" she cried low. "Are you angry?"

"Eh?" Falkayn gathered his will, laughed and relaxed, picked his pipe off the viewport embrasure and took forth his tobacco pouch. The briar hadn't cooled, but he needed something to do. "No. Certainly not, Freelady. Unless I'm angry at circumstance. You see, I'd like to stay, but I have no choice. I have got to go back tomorrow mornwatch, kicking and screaming maybe, but back."

"You said you could spend several days."

"As I told Freeman Kim, that was before I learned old van Rijn's gnawing his whiskers."

"Have you considered taking a position elsewhere? Serendipity can make you a good offer."

"He has my contract and my fealty," Falkayn rapped. "I'm sorry. I'll be glad to confer with you people this whole nightwatch, if you desire. But then I'm off." He shrugged, though his skin prickled. "And what's your rush? I can return at another date, when I do have leisure."

Her look was desolate. "You cannot be persuaded?"

"I'm afraid not."

"Well . . . follow me to the meeting room, please." She thumbed the intercom and spoke a few words he did not recognize. They went down a high, stone-flagged corridor.

Her feet dragged, her head drooped.

Kim met them halfway. He stepped from an intersecting hall with a stun pistol in his grip. "Raise your hands, Captain," he said unemotionally. "You are not leaving soon."

VI

AFTER touching at Djakarta, Delfinburg proceeded by way of Makassar Strait and the Celebes into Pacific waters. At that point, an aircar deposited Nicholas van Rijn. He did not own the town; to be precise, his rights in it consisted of one house, one dock for a largish ketch, and seventy-three percent of the industry. But mayor and skipper agreed with his suggestion that they change course and pass nearer the Marianas than was usual on their circuit.

"Be good for the poor toilers, visiting those nice islands, *nie?*" he beamed, rubbing hairy hands together. "Could be they might also like a little holiday and come cheer their old honorific uncle when he enters the Micronesia Cup regatta on twenty-fourth of this month. That is, I will if we chance to be by the right place no later than twenty-second noon, and need to lay over a few days. I don't want to be you any bother."

The skipper made a quick calculation. "Yes, sir," he reported, "it so happens we'll arrive on the twenty-first." He signaled for an additional three knots. "And you know, you're right, it would be a good idea to stop a while and clean out the catalyst tanks or something."

"Good, good! You make a poor old lonely man very happy, how much he is in need of rest and recreation and maybe right now a gin and tonic to settle his stomach. A lot of settlement to make, hey?" Van Rijn slapped his paunch.

He spent the next week drilling his crew to a degree that would have appalled Captain Bligh. The men didn't really mind—sails dazzling against living, limitless, foam-laced blue across which the sun flung diamond dust; surge, pitch, thrum, hiss at the bows and salt on the lips, while the wind filled lungs with purity—except that he acted hurt when they declined to carouse with him every night. At length he gave them a rest. He wanted them tuned to an exact pitch for the next race, not overstrained. Besides, a business operating across two hundred light-years had inevitably accumulated problems requiring his personal attention. He groaned, cursed, and belched most piteously, but the work did not go away.

"Bah! Pox and pestilence! Work! Four-letter Angular-Saxon word! Why must I, who should be having my otium, should at my age be serene and spewing wisdom on younger generations, why must I use up grindstones against my nose? Have I not got a single deputy whose brain is not all thumbs?"

"You could sell out, for more money than you can spend in ten lifetimes," answered his chief secretary, who was of a warrior caste in a tigerish species and thus required to be without fear. "Or you would finish your tasks in half the time if you stopped whining."

"I let my company, that I built from scratches and got maybe millions of what claim to be thinking beings hanging off it, I let that go crunch? Or I sit meek like my mouth won't smelt butter, and not say pip about vacuum-conscience competitors, subordinates with reverse peristalsis, guilds, brotherhoods, unions, leeches, and"—van Rijn gathered his breath before shouting the ultimate obscenity—*"bureaucrats?* No, no, old and tired and feeble and lonesome I am, but I wield my sword to the last bullet. We get busy, ha?"

An office had been established for him in an upper-level solarium of his mansion. Beyond the ranked phones, computers, recorders, data retrievers, and other portable business equipment, the view was broad, from one many-tiered unit to the next, of that flotilla which comprised Delfinburg. There was not much overt sign of production. You might notice turbulence around the valves of a minerals-extraction plant, or the shadow traces of submarines herding fish, or the appetizing scents from a factory that turned seaweeds into condiments. But most of the work was interior, camouflaged by hanging gardens, shops, parks, schools, recreation centers. Few sportboats were out; the ocean was choppy today, although you could not have told that blindfolded on these stabilized superbarges.

Van Rijn settled his huge body into a lounger. He was clad only in a sarong and a lei; why not be comfortable while he suffered? "Commence!" he bawled. The machines chattered, regurgitating facts, calculations, assessments, summaries, and proposals. The principal phone screen flickered with the first call, from a haggard man who had newly escaped a war ten parsecs distant. Meanwhile a set of loudspeakers emitted Mozart's Eighth Symphony; a scarcely clothed young woman fetched beer; another lit the master's Trichinopoly cigar; a third set forth a trayful of fresh Danish sandwiches in case he got hungry. She came incautiously near, and he swept her to him with one gorilla arm. She giggled and ran her fingers through the greasy black ringlets that fell to his shoulders.

"What you making fumblydiddles about?" van Rijn barked at the image. "Some piglet of a king burns our plantations, we give troops to his enemies what beat him and make terms allowing us poor sat-upon exploited meeters of inflated payrolls enough tiny profit we can live. *Nie?*" The man objected. Van Rijn's beady eyes popped. He tugged his goatee. His waxed mustaches quivered like horns. "What you mean, no local troops can face his? What you been doing these years, selling them maybe jackstraws for deadly weapons?—Hokay, hokay, I authorize you should bring in a division outplanet mercenaries. Try Diomedes. Grand Admiral Delp hyr Orikan, in Drak'ho Fleet, will remember me and may be spare a few restless young chaps what like adventure and booties. In six months, I hear everything is loverly-doverly, or you go find yourself a job scrubbing somebody else's latrines. *Tot weerziens!*" He waved his hand, and an assistant secretary switched to the next caller. Meanwhile he buried his great hook nose in his tankard, came up snorting and blowing foam, and held out the vessel for another liter.

A nonhuman head appeared in the screen. Van Rijn

replied by the same eerie set of whistles and quavers. Afterward, his sloping forehead corrugated with thought, he rumbled, "I hate like taxes admitting it, but that factor is almost competent, him. He settles his present trouble, I think we can knock him up to sector chief, ha?"

"I couldn't follow the discussion," said his chief secretary. "How many languages do you speak, sir?"

"Twenty-thirty bad. Ten-fifteen good. Anglic best of all." Van Rijn dismissed the girl who had been playing with his hair; though friendly meant, his slap to the obvious target as she started off produced a bombshell crack and a wail. "Hu, hu, little chickpea, I am sorry. You go buy that shimmerlyn gown you been wheedling at me about, and maybe tonight we trot out and show you off—you show plenty, shameless way such things is cut, oh, what those bandits charge for a few square centimeters cloth!" She squealed and scampered away before he changed his mind. He glowered at the other members of his current harem. "Don't you waggle at me too. You wait your turns to bleed a poor foolish old man out of what he's got left between him and beggary. . . . Well, who's next?"

The secretary had crossed the deck to study the phone in person. He turned about. "The agenda's been modified, sir. Direct call, Priority Two."

"Hum. Hum-hum." Van Rijn scratched the pelt that carpeted his chest, set down his beer, reached for a sandwich and engulfed it. "Who we got in these parts now, authoritied for using Priority Two?" He swallowed, choked, and cleared his throat with another half-liter draught. But thereafter he sat quite still, cigar to lips, squinting through the smoke, and said with no fuss whatsoever, "Put them on."

The screen flickered. Transmission was less than perfect, when a scrambled beam must leave a moving spaceship, punch through the atmosphere, and stay locked on the solitary station that could unscramble and relay. Van Rijn identified the control cabin of his pioneer vessel *Muddlin' Through,* Chee Lan in the foreground and Adzel behind her. "You got problems?" he greeted mildly.

The pause was slight but noticeable, while electromagnetic radiation traversed the distance between. "I believe we do," Adzel said. Interference hissed around his words. "And we cannot initiate corrective measures. I would give much for those machines and flunkies that surround you to have allowed us a direct contact before today."

"I'll talk," Chee said. "You'd blither for an hour." To van Rijn: "Sir, you'll remember we told you, when reporting on Earth, that we'd proceed to Lunograd and look in on Serendipity, Inc." She described Falkayn's visit there and subsequently to the castle. "That was two weeks ago. He hasn't come back yet. One call arrived after three standard days. Not a real talk—a message sent while he knew we'd be asleep. We kept the record, of course. He said not to worry; he was on to what might be the most promising lead of his career, and he might be quite some time following it up. We needn't stay on Luna, he would take a shuttle-boat to Earth." Her fur stood out, a wild aureole around her countenance. "It wasn't his style. We had voice and somatic analysis done at a detective agency, using several animations of him from different sources. It's him, beyond reasonable doubt. But it's *not* his style."

"Playback," van Rijn ordered. "Now. Before you go on." He watched unblinkingly as the blond young man spoke his piece and signed off. "By damn, you have right, Chee Lan. He should at least grin and ask you give his love to three or four girls."

"We've been pestered by one, for certain," the Cynthian declared. "A spy set on him, who found she couldn't cope with his technique or whatever the deuce he's got. Last call, she actually admitted she'd been on a job, and blubbered she was sorry and she'd never, never, never— You can reconstruct the sequence."

"Play her anyhow." Veronica wept. "*Ja*, a bouncy wench there. Maybe I interview her personal, ho-ho! Somebody got to. Such a chance to get a look inside whoever hired her!" Van Rijn sobered. "What happened next?"

"We fretted," Chee said. "At last even this big lard statue of a saint here decided that enough was too furious much. We marched into the SI office itself and said if we didn't get a more satisfactory explanation, from Dave himself, we'd start disassembling their computers. With a pipe wrench. They quacked about the convenant, not to mention the civil police, but in the end they promised he'd phone us." Grimly: "He did. Here's the record."

The conversation was long. Chee yelled, Adzel expostulated, Falkayn stayed deadpan and unshakable. "—I am sorry. You may never guess how sorry I am, old friends. But nobody gets a choice about how the lightning's going to strike him. Thea's my woman, and there's an end on the matter.

"We'll probably go aroving after we get married. I'll be working for SI. But only in a technical sense. Because what we're really after, what's keeping me here, is something bigger, more fundamental to the whole future, than— No. I can't say more. Not yet. But think about making liaison with a genuinely superior race. The race that's been dreamed about for centuries, and never found—the Elders, the Wise Ones, the evolutionary step beyond us—

"—Yes!" A flicker of irritation. "Naturally SI will refund Solar S & L's wretched payments. Maybe SI should double the sum. Because a fact that I supplied was what started our whole chain of discovery. Though what possible reward could match the service?

"—Good-bye. Good faring."

Silence dwelt, under the wash of sea waves and whisper of stars. Until van Rijn shook himself, animal fashion, and said, "You took into space and called me today when I got available."

"What else could we do?" Adzel groaned. "David may be under psychocontrol. We suspect it, Chee and I. But we have no proof. For anyone who does not know him personally, the weight of credibility is overwhelming on the opposite side, so great that I myself can reach no firm conclusion about what has really happened. More is involved than Serendipity's established reputation. There is the entire covenant. Members of the League do not kidnap and drug each other's agents. Not ever!"

"We did ask the Lunar police about a warrant," Chee said. She jerked her tail at the Wodenite. "Tin Pan Buddha insisted. We were laughed at. Literally. We can't propose a League action—strike first, argue with the law afterward—

not us. We aren't on the Council. You are."

"I can propose it," van Rijn said carefully. "After a month's wringle-wrangle, I get voted no. They won't believe either, SI would do something so bad like that, for some sternly commercial reason."

"I doubt if we have a month, regardless," Chee said. "Think. Suppose Dave has been brainscrubbed. They'll've done it to keep him from reporting to you what he learned from their damned machine. They'll pump him for information and advice too. Might as well. But he is evidence against them. Any medic can identify his condition and cure it. So as soon as possible—or as soon as necessary—they'll get rid of the evidence. Maybe send him off in a spaceship with his new fiancée to control him. Maybe kill him and disintegrate the body. I don't see where Adzel and I had any alternative except to investigate as we did. Nevertheless, our investigations will probably cause SI to speed up whatever timetable it's laid out for Captain Falkayn."

Van Rijn smoked through an entire minute. Then: "Your ship is loaded for bear, also elephant and walrus. You could maybe blast in, you two, and snatch him?"

"Maybe," Adzel said. "The defenses are unknown. It would be an act of piracy."

"Unless he was a prisoner. In what case, we can curry ruffled fur afterward. I bet curried fur tastes terrible. But you turn into heroes."

"What if he is there voluntarily?"

"You turn into pumpkins."

"If we strike, we risk his life," said Adzel. "Quite possibly, if he is not a prisoner, we take several innocent lives. We are less concerned with our legal status than with our shipmate. But however deep our affection for him, he is of another civilization, another species, yes, a wholly different evolution. We cannot tell whether he was in a normal state when he called us. He acted peculiarly, true. But might that have been due to the emotion known as love? Coupled, perhaps, with a sense of guilt at breaking his contract? You are human, we are not. We appeal to your judgment."

"And mix me—old, tired, bothered, sorrowful me, that wants nothing except peace and a little, little profit—you

51

mix me right in with the glue," van Rijn protested.

Adzel regarded him steadily. "Yes, sir. If you authorize us to attack, you commit yourself and everything you own, for the sake of one man who may not even need help. We realize that."

Van Rijn drew on his cigar till the end glowed volcanic. He pitched it aside. "Hokay," he growled. "Is a flousy boss does not stand by his people. We plan a raid, us, ha?" He tossed off his remaining beer and threw the tankard to the deck. "God damn," he bellowed, "I wish I was going along!"

VII

ADZEL paused at the airlock. "You will be careful, won't you?" he asked.

Chee bristled. "You're the one to worry about, running around without a keeper. Watch yourself, you oversized clatterbrain." She blinked. "Rats and roaches! Something in my eyes. Get started—out of my way."

Adzel closed his faceplate. Encased in space armor, he could just fit inside the lock. He must wait until he had cycled through before securing his equipment on his back. It included a small, swivel-mounted automatic cannon.

Muddlin' Through glided from him, low above soaring, jagged desolation. Mottled paint made her hard to see against the patchwork of blinding noon and ink-black shadow. When past the horizon, she climbed.

Adzel stayed patiently put until the seething in his radio earplugs was broken by the Cynthian's voice: "Hello, do you read me?"

"Like a primer," he said. Echoes filled his helmet. He was aware of the mass he carried, protective but heavy; of the smells, machine and organic, already accumulating; of temperature that began to mount and prickle him under the scales.

"Good. This beam's locked onto you, then. I'm stabilized in position, about a hundred and fifty kilometers up. No radar has fingered me yet. Maybe none will. All check, sir?"

"*Ja.*" Van Rijn's words, relayed from a hired maser in Lunograd, sounded less distinct. "I have talked with the police chief here and he is not suspecting. I got my boys set to start a fracas that will make distractions. I got a judge ready to hand out injunctions if I tell him. But he is not a very high judge, even if he is expensive like Beluga caviar, so he can't make long stalls either. Let the Lunar federal police mix in this affair and we got troubles. Ed Garver would sell the soul he hasn't got to jail us. You better be quick like kissing a viper. Now I go aboard my own boat, my friends, and light candles for you in the shrine there, to St. Dismas, and St. Nicholas, and especial to St. George, by damn."

Adzel couldn't help remarking, "In my studies of Terrestrial culture, I have encountered mention of that latter personage. But did not the Church itself, as far back as the twentieth century, decide he was mythical?"

"Bah," said van Rijn loftily. "They got no faith. I need a good fighting saint, who says God can't improve the past and make me one?"

Then there was no time, or breath, or thought for anything except speed.

Adzel could have gone quicker and easier on a gravsled or some such vehicle. But the radiations would have given him away. Afoot, he could come much nearer before detection was certain. He bounded up the Alpine slopes, over razorback ridges, down into ravines and out their other sides, around crater walls and crags. His heart slugged, his lung strained, in deep steady rhythm. He used the forward tendency of his mass—great inertia at low weight—and the natural pendulum-periods of his legs, to drive himself. Sometimes he overleaped obstacles, soaring in an arc and landing with an impact that beat through his bones. He kept to the shade wherever possible. But pitilessly, at each exposure to sunlight, heat mounted within his camouflaged armor faster than his minimal cooling system could shed it. Glare filters did not entirely protect his eyes from the raw sundazzle. No human could have done what he did—hardly anyone, indeed, of any race, except the children of a fiercer star than Sol and a vaster planet than Earth.

Twice he crouched where he could and let a patrol boat slip overhead. After an hour, he wormed his way from shadow to shadow, evading a watchpost whose radar and guns stood skeletal against the sky. And he won to the final peak unheralded.

The castle loomed at the end of an upward road, black witchhatted towers above battlemented walls. With no further chance of concealment, Adzel started openly along the path. For a moment, the spatial silence pressed in so huge that it well-nigh smothered pulse, breath, airpump, foot-thuds. Then: "Who goes there? Halt!" on the standard band.

"A visitor," Adzel replied without slacking his even trot. "I have an urgent matter to discuss and earnestly request admittance."

"Who are you? How did you get here?" The voice was female human, accented, and shrill with agitation. "Stop, I tell you! This is private property. No trespassing."

"I humbly beg pardon, but I really must insist on being received."

"Go back. You will find a gatehouse at the foot of the road. You may shelter there and tell me what you have to say."

"Thank you for your kind offer." Adzel kept advancing. "Freelady...ah...Beldaniel, I believe? It is my understanding that your partners are presently at their office. Please correct me if I am wrong."

"I said go back!" she screamed. "Or I open fire! I have the right. You have been warned."

"Actually my business is with Captain Falkayn." Adzel proceeded. He was quite near the main portal. Its outer valve bulked broad in the fused-stone wall. "If you will be good enough to inform him that I wish to talk to him, viva voce, we can certainly hold our discussion outdoors. Permit me to introduce myself. I am one of his teammates. My claim upon his attention therefore takes precedence over the seclusion of your home. But I have no real wish to intrude, Freelady."

"You're not his companion. Not any more. He resigned. He spoke to you himself. He does not want to see you."

"With profoundest regret and sincerest apologies for any inconvenience caused, I am compelled to require a direct confrontation."

"He...he isn't here. I will have him call you later."

"Since you may conceivably be in error as to his whereabouts, Freelady, perhaps you will graciously allow me to search your premises?"

"No! This is your last warning! Stop this instant or you'll be killed!"

Adzel obeyed; but within the armor, his muscles bunched. His left hand worked the cannon control. In his palm lay a tiny telescreen whose cross hairs centered on the same view as the muzzle. His right hand loosened his blast pistol in its holsters.

"Freelady," he said, "violence and coercion are deplorable. Do you realize how much merit you have lost? I beg of you—"

"Go back!" Half hysterical, the voice broke across. "I'll give you ten seconds to turn around and start downhill. One. Two."

"I was afraid of this." Adzel sighed. And he sprang—but forward. His cannon flung three shaped charges at the main gate. Fire spurted, smoke puffed, shrapnel flew, eerily soundless except for a quiver through the ground.

Two energy beams flashed at him, out of the turrets that flanked the entry port. He had already bounded aside. His cannon hammered. One emplacement went down in a landslide of rubble. Smoke and dust whirled, veiling him from the other. By the time it had settled, he was up to the wall, beneath the gun's reach.

The outer valve sagged, twisted metal. "I'm headed in," he said to Chee Lan, and fired through the chamber. A single shell tore loose the second, less massive barrier. Air gushed forth, momentarily white as moisture froze, vanishing as fog dissipated under the cruel sun.

Inside, an illumination now undiffused fell in puddles on a disarrayed antechamber. Through its shadows, he noticed a few pictures and a brutally massive statue. The artistic conventions were foreign to anything he had encountered in all his wanderings. He paid scant attention. Which way to David, in this damned warren? Like a great steel hound, he cast about for clues. Two hallways led off in opposite directions. But one held empty rooms; the chambers fronting on the other were furnished, albeit sparsely. *Hm, the builders plan on enlarging the castle's population sometime. But with whom, or what?* He galloped down the inhabited corridor. Before long he encountered a bulkhead that had automatically closed when pressure dropped.

Beldaniel's retainers were probably on the other side of it, spacesuited, expecting to give him a full barrage when he cracked through. She herself was no doubt on the phone, informing her partners in Lunograd of the invasion. With luck and management, van Rijn could tie up the police for a while. They must be kept off, because they were bound to act against the aggressor, Adzel. No matter what allegations he made, they would not ransack the castle until warrants had been issued. By that time, if it ever came, the Serendipity gang could have covered their tracks as regarded Falkayn in any of numerous ways.

But Beldaniel herself might attempt that, if Adzel didn't get busy. The Wodenite retreated to the foreroom and unlimbered his working gear. No doubt another chamber, belonging to the adjacent airseal section, lay behind this one. Though gastight, the interior construction was nowhere near as ponderous as the outworks. What he must do was enter unnoticed. He spread out a plastic bubblecloth, stood on it, and stuck its edges to the wall. His cutting torch flared. He soon made a hole, and waited until air had leaked through and inflated to full pressure the tent that now enclosed him. Finishing the incision, he removed the panel he had burned out and stepped into an apartment.

It was furnished with depressing austerity. He took a moment to pull the door off a closet—yes, female garb—and inspect a bookshelf. Many volumes were in a format and symbology he did not recognize; others, in Anglic, were texts describing human institutions for the benefit of visiting extraterrestrials. Boddhisatva! What sort of background did this outfit have, anyway?

He opened his faceplate, removed an earplug, and cautiously stuck his muzzle out into the hall. Clanks and rattles came to him from around a corner where the bulkhead must be. Hoarse words followed. The servants hadn't closed their helmets yet. . . . They were from several scarcely civilized planets, and no doubt even those who were not professional guards were trained in the use of modern weapons as well as household machinery. Cat-silent in his own armor. Adzel went the opposite way.

This room, that room, nothing. *Confound it—yes, I might go so far as to say curse it—David must be somewhere near.... Hold!* His wilderness-trained hearing had picked up the least of sounds. He entered a boudoir and activated its exterior scanner.

A woman went by, tall slacksuited, vigorous-looking in a lean fashion. Her face was white and tense, her breath rapid. From van Rijn's briefing, Adzel recognized Thea Beldaniel. She passed. Had she looked behind her, she would have seen four and a half meters of dragon following on tiptoe.

She came to a door and flung it wide. Adzel peeked around the jamb. Falkayn sat in the chamber beyond, slumped into a lounger. The woman hurried to him and shook him. "Wake up!" she cried. "Oh, hurry!"

"Huh? Uh. Whuzza?" Falkayn stirred. His voice was dull, his expression dead.

"Come along, darling. We must get out of here."

"Uhhh...." Falkayn shambled to his feet.

"Come, I say!" She tugged at his arm. He obeyed like a sleepwalker. "The tunnel to the spaceport. We're off for a little trip, my dear. But run!"

Adzel identified the symptoms. Brainscrub drugs, yes, in their entire ghastliness. You submerged the victim into a gray dream where he was nothing but what you told him to be. You could focus an encephaloductor beam on his head and a subsonic carrier wave on his middle ear. His drowned self could not resist the pulses thus generated; he would carry out whatever he was told, looking and sounding almost normal if you operated him skillfully but in truth a marionette. Otherwise he would simply remain where you stowed him.

In time, you could remodel his personality.

Adzel trod full into the entrance. "Now that is too bloody much!" he roared.

Thea Beldaniel sprang back. Her scream rose, went on and on. Falkayn stood hunched.

A yell answered, through the hallways. *My mistake,*

Adzel realized. *Perhaps not avoidable. But the guards have been summoned, and they have more armament than I do. Best we escape while we may.*

Nonetheless, van Rijn's orders had been flat and loud. "You get films of our young man, right away, and you take blood and spit samples, before anything else. Or I take them off you, hear me, and not in so polite a place neither!" It seemed foolish to the Wodenite, when death must arrive in a minute or two. But so rarely did the old man issue so inflexible a directive that Adzel decided he'd better obey.

"Excuse me, please." His tail brushed the shrieking woman aside and pinned her gently but irresistibly to the wall. He tabled his camera, aimed it at Falkayn, set it on Track, and left it to work while he used needle and pipette on the flesh that had been his comrade. (And would be again, by everything sacred, or else be honorably dead!) Because he was calm about it, the process took just a few seconds. He stowed the sample tubes in a pouch, retrieved the camera, and gathered Falkayn in his arms.

As he came out the door, half a dozen retainers arrived. He couldn't shoot back, when he must shield the human with his own body. He plowed through, scattering a metallic bow wave. His tail sent two of the opposition off on an aerial somersault. Bolts and bullets smote. Chaos blazed around him. Some shots were deflected, some pierced the armor—but not too deeply, and it was self-sealing and he was tough.

None could match his speed down the hall and up the nearest rampway. But they'd follow. He couldn't stand long against grenades or portable artillery. Falkayn, unprotected, would be torn to pieces sooner than that. It was necessary to get the devil out of this hellhole.

Up, up, up! He ended in a tower room, bare and echoing, its viewports scanning the whole savage moonscape. Beldaniel, or someone, must have recovered wits and called in the patrols, because several boats approached swift above the stonelands. At a distance, their guns looked pencil thin, but those were nasty things to face. Adzel set Falkayn down in a corner. Carefully, he drilled a small hole in a viewport through which he could poke the transmitter antenna on his helmet.

Since Chee Lan's unit was no longer locked on his, he broadened the beam and increased the power. "Hello, hello. Adzel to ship. Are you there?"

"No." Her reply was half-sneer, half-sob. "I'm on Mars staging a benefit for the Sweet Little Old Ladies' Knitting and Guillotine Watching Society. What have you bungled now?"

Adzel had already established his location with reference to published photographs of the castle's exterior and van Rijn's arbitrary nomenclature. "David and I are in the top of Snoring Beauty's Tower. He is indeed under brainscrub. I estimate we will be attacked from the ramp within five minutes. Or, if they decide to sacrifice this part of the structure, their flitters can demolish it in about three minutes. Can you remove us beforehand?"

"I'm halfway there already, idiot. Hang on!"

"You do not go aboard, Adzel," van Rijn cut in. "You stay outside and get set down where we agreed, hokay?"

"If possible," Chee clipped. "Shut up."

"I shut up to you," van Rijn said quietly. "Not right away to God."

Adzel pulled back his antenna and slapped a sealing patch on the hole. Little air had bled out. He looked over Falkayn. "I have a spacesuit here for you," he said. "Can you scramble into it?"

The clouded eyes met his without recognition. He sighed. No time to dress a passive body. From the spiraling rampwell, barbaric yells reached his ears. He couldn't use his cannon; in this narrow space, concussion would be dangerous to an unarmored Falkayn. The enemy was not thus restricted. And the patrols were converging like hornets.

And *Muddlin' Through* burst out of the sky.

The spaceship was designed for trouble—if need be, for war. Chee Lan was not burdened by any tenderness. Lightning flashed, briefly hiding the sun. The boats rained molten down the mountain. The spaceship came to a halt on gravfields alongside the turret. She could have sliced through, but that would have exposed those within to hard radiation. Instead, with tractor and pressor beams, she took the walls apart.

Air exploded outward. Adzel had clashed shut his own faceplate. He fired his blaster down the ramp, to discourage the servants, and collected Falkayn. The human was still unprotected, and had lost consciousness. Blood trickled from his nostrils. But momentary exposure to vacuum is not too harmful; deep-sea divers used to survive greater decompressions, and fluids do not begin to boil instantaneously. Abzel pitched Falkayn toward an open airlock. A beam seized him and reeled him in. The valve snapped shut behind him. Adzel sprang. He was caught likewise and clutched to the hull.

Muddlin' Through stood on her tail and grabbed herself some altitude.

Shaken, buffeted, the castle and the mountains spinning beneath him, Adzel still received van Rijn's orders to Chee Lan:

"—You let him down by where I told you. My yacht fetches him inside five minutes and takes us to Lunograd. But you, you go straight on with Falkayn. Maybe he is thick in the noodle, but he can tell you what direction to head in."

"Hoy, wait!" the Cynthian protested. "You never warned me about this."

"Was no time to make fancy plans, critchety-crotchety, for every possible outgo of happenings. How could I tell for sure what would be the circlestances? I thought probable it would be what it is, but maybe could have been better, maybe worse. Hokay. You start off."

"Look here, you fat pirate, my shipmate's drugged, hurt, sick! If you think for one picosecond he's going anywhere except to a hospital, I suggest you pull your head—the pointed one, that is—out of a position I would hitherto have sworn was anatomically impossible, and—"

"Whoa down, my furry friendling, easy makes it. From what you describe, his condition is nothing you can't cure en route. We fixed you with a complete kit and manual for unscrubbing minds and making them dirty again, not so? And what it cost, yow, would stand your hair on end so it flew out of the follicles! Do listen. This is big. Serendipity puts its whole existing on stake for whatever this is. We got to do the same."

"I like money as well as you do," Chee said with unwonted slowness. "But there are other values in life."

"Ja, ja." Adzel grew dizzy from the whirling away of the land beneath. He closed his eyes and visualized van Rijn in the transmitter room, churchwarden in one fist, chins wobbling as he ripped off words, but somehow acrackle. "Like what Serendipity is after. Got to be more than money.

"Think hard, Chee Lan. You know what I deducted from the facts? Davy Falkayn *had* to be under drugs, a prisoner chained worse than with irons. Why? Because a lot of things, like he wouldn't quit on me sudden . . . but mainly, he is human and I is human, and I say a healthy lecherous young man that would throw over Veronica—even if he didn't think Veronica is for anything except fun—what would throw over a bouncer-bouncer like that for a North Pole like Thea Beldaniel, by damn, he got something wrong in his upper story and maybe in his lower story too. So it looked probabilistic he was being mopped in the head.

"But what follows from this? Why, Serendipity was breaking the convenant of the Polesotechnic League. And that meant something big was on foot, worth the possible consequentials. Maybe worth the end of Serendipity itself—which is for sure now guaranteed!

"And what follows from that, little fluffymuff? What else, except the purpose was not commercial? For money, you play under rules, because the prize is not worth breaking them if you got the sense you need to be a strong player. But you could play for different things—like war, conquest, power—and those games is not nice, ha? The League made certain Serendipity was not doing industrial espionaging. But there is other kinds. Like to some outsider—somebody outside the whole of civilizations we know about—somebody hidden and ergo very, very likely our self-appointed enemy. *Nie?"*

Adzel's breath sucked in between his teeth.

"We got no time for fumblydiddles," van Rijn went on.

"They sent off a messenger ship two weeks ago. Leastwise, Traffic Control records clearing it from the castle with two of the partners aboard personal. Maybe you can still beat their masters to wherever the goal is. In every case, you and Falkayn makes the best we got, right now in the Solar System, to go look. But you wait one termite-bitten hour, the police is in action and you is detained for material witnesses.

"No, get out while you can. Fix our man while you travel. Learn what gives, yonderwards, and report back to me, yourselfs or by robocourier. Or mail or passenger pigeon or whatever is your suits. The risk is big but maybe the profits is in scale. Or maybe the profit is keeping our lives or our freedom. Right?"

"Yes," said Chee faintly, after a long pause. The ship had crossed the mountains and was descending on the rendez-vous. Mare Frigoris lay darkling under a sun that stood low in the south. "But we're a team. I mean, Adzel—"

"Can't go, him," van Rijn said. "Right now, we are also ourselfs making crunch of the covenant and the civil law. Bad enough you and Falkayn leave. Must be him, not Adzel, because he's one of the team is trained special for working with aliens, new cultures, diddle and counterdiddle. Serendipity is clever and will fight desperate here on Luna. I got to have evidences of what they done, proofs, eyewitness-ing. Adzel was there. He can show big, impressive testimoni-als."

"Well—" The Wodenite had never heard Chee Lan speak more bleakly. "I suppose. I didn't expect this."

"To be alive," said van Rijn, "is that not to be again and again surprised?"

The ship set down. The tractor beam released Adzel. He stumbled off over the lava. "Fare you well," said Chee. He was too shaken for any articulate answer. The ship rose anew. He stared after her until she had vanished among the stars.

Not much time passed before the merchant's vessel arrived; but by then, reaction was going at full tide through Adzel. As if in a dream, he boarded, let the crew divest him of his gear and van Rijn take over his material from the castle.

63

He was only half conscious when they made Lunograd port, and scarcely heard the outraged bellows of his employer—was scarcely aware of anything except the infinite need for sleep and sleep and sleep—when he was arrested and led off to jail.

VIII

THE phone announced, "Sir, the principal subject of investigation has called the office of Mendez and is demanding immediate conference with him."

"Exactly as I expected," Edward Garver said with satisfaction, "and right about at the moment I expected, too." He thrust out his jaw. "Go ahead, then, switch him to me."

He was a short man with thinning hair above a pugdog face; but within a severe gray tunic, his shoulders were uncommonly wide. The secretarial machines did not merely surround him as they would an ordinary executive or bureaucrat; somehow they gave the impression of standing guard. His desk bore no personal items—he had never married—but the walls held numerous pictures, which he often animated, of himself shaking hands with successive Premiers of the Solar Commonwealth, Presidents of the Lunar Federation, and other dignitaries.

His words went via wire to a computer, which heard and obeyed. A signal flashed through electronic stages, became a maser beam, and leaped from a transmitter perched above Selenopolis on the ringwall of Copernicus. It struck a satellite and was relayed north, above barren sun-beaten ruggedness, until it entered a receiver at Plato. Coded for destination, it was shunted to another computer, which closed the appropriate connections. Because this moon is a busy place with heavy demands on its communication lines, the entire process took several milliseconds.

A broad countenance, mustached and goateed, framed in

the ringleted mane that had been fashionable a generation ago, popped into Garver's phone screen. Little jet eyes, close set to an enormous crag of a nose, widened. "Pox and pestilence!" exclaimed Nicholas van Rijn. "I want Hernando Mendez, police chief for Lunograd. What you doing here, you? Not enough busybodying in the capital for keeping you happy?"

"I am in the capital . . . still," Garver said. "I ordered any call from you to him passed directly to me."

Van Rijn turned puce. "You the gobblehead told them my Adzel should be arrested?"

"No *honest* police official would let a dangerous criminal like that go loose."

"Who you for calling him criminals?" van Rijn sputtered. "Adzel got more milk of human kindness, *ja,* with plenty butterfat too, than what thin, blue, sour yechwater ever oozes from you, by damn!"

The director of the Federal Centrum of Security and Law Enforcement checked his temper. "Watch your language," he said. "You're in bad trouble yourself."

"We was getting out of trouble, us. Self-defense. And besides, was a local donnerblitz, no business of yours." Van Rijn tried to look pious. "We come back, landed in my yacht, Adzel and me, after he finished. We was going straight like arrows with crow feathers to Chief Mendez and file complaints. But what happened? He was busted! Marched off the spacefield below guard! By whose commandments?"

"Mine," Garver said. "And frankly, I'd have given a lot to include you, Freeman."

He paused before adding as quietly as possible, "I may get what I need for that very shortly, too. I'm coming to Lunograd and take personal charge of investigating this affair. Consider yourself warned. Do not leave Federation territory. If you do, my office will take it as prima-facie evidence sufficient for arrest. Maybe we won't be able to extradite you from Earth, or wherever you go, on a Commonwealth warrant—though we'll try. But we'll slap a hold on everything your Solar Spice & Liquors Company owns here, down to the last liter of vodka. And your Adzel will serve a mighty long term of correction whatever you do,

Freeman. Likewise his accomplices, if they dare come back in reach."

His voice had gathered momentum as he spoke. So had his feelings. He knew he was being indiscreet, even foolish, but the anger of too many years was upon him, now when at least a small victory was in sight. Almost helpless to do otherwise, he leaned forward and spoke staccato:

"I've been waiting for this chance. For years I've waited. I've watched you and your fellow plutocrats in your Polesotechnic League make a mockery of government—intrigue, bribe, compel, corrupt, ignore every inconvenient law, make your private deals, set up your private economic systems, fight your private battles, act like barons of an empire that has no legal existence but that presumes to treat with whole civilizations, make vassals of whole worlds—bring back the rawest kind of feudalism and capitalism! This 'freedom' you boast about, that your influence has gotten written into our very Constitution, it's nothing but license. License to sin, gamble, indulge in vice ... and the League supplies the means, at a whopping profit!

"I can't do much about your antics outside the Commonwealth. Nor much about them anyplace, I admit, except on Luna. But that's a beginning. If I can curb the League here in the Federation, I'll die glad. I'll have laid the cornerstone of a decent society everywhere. And you, van Rijn, are the beginning of the beginning. You have finally gone too far. I believe I've got you!"

He sat back, breathing hard.

The merchant had turned impassive. He took his time about opening a snuffbox, inhaling, sneezing, and dribbling a bit on the lace of his shirtfront. Finally, mild as the mid-oceanic swell of a tsunami, he rumbled, "Hokay. You tell me what you think I done wrong. Scripture says sinful man is prone to error. Maybe we can find out whose error."

Garver had gathered calm. "All right," he said. "No reason why I should not have the pleasure of telling you personally what you could find out for yourself.

"I've always had League activities watched, of course, with standing orders that I'm to be told about anything unusual. Slightly less than a week ago, Adzel and the other xeno teamed with him—yes, Chee Lan of Cynthia—applied for a warrant against the information brokers, Serendipity, Inc. They said their captain, David Falkayn, was being held prisoner under brainscrub drugs in that Alpine castle the SI partners keep for a residence. Naturally, the warrant was refused. It's true the SI people are rather mysterious. But what the flame, you capitalists are the very ones who make a fetish of privacy and the right to keep business details confidential. And SI is the only member of the League that nothing can be said against. All it does, peacefully and lawfully, is act as a clearinghouse for data and a source of advice.

"But the attempt did alert me. Knowing what you freebooters are like, I thought violence might very well follow. I warned the partners and suggested they call me directly at the first sign of trouble. I offered them guards, but they said they had ample defenses." Garver's mouth tightened. "That's another evil thing you Leaguers have brought. Self-defense, you call it! But since the law does say a man may keep and use arms on his own property—" He sighed. "I must admit SI has never abused the privilege."

"Did they tell you their story about Falkayn?" van Rijn asked.

"Yes. In fact, I talked to him myself on the phone. He explained he wanted to marry Freelady Beldaniel and join her outfit. Oh, sure, he *could* have been drugged. I don't know his normal behavior pattern. Nor do I care to. Because it was infinitely more plausible that you simply wanted him snatched away before he let his new friends in on your dirtier secrets.

"So." Garver bridged his fingers and grinned. "Today, about three hours ago, I got a call from Freeman Kim at the SI offices. Freelady Beldaniel had just called him. A space-armored Wodenite, obviously Adzel, had appeared at the castle and demanded to see Falkayn. When this was denied him, he blasted his way in, and was rampaging loose at that moment.

"I instructed Chief Mendez to send out a riot detachment. He said he was already preoccupied with a riot—a brawl, at least—among men of yours, van Rijn, at a warehouse of yours. Don't tell me that was a coincidence!"

"But it was," van Rijn said. "Ask them. They was bad boys. I will scold them."

"And slip them a fat bonus after they get out of jail."

"Well, maybe for consoling them. Thirty days on britches of the peace charges makes them so sad my old gray heart is touched. . . . But go on, Director. What did you do?"

Garver turned livid. "The next thing I had to do was get an utterly baseless injunction quashed. One of your kept judges? Never mind now; another thing to look into. The proceedings cost me a whole hour. After that, I could dispatch some men from my Lunograd division. They arrived too late. Adzel had already gotten Falkayn. The damage was done."

Again he curbed his wrath and said with bitter control, "Shall I list the different kinds of damage? SI's private, but legitimate, patrollers had been approaching the tower where Adzel was, in their gravboats. Then a spaceship came down. Must have been a spaceship, fully armed, acting in closely planned coordination with him. It wiped out the boats, broke apart the tower, and fled. Falkayn is missing. So is his one-time partner Chee Lan. So is the vessel they habitually used—cleared from Lunograd spaceport several standard days ago. The inference is obvious, don't you agree? But somehow, Adzel didn't escape. He must have radioed you to pick him up, because you did, and brought him back. This indicates that you have also been in direct collusion, van Rijn. I know what a swarm of lawyers you keep, so I want a little more evidence before arresting you yourself. But I'll get it. I'll do it."

"On what charges?" the other man asked tonelessly.

"For openers, those brought by the Serendipity partners, with eyewitness corroboration from Freelady Beldaniel and the castle staff. Threat. Mayhem. Invasion of privacy. Malicious mischief. Extensive destruction of property. Kidnapping. Murder."

"Whoa, horsey! Adzel told me, maybe he banged up those servants and guards a little, but he's a Buddhist and was careful not to kill anybody. That gun tower he shot out, getting in, was a standard remote-control type."

"Those patrol boats were not. Half a dozen one-seaters, smashed by energy beams. Okay, the pilots, like the rest of the castle staff, were nonhuman, noncitizen hirelings. But they were sophonts. Killing them in the course of an illegal invasion was murder. Accessories are equally guilty. This brings up the charge of conspiracy and—"

"Never mind," van Rijn said. "I get a notion somehow you don't like us much. When you coming?"

"I leave as soon as I can set matters in order here. A few hours." Garver peeled lips up from his teeth again. "Unless you care to record a confession at once. You'd save us trouble and might receive a lighter sentence."

"No, no. I got nothings to confess. This is such a terrible mistake. You got the situation all arsey-free versey. Adzel is gentle like a baby, except for some babies I know what are frightening ferocious. And me, I am a poor lonely old fat man only wanting a tiny bit profit so he does not end up like a burden on the welfare."

"Stow it," Garver said, and moved to break the connection.

"Wait!" van Rijn cried. "I tell you, everything is upwhirled. I got to unkink things, I see, because I try hard for being a good Christian that loves his fellow man and not let you fall on your ugly flat face and get laughed at like you deserve. I go talk with Adzel, and with Serendipity, too, before you come, and maybe we straighten out this soup you have so stupid-like brewed."

A muscle jumped at the corner of Garver's mouth. "I warn you," he said, "if you attempt any threat, bribery, blackmail—"

"You call me names," van Rijn huffed. "You implicate my morals. I don't got to listen at your ungentlemanly language. Good day for you, Gorgonzola brain." The screen blanked.

Luna being a focal point for outsystem traffic, the jails of the Federation's member cities are adjustable to the needs of a wide variety of species. Adzel's meticulous fairness compelled him to admit that with respect to illumination, temperature, humidity, pressure, and weight, he was more at home in his cell than under Earth conditions. But he didn't mind the latter. And he did mind the food here, a glutinous swill put together according to what some fink of a handbook said was biologically correct for Wodenites. Still more did he suffer from being too cramped to stretch his tail, let alone exercise.

The trouble was, individuals of his race were seldom met off their planet. Most were primitive hunters. When he was brought in, by an understandably nervous squad of policemen, the warden had choked. *"Ullah akhbar!* We must house this cross between a centaur and a crocodile? And every elephant-size unit already filled because of that cursed science fiction convention—"

Thus it was with relief, hours later, that Adzel greeted the sergeant in the phonescreen who said, "Your, uh, legal representative is here. Wants a conference. Are you willing?"

"Certainly. High time! No reflection on you, officer," the prisoner hastened to add. "Your organization has treated me with correctness, and I realize you are bound to your duty as to the Wheel of Karma." The sergeant in his turn made haste to switch over.

Van Rijn's image squinted against a glare too faithfully reproduced. Adzel was surprised. "But . . . but I expected a lawyer," he said.

"Got no time for logic choppers," his boss replied. "We chop our own logics, *ja,* and split and stack them. I mainly should tell you, keep your turnip hatch dogged tight. Don't say one pip. Don't even claim you is innocent. You are not legally requisitioned to tell anybody anything. They want the time of day, let them send out their flatfeetsers and investigate."

"But what am I doing in this kennel?" Adzel protested.

"Sitting. Loafing. Drawing fat pay off me. Meanwhiles I run around sweating my tired old legs down to the knees. Do you know," van Rijn said pathetically, "for more than an hour I have had absolute no drink? And it looks like I might miss lunch, that today was going to be Limfjord oysters and stuffed Pacific crab à la—"

Adzel started. His scales crashed against unyielding walls. "But I don't belong here!" he cried. "My evidence—"

Van Rijn achieved the amazing feat for a human of

outshouting him. "*Quiet!* I said upshut you! Silence!" He dropped his tone. "I know this is supposed to be a sealed circuit, but I do not put past that Garver he plugs one of his trained seals in the circuit. We keep what trumps we hold a while yet, play them last like Gabriel. Last trump—Gabriel—you understood me? Ha, ha!"

"Ha," said Adzel hollowly, "ha."

"You got privacy for meditating, plenty chances to practice asceticisms. I envy you, I wish I could find a chance for sainthood like you got there. You sit patient. I go talk with the people at Serendipity. Toodle oodle." Van Rijn's features vanished.

Adzel crouched motionless for a long while.

But I had the proof! he thought, stunned. *I took those photographs, those body-fluid samples, from David in the castle...exactly as I'd been told to...proof that he was, indeed, under brainscrub. I handed the material over to Old Nick when he asked for it. For certainly that would justify my breaking in. This civilization has a horror of personality violations. But he—the leader I trusted—he hasn't mentioned it!*

When Chee Lan and a cured Falkayn returned they could testify, of course. Without the physical evidence Adzel had obtained, their testimony might be discounted, even if given torporifically. There were too many ways of lying under those drugs and electropulses that interrogators were permitted to use on volunteers: immunization or verbal conditioning, for instance.

At best, the situation would remain difficult. How could you blink the fact that intelligent beings had been killed by unauthorized raiders? (Though Adzel had more compunctions about fighting than the average roamer of today's turbulent frontiers, he regretted this particular incident only mildly in principle. A private war remained a war, a type of conflict that was occasionally justifiable. The rescue of a shipmate from an especially vile fate took priority over hard-boiled professional weapon-wielders who defended the captors of that shipmate. The trouble was, however, Commonwealth law did not recognize private wars.) But there was a fair chance the authorities would be sufficiently convinced that they would release, or convict and then pardon, the raiders.

If the proof of brainscrubbing was laid before them. And if Chee and Falkayn came back to tell their story. They might not. The unknowns for whom Serendipity had been an espionage front might find them and slay them before they could learn the truth. *Why did van Rijn not let me go too?* Adzel chafed. *Why, why, why?*

Alone, the exhibits would at least get him out on bail. For they would show that his attack, however illegal, was no wanton banditry. It would also destroy Serendipity by destroying the trust on which that organization depended—overnight.

Instead, van Rijn was withholding the proof. He was actually off to dicker with Falkayn's kidnappers.

The walls seemed to close in. Adzel was born to a race of rangers. A spaceship might be cramped, but outside burned the stars. Here was nothing other than walls.

Oh, the wide praries of Zatlakh, earthquake hoofbeats, wind whooping off mountains ghost-blue above the great horizon! After dark, fires beneath a shaken aurora; the old songs, the old dances, the old kinship that runs deeper than blood itself. Home is freedom. Ships, outfarings, planets, and laughter. Freedom is home. Am I to be sold for a slave in his bargain?

Shall I let him sell me?

IX

PUFFING like an ancient steam locomotive, Nicholas van Rijn entered the central office. He had had previous dealings with Serendipity, in person as well as through subordinates. But he had never been in this particular room before, nor did he know anyone besides the owners who had.

Not that it differed much from the consultation cubicles, except for being larger. It was furnished with the same expensive materials in the same cheerlessly functional style, and the same strong white light spilled from its fluoropanels. Instead of a desk there was a large table around which several beings could sit; but this was equipped with a full battery of secretarial machines. Weight was set at Earth standard, atmosphere a little warmer.

Those partners who remained on Luna awaited him in a row behind the table. Kim Yoon-Kun was at the middle, slight, stiff, and impassive. The same wary expressionlessness marked Anastasia Herrera and Eve Latimer, who flanked him. Thea Beldaniel showed a human touch of weariness and shakenness—eyes dark-shadowed, the fine lines deepened in her face, hands not quite steady—but less than was normal for a woman who, a few hours ago, had seen her castle stormed by a dragon.

Van Rijn halted. His glance flickered to the pair of great gray-furred four-armed tailed bipeds, clad alike in traditional mail and armed alike with modern blasters, who stood against the rear wall. Their yellow eyes, set beneath bony prominences that looked like horns, glowered back out of the coarse faces. "You did not need to bring your Gorzuni goons," he said. His cloak swirled as he spread his hands wide, then slapped them along his tight plum-colored culottes. "I got no arsenal, me, and I come alone, sweet and innocent like a pigeon of peace. You know how pigeons behave."

"Colonel Melkarsh heads the patrol and outpost crews on our grounds," Kim stated. "Captain Urugu commands the interior guards and therefore the entire household servant corps. They have the right to represent their people, on whom your agents have worked grievous harm."

Van Rijn nodded. You can preserve secrets by hiring none except nonhumans from barbarian cultures. They can be trained in their jobs and in no other aspects of Technic civilization. Hence they will keep to themselves, not mix socially with outsiders, blab nothing, and at the end of their contracts go home and vanish into the anonymity of their seldom-visited planets. But if you do this, you must also accept their codes. The Siturushi of Gorzun make fine mercenaries—perhaps a little too fierce—and one reason is the bond of mutual loyalty between commanders and troops.

"Hokay," the merchant said. "Maybe best. Now we make sure everybody gets included in the settlement we reach." He sat down, extracted a cigar, and bit off the end.

"We did not invite you to smoke," Anastasia Herrera said frigidly.

"Oh, that's all right, don't apologize, I know you got a lot on your minds." Van Rijn lit the cigar, leaned back, crossed his legs, and exhaled a blue cloud. "I am glad you agreed to meet private with me. I would have come out to your home if you wanted. But better here, *nie?* What with police swarming around grounds and trying to look efficient. Here is maybe the one place in Lunograd we can be sure nobody is dropping eaves."

Melkarsh growled, deep in his throat. He probably knew some Anglic. Kim said, "We are leaning backward to be accommodating, Freeman van Rijn, but do not overstrain our patience. Whatever settlement is reached must be on our terms and must have your full cooperation. And we cannot guarantee that your agents will go unpunished by the law."

The visitor's brows climbed, like black caterpillars, halfway up his slanted forehead. "Did I hear you right?" He cupped one ear. "Maybe, in spite of what extrarageous fees I pay for antisenescence treating, maybe at last in my old age I grow deaf? I hope you are not crazy. I hope you know this wowpow is for your sakes, not mine, because I don't want to squash you flat. Let us not beat around the barn." He pulled a stuffed envelope from his waistcoat pocket and threw it on the table. "Look at the pretty pictures. They are duplicates, natural. Originals I got someplace else, addressed to police and will be mailed if I don't come back in a couple of hours. Also biological specimens—what can positive be identified for Falkayn's, because on Earth is medical records of him what include his chromosome patterns. Radioisotope tests will prove samples was taken not many hours ago."

The partners handed the photographs around in a silence that grew deeper and colder. Once Melkarsh snarled and took a step forward, but Urugu restrained him and both stood glaring.

"You had Falkayn under brainscrub," van Rijn said. He wagged a finger. "That was very naughty. No matter what we Solar Spicers may be guilty of, police going to investigate you from guzzle to zorch. And no matter what is then done with you, Serendipity is finished. Just the suspicion that you acted not so nice will take away your customers and their money."

They looked back at him. Their faces were metal-blank, aside from Thea Beldaniel's, on which there flickered something akin to anguish. "We *didn't*—" she half sobbed; and then, slumping back: "Yes. But I ... we ... meant him no real harm. We had no choice."

Kim waved her to silence. "You must have had some reason for not introducing this material officially at the outset," he said, syllable by syllable.

"Ja, ja," van Rijn answered. "Don't seem my boy was permanent hurt. And Serendipity does do a real service for the whole Polesotechnic League. I carry no big grudge. I try my best to spare you the worst. Of course, I can't let you go without some loss. Is not possible. But you was the ones brought in the policemen, not me."

"I admit no guilt," Kim said. His eyes kindled. "We serve another cause than your ignoble money-grubbing."

"I know. You got bosses somewhere out in space don't like us. So we can't so well let your outfit continue for a spy and maybe someday a saboteur. But in spirit of charity, I do want to help you escape terrible results from your own foolishness. We start by calling off the law dogs. Once they got their big sticky teeth out of our business—"

"Can they be called off . . . now?" Thea Beldaniel whispered.

"I think maybe so, if you cooperate good with me. After all, your servants inside the castle did not suffer more from Adzel than some bruises, maybe a bone or two broken, right? We settle damage claims out of court with them, a civil and not a criminal matter." Van Rijn blew a thoughtful smoke ring. "You do the paying. Now about those patrol boats got clobbered, who is left that saw any spaceship hit them? If we—"

Melkarsh shook off his companion's grasp, jumped forward, raised all four fists and shouted in the dog Latin that has developed from the League's common tongue, "By the most foul demon! Shall my folk's heads lie unavenged?"

"Oh, you get weregild you can take to their relatives," van Rijn said. "Maybe we add a nice sum for you personal, ha?"

"You believe everything is for sale," Melkarsh rasped. "But honor is not. Know that I myself saw the spaceship from afar. It struck and was gone before I could arrive. But I know the type for one that you companies use, and I will so declare to the Federation's lawmen."

"Now, now," van Rijn smiled. "Nobody is asking you should perjure. You keep your mouth shut, don't volunteer information you saw anything, and nobody will ask you. Especial since your employers is going to send you home soon—next available ship, or maybe I myself supply one— with pay for your entire contract and a fat bonus." He nodded graciously at Urugu. "Sure, my friend, you too. Don't you got generous employers?"

"If you expect I will take your filthy bribe," Melkarsh said, "when I could avenge my folk by speaking—"

"Could you?" van Rijn answered. "Are you sure you pull

me down? I don't pull down easy, with my big and heavy foundation. You will for certain destroy your employers here, what you gave your word to serve faithful. Also, you and yours will be held for accessories to kidnap and other bad behavings. How you help your folk, or your own honor, in a Lunar jail? Ha? Far better you bring back weregild to their families and story of how they fell nobly in battle like warriors should."

Melkarsh snatched for air but could speak no further. Thea Beldaniel rose, went to him, stroked his mane, and murmured, "He's right, you know, my dear old friend. He's a devil, but he's right."

The Gorzuni gave a jerky nod and stepped backward.

"Good, good!" van Rijn beamed. He rubbed his hands. "How glad I am for common sense and friendliness. I tell you what plans we make together." He looked around. "Only I'm terrible thirsty. How about you send out for a few bottles beer?"

X

REACHING Lunograd, Edward Garver went directly to the police complex. "Bring that Wodenite prisoner to an interrogation room," he ordered. With a nod at the three hard-countenanced men who accompanied him: "My assistants and I want to grill him ourselves. Make his environment as uncomfortable as the law allows—and if the law should happen to get stretched a trifle, this case is too big for recording petty details."

He did not look forward to the prospect. He was not a cruel man. And intellectually he despised his planned approach. Guilt should be determined by logical reasoning from scientifically gathered evidence. What could you do, though, when the League paid higher salaries than you were able to offer, thus getting technicians more skilled and reasoners more glib? He had spent a career building the Centrum into an efficient, high-morale organization. His pride was how well it now functioned against the ordinary criminal. But each time he saw his agents retreat, baffled and disheartened, from a trail that led to the League, that pride became ashen within him.

He had studied the apologetics of the modern philosophers. "Government is that organization which claims the right to command all individuals to do whatever it desires and to punish disobedience with loss of property, liberty, and ultimately life. It is nothing more. The fact is not changed by its occasional beneficence. Possessing equal or greater power, but claiming no such right of compulsion, the Polesotechnic League functions as the most effective check

upon government which has yet appeared in known history."
He did not believe a word of it.

Thus Adzel found himself in air stranglingly thin and wet,
cold enough for his scales to frost over, and in twice the
gravity of his home planet. He was almost blind beneath the
simulated light of a distant red dwarf sun, and could surely
not look through the vitryl panel behind which Garver's
team sat under Earth conditions. As time passed, no one
offered food or drink. The incessant questions were
projected shrill, on a frequency band painful to eardrums
adapted for low notes.

He ignored them.

After half an hour, Garver realized this could go on
indefinitely. He braced his mind for the next stage. It
wouldn't be pleasant for anyone, but the fault was that
monster's own.

Inflating his lungs, he roared, "Answer us, damn you! Or
do you want to be charged with obstructing justice, on top of
everything else?"

For the first time, Adzel replied. "In point of fact," he
said, "yes. As I am merely standing upon my right to keep
silent, such an accusation would cap the ridiculousness of
these proceedings."

Garver jabbed a button. Adzel must needs wince. "Is
something wrong?" asked the team member who had been
assigned the kindliness role.

"I suffered quite a severe electric shock through the
floor."

"Dear me. Perhaps a wiring defect. Unless it was your
imagination. I realize you're tired. Why don't we finish this
interview and all go get some rest?"

"You are making a dreadful mistake, you know," Adzel
said mildly. "I admit I was somewhat irritated with my
employer. Now I am far more irritated with you. Under no
circumstances shall I cooperate. Fortunately, my spacefar-
ing has accustomed me to exotic surroundings. And I regard
this as an opportunity to gain merit by transcending physical
discomfort." He assumed the quadrupedal equivalent of the
lotus position, which is quite a sight. "Excuse me while I say
my prayers."

"Where were you on the evenwatch of—"

"Om mani padme hum."

An interrogator switched off the speaker system. "I don't know if this is worth our trouble, Chief," he said.

"He's a live organism," Garver growled. "Tough, yeh, but he's got his limits. We'll keep on, by God, in relays, till we grind him down."

Not long afterward, the phone buzzed in the chamber and Mendez's image said deferentially, "Sir, I regret the interruption, but we've received a call. From the Serendipity people." He gulped. "They... they're dropping their complaint."

"What?" Garver leaped from his chair. "No! They can't! I'll file the charges myself!" He stopped. The redness ebbed from his cheeks. "Put them on," he said coldly.

Kim Yoon-Kun looked out of the screen. Was he a shade less collected than before? At his back loomed van Rijn. Garver suppressed most of his automatic rage at glimpsing that man. "Well?" he said. "What is this nonsense?"

"My partners and I have conferred with the gentleman here," Kim said. Each word seemed to taste individually bad; he spat them out fast. "We find there has been a deplorable misunderstanding. It must be corrected at once."

"Including bringing the dead back to life?" Garver snorted. "Never mind what bribes you've been tempted by. I have proof that a federal crime was committed. And I warn you, sir, trying to conceal anything about it will make you an accessory after the fact."

"But it was no crime," Kim said. "It was an accident."

Garver stared past him, at van Rijn. If the old bastard tried to gloat—! But van Rijn only smiled and puffed on a large cigar.

"Let me begin from the beginning," Kim said. "My partners and I would like to retire. Because Serendipity, Inc., does satisfy a genuine need, its sale will involve considerable sums and many different interests. Negotiations are accordingly delicate. This is especially true when you consider that the entire value of our company lies in the fact that its services are rendered without fear or favor. Let its name be tainted with the least suspicion of undue influence om outside, and it will be shunned. Now everyone knows that we are strangers here, aloof from society. Thus we are unfamiliar with the emotional intricacies that may be involved. Freeman van Rijn generously"—Kim had a fight to get the adverb out—"offered us advice. But his counseling must be done with extreme discretion, lest his rivals assume that he will turn Serendipity into a creature of his own."

"You—you—" Garver heard himself squeak, as if still trying to grill Adzel, "you're selling out? To who?"

"That is the problem, Director," Kim said. "It must be someone who is not merely able to pay, but is capable of handling the business and above suspicion. Perhaps a consortium of nonhumans? At any rate, Freeman van Rijn will, *sub rosa,* be our broker."

"At a fat commission," Garver groaned.

Kim could not refrain from groaning back, "Very fat." He gathered himself and plowed on:

"Captain Falkayn went as his representative to discuss matters with us. To preserve the essential secrecy, perforce he misled everyone, even his long-time shipmates. Hence that story about his betrothal to Freelady Beldaniel. I see now that this was a poor stratagem. It excited their suspicions to the point where they resorted to desperate measures. Adzel entered violently, as you know. But he did no real harm, and once Captain Falkayn had explained the situation to him, we were glad to accept his apologies. Damage claims will be settled privately. Since Captain Falkayn had completed his work at our home anyhow, he embarked with Chee Lan on a mission related to finding a buyer for us. There was nothing illegal about his departure, seeing that no laws had been broken. Meanwhile Freeman van Rijn was kind enough to fetch Adzel in his personal craft."

"No laws broken? What about the laws against murder?" Garver yelled. His fingers worked, as if closing on a throat. "I've got them—you—for that!"

"But no, Director," Kim said. "I agree the circumstances looked bad, for which reason we were much too prompt to prefer charges. By 'we' I mean those of us who were not present at the time. But now a discussion with Freelady

Beldaniel, and a check of the original plans of the castle, have shown what actually happened.

"You know the place has automatic as well as manned defenses. Adzel's disruptive entry alerted the robots in one tower, which then overreacted by firing on our own patrol boats as these came back to help. Chee Lan, in her spaceship, demolished the tower in a valiant effort to save our people, but she was too late.

"A tragic accident. If anyone is to blame, it is the contractor who installed those machines with inadequate discriminator circuits. Unfortunately, the contractor is nonhuman, living far beyond the jurisdiction of the Commonwealth..."

Garver sat.

"You had better release Adzel immediately," Kim said. "Freeman van Rijn says he may perhaps be induced not to generate a great scandal about false arrest, provided that you apologize to him in person before a public newscaster."

"You have made your own settlement—with van Rijn?" Garver whispered.

"Yes," said Kim, like one up whom a bayonet has been rammed.

Garver rallied the fragments of his manhood. "All right," he got out. "So be it."

Van Rijn looked over Kim's shoulder. "Gloat," he said and switched off.

The space yacht lifted and swung toward Earth. Stars glittered in every viewport. Van Rijn leaned back in his lounger, hoisted a foamful mug, and said, "By damn, we better celebrate fast. No sooner we make planetfall but we will be tongue-dragging busy, you and me."

Adzel drank from a similar mug which, however, was filled with prime whisky. Being large has some advantages. His happiness was limited. "Will you let the Serendipity people go scot-free?" he asked. "They are evil."

"Maybe not evil. Maybe plain enemies, which is not necessarily same thing," van Rijn said. "We find out. For sure not scot-free, though, any more than what you glug down at my expense like it was beer is free Scotch. No, you see, they has lost their company, their spy center, which was their whole *raison d'être*. Off that loss, I make a profit, since I handle the selling."

"But you must have some goal besides money!" Adzel exclaimed.

"Oh, *ja, ja,* sure. Look, I did not know what would happen after you rescued Davy boy. I had to play on my ear. What happened was, Serendipity tried striking back at us through the law. This made special dangers, also special opportunities. I found four things in my mind."

Van Rijn ticked the points off on his fingers. "One," he said, "I had to get you and my other loyal friends off the hook. That was more important by itself than revenge. But so was some other considerates.

"Like two, I had to get the government out of this business. For a while at least. Maybe later we must call it back. But for now, these reasons to keep it out. Alpha, governments is too big and cumbersome for handling a problem with so many unknowns as we got. Beta, if the public in the Commonwealth learned they have a powerful enemy some place we don't know, they could get hysterical and this could be bad for developing a reasonable type policy, besides bad for business. Gamma, the longer we can work private, the better chance for cutting ourselves a share of whatever pies may be floating around in space, in exchange for our trouble."

He paused to breathe and gulp. Adzel looked from this comfortable saloon, out the viewport to the stars that were splendid but gave no more comfort than life could seize for itself; and no life was long, compared to the smallest time that any of those suns endured. "What other purposes have you?" he asked mutedly.

"Number three," van Rijn said, "did I not make clear Serendipity is in and for itself a good idea, useful to everybody? It should not be destroyed, only passed on into honest hands. Or tentacles or paws of flippers or whatever. Ergo, we do not want any big hurray about it. For that reason too, I must bargain with the partners. I did not want them to feel like Samson, no motive not to pull down the whole barbershop.

"And four." His tone turned unwontedly grave. "Who are these X beings? What do they want? Why are they secret? Can we maybe fix a deal with them? No sane man is after a war. We got to learn more so we can know what is best to do. And Serendipity is our one lonesome lead to its masters."

Adzel nodded. "I see. Did you get any information?"

"No. Not really. That I could not push them off of. They would die first. I said to them, they must go home and report to their bosses. If nothings else, they got to make sure their partners who has already left is not seized on returning to Luna and maybe put in the question. So hokay, they start, I have a ship that trails theirs, staying in detection range the whole way. Maybe they can lure her into a trap, maybe not. Don't seem worth the trouble, I said, when neither side is sure it can outfox the other. The most thickly sworn enemies always got *some* mutual interests. And supposing you intend to kill somebody, why not talk at him first? For worst, you have wasted a little time; for best, you learn you got no cause to kill him."

Van Rijn drained his mug. "Ahhhh! Well," he said, "we made a compromise. They go away, except one of them, in a ship that is not followed. Their own detectors can tell them this is so. The one stays behind and settles legal details of transferring ownership. That is Thea Beldaniel. She was not too unwilling, and I figure she is maybe more halfway human than her friends. Later on, she guides one ship of ours to a rendezvous agreed on, some neutral spot, I suppose, where maybe we can meet her bosses. They should be worth meeting, what made so brilliant a scheme like Serendipity for learning all about us. *Nie?*"

Adzel lifted his head with a jerk. "I beg your pardon?" he exclaimed. "Do you mean that you personally and—and I—"

"Who else?" van Rijn said. "One reason I kept you back. I need to be sure some fellow besides me will be around I can trust. It is going to be a cold journey, that one. Like they used to say in Old Norse and such places, 'Bare is brotherless back.'" He pounded the table. "Cabin boy!" he thundered. "Where in hell's name is more beer?"

XI

IN the decade or so that had passed since the Lemminkainenites found it, the rogue had fallen a long way. Watching Beta Crucis in the bow viewscreen, Falkayn whistled, low and awed. "Can we even get near?" he asked.

Seated amidst the control boards, flickering and blinking and clicking instruments, soft power-throb and quiver, of *Muddlin' Through*'s bridge, he did not look directly at the star, nor at a true simulacrum. Many astronomical units removed, it would still have burned out his eyes. The screen reduced brightness and magnified size for him. He saw an azure circle, spotted like a leopard, wreathed in an exquisite filigree of ruby, gold, and opal, a lacework that stretched outward for several times its diameter. And space behind was not dark, but shimmered with pearliness through a quarter of the sky before fading into night.

Falkayn's grip tautened on the arms of his chair. The heart thuttered in him. Seeking comfort for a rising, primitive dread, he pulled his gaze from the screen, from all screens, to the homely traces of themselves that his team had put on used patches of bulkhead. Here Chee Lan had hung one of those intricate reticulations that her folk prized as art; there he himself had pasted up a girlie picture; yonder Adzel kept a bonsai tree on a shelf—*Adzel, friend, now when we need your strength, the strength in your very voice, you are two light-centuries behind us.*

Stop that, you nit! Falkayn told himself. *You're getting spooked. Understandable, when Chee had to spend most of our voyage time nursing me out of half-life—*

His mind halted. He gasped for air. The horror of what had been done to him came back in its full strength. All stars receded to an infinite radius. He crouched alone in blackness and ice.

And yet he could not remember clearly what the enslavement of his mind had been like. It was as if he tried to reconstruct a fever dream. Everything was vague and grotesque; time twisted smokily about, dissolved and took new evanescent shapes; he had been trapped in another universe and another self, and they were not his own, and he could not bring himself to confront them again in memory, even were he able. He had desired Thea Beldaniel as he had desired no other woman since his first youth; he had adored the undefined Elder Race as he had adored no gods in his life; he had donned a cool surface and a clear logical mind at need, and afterward returned to his dim warm abyss. Yet somehow it was not he who did these things, but others. They used him, entered and wore him.... How could he find revenge for so inward a rape?

That last thought was born as a solitary spark in his night. He seized it, held it close, blew his spirit upon it and nursed it to flame. Fury followed, blinding as yonder great sun, burning him clean again. He might have been reliving ancient incarnations as he swung a Viking ax, galloped torch in hand on a Tartar pony, unleashed the guns that smash cities to rubble. It gave strength, which in turn gave sanity.

Minutes after the seizure began, he was calm once more. His muscles slackened their hurtful knots, pulse and breath slowed, the sweat dried on him though he was aware of its lingering sourness.

He thought harshly: *Let's get on with the work we've got here. And to begin with, let's not be so bloody reverential about it. I've seen bigger, brighter stars than this one.*

Only a few, of course. The blue giants are also monsters in their rarity. And the least of them is terrifying to contemplate. Those flecks on the photosphere were vortices that could each have swallowed a planet like Jupiter. That arabesque of filaments comprised the prominences—the mass equivalents of whole Earths, vaporized, ionized, turned to incandescent plasma, spewed millions of kilometers into space, some forever lost and some raining back—yet given its faerie patterns by magnetic fields great enough to wrestle with it. The corona fluoresced across orbital distances because its gas was sleeted through and through by the particles, stripped atoms, hard and soft quanta of a star whose radiance was an ongoing storm, eight hundred and fifty times the measure of Sol's, a storm so vast that it could endure no longer than a hundred megayears before ending in the thunderclap of a supernova. Falkayn looked upon its violence and shivered.

He grew aware that the ship's computer had spoken. "I beg your pardon?" he said automatically.

"I am not programmed to take offense; therefore apologies to me are superfluous," said the flat artificial voice. "However, I have been instructed to deal as circumspectly with you as my data banks and ideational circuits allow, until you have fully recovered your nervous equilibrium. Accordingly, it is suggested that you consider indulgence as having been granted you as requested."

Falkayn relaxed. His chuckle grew into a guffaw. "Thanks, Muddlehead," he said. "I needed that." Hastily: "Don't spoil it by telling me you deduced the need and calculated your response. Just start over."

"In reply to your question as to whether we can come near, the answer depends upon what is meant by 'near.' Context makes it obvious that you wish to know whether we can reach the planet of destination with an acceptable probability of safety. Affirmative."

Falkayn turned to Chee Lan, who hunkered in her own chair—it looked more like a spiderweb—on his right. She must have sensed it when the horror came upon him but, characteristically, decided not to intervene. Because he still needed distraction, he said:

"I distinctly remember telling Muddlehead to lay off that stupid 'affirmative, negative' business, when a plain 'yes' or 'no' was good enough for Churchill. Why did you counter-mand?"

"I didn't," the Cynthian answered. "I don't care either way. What are the nuances of the Anglic language to me? If it has any," she sneered. "No, blame Adzel."

"Why him?"

"The ship came new to us from the yard, you recall, so the computer's vocabulary was engineerese. It's gotten modified in the course of work with us. But you may recall too that while we were on Luna, we ordered a complete inspection. You were hot on the tail of your Veronica creature, which left Adzel and me to make arrangements. Old butterheart was afraid the feelings of the engineers would be hurt, if they noticed how little use we have for their dialect. He instructed Muddlehead—"

"Never mind," Falkayn said. He felt he had now gotten enough distraction to last him for quite a while. To the ship: "Revert to prior linguistic pattern and give us some details about our next move."

"Instrumental observation appears to confirm what you were told of the planet itself," said the machine. Falkayn nodded. Though he had only recovered the full use of his free-will in the past several days, Chee had been able to get total-recollection answers from him very early in the trip. "However, the noise level is too high for exactitude at our present distance. On the other hand, I have determined the orbit with sufficient precision. It is, indeed, a hyperbola of small eccentricity. At present, the rogue is near periastron, the radius vector having a length of approximately one-point-seven-five astronomical units. It will make the closest approach, approximately zero-point-nine-three astronomical units, in approximately twenty-seven-point-three-seven days, after which it will naturally return to outer space along the other arm of the hyperbola. There is no evidence of any companion body of comparable size. Thus the dynamics of the situation are simple and the orbit almost perfectly symmetrical."

Chee put a cigarette in an interminable ivory holder and puffed it alight. Her ears twitched, her whiskers bristled. "What a time to arrive!" she snarled. "It couldn't be when the planet's decently far off from that bloated fire balloon. Oh, no! That'd be too easy. It'd put the gods to the trouble of finding somebody else to dump their garbage on. We get to go in while the radiation peaks."

"Well," Falkayn said, "I don't see how the object

could've been found at all, if it hadn't happened to be coming in, close enough to reflect a detectable amount of light off its cryosphere. And then there was the galactic communications lag. Sheer luck that I ever heard about the discovery."

"You could have heard a few years earlier, couldn't you?"

"In that event," Muddlehead said, "the necessity would have remained of making later, short-range observations, in order to ascertain whether surface conditions are indeed going to become suitable for an industrial base. The amount and the composition of frozen material could not have been measured accurately. Nor could its behavior have been computed beforehand in sufficient detail. The problem is too complex, with too many unknowns. For example, once a gaseous atmosphere has begun to form, other volatile substances will tend to recondense at high altitudes, forming clouds which will in time disappear but which, during their existence, may reflect so much input radiation that most of the surface remains comparatively cold."

"Oh, dry up," Chee said.

"I am not programmed or equipped to—"

"And blow away." Chee faced the human. "I see your point, Dave, as well as Muddlehead's. And of course the planet's accelerating as it moves inward. I got a preliminary orbital estimate a few watches back, while you were asleep, that says the radius vector changes from three to one a.u. in about ten standard weeks. So little time, for the irradiation to grow ninefold!—But I do wish we could've arrived later, anyhow, when the thing's outward bound and cooling off."

"Although not prepared for detailed meteorological calculations," Muddlehead said, "I can predict that the maximum atmospheric instability will occur after periastron passage. At present, most of the incident stellar energy is being absorbed by heats of fusion, vaporization, et cetera. Once this process has been completed, energy input will continue large. For example, at thirty astronomical units the planet will still be receiving approximately as much irradiation as Earth; and it will not get that far out for a number of years. Thus temperatures can be expected to soar, and storms of such magnitude will be generated that no vessel dares land. Ground observation may as yet be feasible for us, given due precautions."

Falkayn grinned. He felt better by the minute: if not able to whip the cosmos, at least to let it know it had been in a fight. "Maybe our luck is the best possible," he said.

"I wouldn't be the least bit surprised," Chee replied sourly. "Well, Muddlehead, how do we make rendezvous?"

"The force-screens can of course ward off more particle radiation than we will receive, even if a stellar storm occurs," said the computer. "Electromagnetic input is the real problem. Our material shielding is insufficient to prevent an undesirable cumulative X-ray dosage in the period required for adequate study. The longer wavelengths could similarly overload our thermostatting capabilities. Accordingly, I propose to continue under hyperdrive."

Falkayn drew his pipe from a pocket of his gray coveralls. "That's a pretty close shave, so few a.u. at faster-than-light," he warned. He left unspoken the possibilities: imperfect intermesh with the star's gravitational field tearing the ship asunder; a brush with a solid body, or a moderately dense gas, producing a nuclear explosion as atoms tried to occupy the same volume.

"It is within the one percent safety margin of this vessel and myself," Muddlehead declared. "Besides spending less time in transit, during that transit we will not interact significantly with ambient photons or material particles."

"Good enough," Chee said. "I don't fancy the nasty little things buzzing through my personal cells. But what about when we reach the planet? We can take station in its shadow cone and let its bulk protect us—obviously—but what can we then observe of the surface?"

"Adequate instruments are available. As a trained planetologist, Adzel could make the most effective use of them. But no doubt you two with my assistance can manage. Furthermore, it should be possible to pay brief visits to the daylight side."

"Bully-o," Falkayn said. "We'll grab some lunch and a nap and be on our way."

"You can stuff your gut and wiggle your epiglottis later," Chee said. "We proceed *now*."

"Huh? Why?"

"Have you forgotten that we have rivals? That messengers departed weeks ago to inform them? I don't know how long the word took to get back there, or how fast they can send an expedition here, but I don't expect them to dawdle very much or be overly polite if they find us." Chee jerked her tailtip and spread her hands, a shrugging gesture. "We might or might not be able to take them in a fight, but I'd really rather delegate the job to a League battle fleet. Let's get our data and out."

"M-m-m...yes. I read. Carry on, Muddlehead. Keep every sensor alert for local dangers, though. There're bound to be some unpredictable ones." Falkayn loaded his pipe. "I'm not sure van Rijn would call for a fleet action at that," he murmured to the Cynthian. "It might impair his claim to the planet. He might have to share some of the profit."

"He'll squeeze every millo he can out of this," she said. "Of course. But for once, he's seen something bigger than money. And it scares him. He thinks the Commonwealth—maybe the whole of Technic civilization—is at war and doesn't realize the fact. And if this rogue is important enough to the enemy that they risked, and lost, a spy organization they'd spent fifteen years developing, it's equally important to us. He'll call in the League; even the different governments and their navies, if he must. I talked to him, after we'd hooked you from the castle."

The humor dropped out of Falkayn. His mouth drew taut. *I know what kind of conflict this is!*

Barely in time, he choked the mood. *No more blue funks. I did get free. I will get revenge. Let's think about what's to be done now.*

He forced lightness back into voice and brain. "If Old Nick really does end up having to settle for a fraction of the wealth, hoo-hah! They'll hear his screams in the Magellanic Clouds. But maybe we can save his bacon—and French toast and scrambled eggs and coffee royal and, uh, yes, it was coconut cake, last time I had breakfast with him. Ready, Muddlehead?"

"Stand by for hyperdrive," said the computer.

The power-hum deepened. Briefly, the screened sky

became a blur. Then the system adjusted, to compensate for billions of quantum microjumps per second. Stars aft assumed their proper colors and configurations. Forward, where Beta Crucis drowned them out, its disc swelled, until it seemed to leap with its flames into the ship. Falkayn crouched back in his seat and Chee Lan bared her fangs.

The moment passed. The vessel resumed normal state. She must swiftly attain the proper position and kinetic velocity, before the heightened power of the sun blasted through her defenses. But her internal gee-fields were manipulated with such suppleness by the computer that the two beings aboard felt no change of weight. In minutes, a stable condition was established. The ship lay two radii from the rogue's ground level, balancing gravitational and centrifugal forces with her own thrust. Her riders peered forth.

The wide-angle screen showed an immense black circle, rimmed with lurid white where the star's rays were refracted through the atmosphere. Behind this, in turn, glowed corona, and wings of zodiacal light. The planetary midnight was not totally unrelieved. Auroras flung multicolored banners from the poles; a wan bluishness flickered elsewhere, as the atoms and ions of sun-split molecules recombined in strange ways; lightning, reflected by immense cloud banks farther down, created the appearance of running will-o'-the-wisps; here and there glowered a red spark, the throat of a spouting volcano.

In the near-view screens, mere fractions of the globe appeared, shouldering into heaven. But there you saw, close and clear, the pattern of weather, the rage of rising mountains and newborn oceans. Almost, Falkayn imagined he could hear the wind-shriek, rain-roar, thunder-cannonade, that he could feel the land shake and split beneath him, the gales whirl boulders through a blazing sky. It was long before he could draw his gaze free of that scene.

But work was on hand, and in the watches that followed, he inevitably lost some of his awe amidst the instruments. With it vanished the weakness that his imprisonment had left in him. The basic anger, the drive to scrub out his humiliation in blood, did not go; but he buried it deep while he studied and calculated. What he was witnessing must be unique in the galaxy—perhaps in the cosmos—and fascinated him utterly.

As the Lemminkainenites had concluded, this was an ancient world. Most of its natural radioactivity was long spent, and the chill had crept near its heart. But part of the core must remain molten, to judge from the magnetism. So stupendous an amount of heat, insulated by mantle and crust and frozen oceans and a blanket of frozen atmosphere averaging ten or twenty meters thick, was slow to dissipate. Nevertheless, for ages the surface had lain at a temperature not far above absolute zero.

Now the cryosphere was dissolving. Glaciers became torrents, which presently boiled away and became storm-winds. Lakes and seas, melting, redistributed incredible masses. Pressures within the globe were shifted; isostatic balance was upset; the readjustments of strata, the changes of allotropic structure, released catastrophic, rock-melting energy. Quakes rent the land and shocked the waters. Volcanoes awoke by the thousands. Geysers spouted above the ice sheath that remained. Blizzard, hail, and rain scourged the world, driven by tempests whose fury mounted daily until words like "hurricane" could no more name them. Hanging in space, Falkayn and Chee Lan took measurements of Ragnarök.

And yet—and yet—what a prize this was! What an incredible all-time treasure house!

XII

"FRANKLY," Chee Lan said, "speaking between friends and meaning no offense, you're full of fewmets. How can one uninhabitable piece of thawed hell matter that much to anybody?"

"Surely I explained, even in my wooze," Falkayn replied. "An industrial base, for the transmutation of elements."

"But they do that at home."

"On a frustratingly small scale, compared to the potential market." Falkayn poured himself a stiff whisky and leaned back to enjoy digesting his dinner. He felt he had earned a few hours' ease in the saloon. "Tomorrow" they were to land, having completed their investigations from orbit, and things could get shaggy. "How about a poker game?"

The Cynthian, perched on the table, shook her head. "No, thanks! I've barely regained my feeling for four-handed play, after Muddlehead got rich enough in its own right to bluff big. Without Adzel, the development's apt to be too unfamiliar. The damned machine'll have our hides." She began grooming her silken fur. "Stick to business, you. I'm a xenologist. I never paid more attention than I could help to your ugly factories. I'd like a proper explanation of why I'm supposed to risk my tailbone down there."

Falkayn sighed and sipped. He would have taken for granted that she could see the obvious as readily as he. But to her, with her biological heritage, cultural background, and special interests, it was not obvious. *I wonder what she sees that I miss? How could I even find out?* "I don't have the statistics in my head," he admitted. "But you don't need anything except a general knowledge of the situation. Look, there isn't an element in the periodic table, nor hardly a single isotope, that doesn't have some use in modern technology. And when that technology operates on hundreds of planets, well, I don't care how minor a percentage of the consumption is Material Q. The total amount of Q needed annually is going to run into tons at a minimum—likelier into megatons.

"Now nature doesn't produce much of some elements. Even in the peculiar stars, transmutation processes have a low yield of nuclei like rhenium and scandium—two metals I happen to know are in heavy demand for certain alloys and semiconductors. Didn't you hear about the rhenium strike on Maui, about twenty years ago? Most fabulous find in history, tremendous boom; and in three years the lodes were exhausted, the towns deserted, the price headed back toward intergalactic space. Then there are the unstable heavy elements, or the shorter-lived isotopes of the lighter ones. Again, they're rare, no matter how you scour the galaxy. When you do find some, you have to mine the stuff under difficult conditions, haul it a long way home . . . and that also drives up the cost."

Falkayn took another swallow. He had been very sober of late, so this whisky, on top of cocktails before dinner and wine with, turned him loquacious. "It isn't simply a question of scarcity making certain things expensive," he added. "Various projects are *impossible* for us, because we're bottlenecked on materials. We could progress a lot faster in interstellar exploration, for instance—with everything that that implies—if we had sufficient hafnium to make sufficient polyergic units to make sufficient computers to pilot a great many more spaceships than we can build at present. Care for some other examples?"

"N-no. I can think of several for myself," Chee said. "But any kind of nucleus can be made to order these days. And is. I've seen the bloody transmutation plants with my own bloody eyes."

"What had you been doing the night before to make your eyes bloody?" Falkayn retorted. "Sure, you're right as far as you go. But those were pygmy outfits you saw. They can't even keep up with the demand. Build them big enough, and their radioactive waste alone would sterilize whatever planets they're on. Not to mention the waste heat. An exothermic reaction gives it off directly. But so does an endothermic one...indirectly, via the power-source that furnishes the energy to make the reaction go. These are nuclear processes, remember. E equals m c squared. One gram of difference, between raw material and final product, means nine times ten to the thirteenth joules. A plant turning out a few tons of element per day would probably take the Amazon River in at one end of its cooling system and blow out a steam jet at the other end. How long before Earth became too hot for life? Ten years, maybe? Or any life-bearing world? Therefore we can't use one, whether or not it's got sophont natives. It's too valuable in other ways—quite apart from interplanetary law, public opinion, and common decency."

"I realize that much," Chee said. "This is why most existing transmuters are on minor, essentially airless bodies. Of course."

"Which means they have to install heat exchangers, feeding into the cold mass of the planetoid." Falkayn nodded. "Which is expensive. Worse, it puts engineering limitations on the size of a plant, and prohibits some operations that the managers would dearly love to carry out."

"I hadn't thought about the subject before," Chee said. "But why not use sterile worlds—new ones, for instance, where life has not begun to evolve—that have reasonable atmospheres and hydrospheres to carry off the heat for you?"

"Because planets like that belong to suns, and circle 'em fairly close," Falkayn answered. "Otherwise their air would be frozen, wouldn't it? If they have big orbits, they might retain hydrogen and helium in a gaseous state. But hydrogen's nasty. It leaks right in between the molecules of any material shielding you set up, and bollixes your nuclear reactions good. Therefore you need a world about like Earth or Cynthia, with reasonably dense air that does not include free hydrogen, and with plenty of liquid water. Well, as I said, when you have a nearby sun pouring its own energy into the atmosphere, a transmutation industry of any size will cook the planet. How can you use a river if the river's turned to vapor? Oh, there have been proposals to orbit a dust cloud around such a world, raising the albedo to near 100. But that'd tend to trap home-grown heat. Cost-effectiveness studies showed it would never pay. And furthermore, new-formed systems have a lot of junk floating around. One large asteroid, plowing into your planet, stands a good chance of wrecking every operation on it."

Falkayn refreshed his throat. "Naturally," he continued, "once a few rogues have been discovered, people thought about using them. But they were *too* cold! Temperatures near absolute zero do odd things to the properties of matter. It'd be necessary to develop an entire new technology before a factory could be erected on the typical rogue. And then it wouldn't accomplish anything. Remember, you need liquid water and gaseous atmosphere—a planet's worth of both—for your coolants. And you can't fluidify an entire cryosphere. Not within historical time. No matter how huge an operation you mount. The energy required is just plain too great. Figure it out for yourself sometime. It turns out to be as much as all Earth gets from Sol in quite a few centuries."

Falkayn cocked his feet on the table and elevated his glass. "Which happens to be approximately what our planet here will have received, in going from deep space to Beta C. and back again," he finished. He tossed off his drink and poured another.

"Don't sound that smug," Chee grumbled. "You didn't cause the event. You are not the Omnipotent: a fact which often reconciles me to the universe."

Falkayn smiled. "You'd prefer Adzel, maybe? Or Muddlehead? Or Old Nick? Hey, what a thought, creation operated for profit!— But at any rate, you can see the opportunity we've got now, if the different factors do turn out the way we hope; and it looks more and more like they will. In another ten years or so, this planet ought to have calmed down. It won't be getting more illumination than your home world or mine; the cold, exposed rocks will have blotted up what excess heat didn't get reradiated; temperature will be reasonable, dropping steadily but not too fast. The transmutation industry can begin building, according to surveys and plans already made. Heat output can be kept in balance with heat loss: the deeper into space the planet moves, the more facilities go to work on it. Since the air will be poisonous anyway, and nearly every job will be automated, radioactive trash won't pose difficulties either.

"Eventually, some kind of equilibrium will be reached. You'll have a warm surface, lit by stars, lamps here and there, radio beacons guiding down the cargo shuttles; nuclear conversion units on every suitable spot; tons of formerly rare materials moving out each day, to put some real muscle in our industry—" The excitement caught him. He was still a young man. His fist smacked into his other palm. "And *we* brought it about!"

"For a goodly reward," Chee said. "It had better be goodly."

"Oh, it will be, it will be," Falkayn burbled. "Money in great, dripping, beautiful gobs. Only think what a franchise to build here will be worth. Especially if Solar S & L can maintain rights of first reconnaissance and effective occupation."

"As against commercial competitors?" Chee asked. "Or against the unknown rivals of our whole civilization? I think they'll make rather more trouble. The kind of industry you speak of has war potentials, you know."

The planet rotated in a little over thirteen hours. Its axis was tilted about eleven degrees from the normal to the plane of its hyperbolic orbit. *Muddlin' Through* aimed for the general area of the arctic circle, where the deadly day would be short, though furnishing periodic illumination, and conditions were apparently less extreme than elsewhere.

When the ship spiraled the globe at satellite altitude and slanted downward, Falkayn drew a sharp breath. He had glimpsed the sun side before, but in brief forays when he was preoccupied with taking accurate measurements. And Beta Crucis had not been this near. At wild and ever mounting velocity, the rogue would soon round the blue giant. They were not much farther apart now than are Earth and Sol.

With four times the angular diameter, this sun raged on the horizon, in a sky turned incandescent. Clouds roiled beneath, now steaming white, now gray and lightning-riven, now black with the smoke of volcanoes seen through rents in their reaches. Elsewhere could be glimpsed stony plains, lashed by terrible winds, rain, earthquake, flood, under mountain ranges off whose flanks cascaded the glacial melt. Vapors decked half a continent, formed into mist by the chill air, until a tornado cut them in half and a pack of gales harried the fragments away. On a gunmetal ocean, icebergs the size of islands crashed into each other; but spume and spindrift off monstrous waves hid most of their destruction. As the spaceship pierced the upper atmosphere, thin though it was, she rocked with its turbulence, and the first clamor keened through her hull plates. Ahead were stacked thunderstorms.

Falkayn said between his teeth, "I've been wondering what we should name this place. Now I know." But then they were in blindness and racket. He lacked any chance to speak further.

The internal fields held weight steady, but did not keep out repeated shocks nor the rising, raving noise. Muddlehead did the essential piloting—the integration of the whole intricate system which was the ship—while the team waited to make any crucial decisions. Straining into screens and meters, striving to make sense of the chaos that ramped across them, Falkayn heard the computer speak through yells, roars, whistles, and bangs:

"The condition of clear skies over the substellar point and in early tropical afternoons prevails as usual. But this continues to be followed by violent weather, with wind velocities in excess of 500 kilometers per hour and rising daily. I note in parentheses that it would already be dangerous to enter such a meteorological territory, and that at any moment it could become impossible even for the most well-equipped vessel. Conditions in the polar regions are much as previously observed. The antarctic is undergoing heavy rainfall with frequent supersqualls. The north polar country remains comparatively cold; thus a strong front, moving southward, preserves a degree of atmospheric tranquillity at its back. I suggest that planetfall be made slightly below the arctic circle, a few minutes in advance of the dawn line, on a section of the larger northern continent which appears to be free of inundation and, judging from tectonic data, is likely to remain stable."

"All right," Chee Lan said. "You pick it. Only don't let the instruments overload your logic circuits. I guess they're feeding you information at a fantastic rate. Well, don't bother processing and evaluating it for now. Just stash it in your memory and concentrate on getting us down safe!"

"Continuous interpretation is necessary, if I am to understand an unprecedented environment like this and conduct us through it," Muddlehead answered. "However, I am already deferring consideration of facts that do not seem to have immediate significance, such as the precise reflection spectra off various types of ice fields. It is noteworthy that—" Falkayn didn't hear the rest. A bombardment of thunder half deafened him for minutes.

And they passed through a wild whiteness, snow of some kind driven by a wind that made the ship reel. And they were in what felt, by contrast, like utter peace. It was night, very dark. Scanner beams built up the picture of a jagged highland, while the ship flew on her own inorganic senses.

And landed.

Falkayn sagged a moment in his chair, simply breathing. "Cut fields," he said, and unharnessed himself. The change to planetary weight wasn't abrupt; it came within five percent of Earth pull, and he was used to bigger differences. But the silence rang in his ears. He stood, working the tension out of his muscles, before he considered the viewscreens again.

Around the ship lay a rough, cratered floor of dark rock. Mountains rose sheer in the north and east. The former began no more than four kilometers away, as an escarpment roofed with crags and streaked with the white of glaciers. Stars lit the scene, for the travelers had passed beneath the clouds, which bulked swart in the south. Alien constellations shone clear, unwavering, through wintry air. Often across them streaked meteors; like other big, childless suns, Beta

Crucis was surrounded by cosmic debris. Aurora danced glorious over the cliffs, and southeastward the first luster of morning climbed into heaven.

Falkayn examined the outside meters. The atmosphere was not breathable—CO, CO_2, CH_4, NH_4, H_2S, and such. There was some oxygen, broken loose from water molecules by solar irradiation, retained when the lighter hydrogen escaped into space, not yet recombined with other elements. But it was too little for him, and vilely cold to boot, not quite at minus 75 degrees Celsius. The ground was worse than that, below minus 200. The tropics had warmed somewhat more. But an entire world could not be brought from death temperature to room temperature in less than years—not even by a blue giant—and conditions upon it would always vary from place to place. No wonder its weather ran amok.

"I'd better go out," he said. His voice dropped near a whisper in the frozen quietness.

"Or I." Chee Lan seemed equally subdued.

Falkayn shook his head. "I thought we'd settled that. I can carry more gear, accomplish more in the available time. And somebody's got to stand by in case of trouble. You take the next outing, when we use a gravsled for a wider look around."

"I merely wanted to establish my claim to an exterior mission before I go cage-crazy," she snapped.

That's more like the way we ought to be talking. Heartened, Falkayn proceeded to the airlock. His suit and his equipment were ready for him. Chee helped him into the armor. He cycled through and stood upon a new world.

An old one, rather: but one that was undergoing a rebirth such as yonder stars had never seen before.

He breathed deeply of chemical-tainted recycled air and strode off. His movements were a trifle clumsy, he stumbled now and then, on the thick soles attached to his boots. But without them, he would probably have been helpless. *Muddlin' Through* could pump heat from her nuclear powerplant into her landing jacks, to keep them at a temperature their metal could stand. But the chill in these rocks would suck warmth straight through any ordinary space brogan. His feet could freeze before he knew it. Even with extra insulation, his stay outdoors was sharply limited.

The sun bounded him more narrowly, though. Day was strengthening visibly, fire and long shadows across desolation. The shielding in his armor allowed him about half an hour in the full radiance of Beta Crucis.

"How are things?" Chee's voice sounded faint in his earplugs, through a rising buzz of static.

"Thing-like." Falkayn unlimbered a counter from his backpack and passed it above the ground. The readoff showed scant radioactivity. Much of what there was, was probably induced by solar wind in the past decade, before the atmosphere thickened. (Not that its insignificant ozone layer was a lot of protection at present.) No matter, men and the friends of men would make their own atoms here. Falkayn hammered in a neutron-analysis spike and continued on his way.

That looked like an interesting outcrop. He struck loose a sample.

The sun lifted into view. His self-darkening faceplate went almost black. Gusts moaned down off the mountains, and vapors began to swirl above the glacial masses.

Falkayn chose a place for a sonic probe and began to assemble the needful tripod. "Better not dawdle," said Chee's distorted tone. "The radiation background's getting foul."

"I know, I know," the Hermetian said. "But we want some idea about the underlying strata, don't we?" The combination of glare and protection against it handicapped his eyes, making delicate adjustments difficult. He swore picturesquely, laid tongue on lip, and slogged ahead with the job. When at last he had the probe in action, transmitting data back to the ship, his safety margin was ragged.

He started his return. The vessel looked unexpectedly small, standing beneath those peaks that also enclosed him on the right. Beta Crucis hurled wave upon wave of heat at his back, to batter past reflecting paint and refrigerating unit. Sweat made his undergarments soggy and stank in his nostrils. Simultaneously, cold stole up into his boots, until toenails hurt. He braced himself, beneath the weight of armor and gear, and jogtrotted.

A yell snatched his gaze around. He saw the explosion on the clifftop, like a white fountain. A moment later, the bawl of it echoed in his helmet and the earth shock threw him to his knees. He staggered erect and tried to run. The torrent—part liquid flood, part solid avalanche—roared and leaped in pursuit. It caught him halfway to the ship.

XIII

REFLEX cast him down and rolled him into a ball an instant before the slide arrived. Then he was in darkness and bass noise, tumbled about, another object among the boulders and ice chunks that smashed against his armor.

Concussion struck through metal and padding. His head rocked in the helmet. Blow after blow kicked him loose from awareness.

The cataract ground to a halt. Falkayn realized dazedly that he was buried in it. His knees remained next his belly, his arms across the faceplate. He mumbled at the pain that throbbed through him, and tried to stir. It was impossible. Terror smote. He yelled and strained. No use. Sheer surrounding bulk locked him into his embryonic crouch.

The freezing began. Radiation is not an efficient process. Conduction is, especially when the stuff around drinks every calorie that a far higher temperature will supply. Falkayn's heating coils drained their powerpack before he had recovered consciousness. He could not thresh about to keep warm by effort. He tried to call on his radio, but it seemed to be knocked out; silence filled his skull, darkness his vision, cold his body.

The thought trickled: *I'm helpless. There is not one goddamned thing in the continuum I can do to save myself. It's an awful feeling.*

Defiance: *At least my mind is my own. I can go out thinking, reliving memories, like a free man.* But nothing came to mind save blackness, stillness, and cold.

He clamped his jaws together against the clatter of teeth

and hung bulldog-wise onto the resolution that he would not panic again.

He was lying thus, no more than a spark left in his brain, when the glacial mass steamed away from him. He sprawled stupid in the fog and evaporating liquid. Beta Crucis burned off the mists and beat on his armor. Elsewhere the avalanche was boiling more gradually off the valley floor. But *Muddlin' Through* cruised overhead, slowly, fanning a low-level energy beam across the snows. When her scanners detected Falkayn, a tractor beam extended. He was snatched up, hauled through a cargo port, and dumped on deck for Chee Lan's profane ministrations.

A couple of hours later he sat in his bunk, nursing a bowl of soup, and regarded her with clear eyes. "Sure, I'm fine now," he said. "Give me a nightwatch's sleep and I'll be my old self."

"Is that desirable?" the Cynthian snorted. "If I were so tubeheaded as to go out on dangerous terrain without a gravbelt to flit me aloft, I'd trade myself in on a newer model."

Falkayn laughed. "You never suggested it either," he said. "It'd have meant I could carry less gear. What did happen?"

"*Ying-ng-ng* . . . the way Muddlehead and I reconstruct it, that glacier wasn't water. It was mostly dry ice—solid carbon dioxide—with some other gases mixed in. Local temperature has finally gotten to the sublimation point, or a touch higher. But the heat of vaporization must be fed in. And this area chills off fast after dark; and daylight lasts just a few hours; and, too, I suspect the more volatile components were stealing heat from the main frozen mass. The result was an unstable equilibrium. It happened to collapse precisely when you were outside. How very like the fates! A major part of the ice pack sublimed, explosively, and dislodged the rest from the escarpment. If only we'd thought to take reflection spectra and thermocouple readings—"

"But we didn't," Falkayn said, "and I for one don't feel too guilty. We can't think of everything. Nobody can. We're bound to do most of our learning by trial and error."

"Preferably with someone standing by to retrieve us when it really hits the fan."

"Uh-huh. We ought to be part of a regular exploratory fleet. But under present circumstances, we aren't, that's all." Falkayn chuckled. "At least I've had my opinion strengthened as to what this planet should be named. Satan."

"Which means?"

"The enemy of the divine, the source of evil, in one of our terrestrial religions."

"But any reasonable being can see that the divine itself is— Oh, well, never mind. I thought you humans had run out of mythological names for planets. Surely you've already christened one Satan."

"M-m, I don't remember. There's Lucifer, of course, and Ahriman, and Loki, and— Anyhow, the traditional Satan operates an underworld of fire, except where it's icy, and amuses himself thinking up woes for wicked souls. Appropriate, no?"

"If he's like some other antigods I've met," Chee said, "he can make you rich, but you always find in the end that it was not a good idea to bargain with him."

Falkayn shrugged. "We'll see. Where are we at the moment?"

"Cruising over the night side, taking readings and pictures. I don't see any point in lingering. Every indication we've gotten, every extrapolation we can make, indicates that the course of events will gladden van Rijn to the clinkered cockles of his greedy heart. That is, the whole cryosphere will fluidify, and in a decade or so conditions will be suitable for industry. Meanwhile, however, things are getting more dangerous by the hour."

As if to underline Chee's words, the ship lurched and her wind-smitten hull plates belled. She was through the storm in a minute or two. But Falkayn reflected what that storm must be like, thus to affect a thermonuclear-powered, gravity-controlling, force-screened, sensor-guided, and computer-piloted vessel capable of crossing interstellar space and fighting a naval engagement.

"I agree," he said. "Let's collect as much more data as we

safely can in—oh, the next twenty-four hours—and then line out for home. Let somebody else make detailed studies later. We'll need a combat group here anyway, I suppose, to mount guard on this claim."

"The sooner Old Nick learns it's worth his while to send that group, the better." Chee switched her tail. "If enemy pickets are posted when it arrives, we've all got troubles."

"Don't worry," Falkayn said. "Our distinguished opponents must live quite a ways off, seeing they haven't even gotten a scout here yet."

"Are you certain their advance expedition did not come and go while we were en route?" Chee asked slowly.

"It'd still be around. We spent a couple of weeks in transit and a bit longer at work. We're quitting early because two beings in one ship can only do so much—not because we've learned everything we'd like to know—and because we've a sense of urgency. The others, having no reason to suspect we're on to their game, should logically have planned on a more leisurely and thorough survey." Falkayn scratched his chin. The stubble reminded him that he was overdue for a dose of antibeard enzyme. "Of course," he said, "their surveyors may have been around, detected us approaching, and run to fetch Daddy. Who might be on his way as of now, carrying a rather large stick." He raised his voice, jocularly. "You don't spot any starships, do you, Muddlehead?"

"No," said the computer.

"Good." Falkayn eased back on his pillows. This craft was equipped to register the quasi-instantaneous "wake" of troubled space that surrounded an operating hyperdrive, out almost to the theoretical limit of about one light-year. "I hardly expected—"

"My detectors are turned off," Muddlehead explained.

Falkayn jerked upright. The soup spilled from his bowl, across Chee Lan, who went into the air with a screech. *"What?"* the man cried.

"Immediately before our run to take orbit, you instructed me to keep every facility alert for local dangers," Muddlehead reminded him. "It followed that computer capability should not be tied up by monitoring instruments directed at interstellar space."

"Judas in a reactor," Falkayn groaned. "I thought you'd acquired more initiative than that. What'd those cookbook engineers on Luna do when they overhauled you?"

Chee shook herself, dog fashion, spraying soup across him. *"Ya-t'in'chai-ourh,"* she snarled, which will not bear translation. "Get cracking on those detectors!"

For a moment, silence hummed, under the shriek outside. The possessions that crowded Falkayn's cabin—pictures, books, taper and spools and viewer, a half-open closet jamful of elegant garments, a few souvenirs and favorite weapons, a desk piled with unanswered letters—became small and fragile and dear. Human and Cynthian huddled together, not noticing that they did so, her fangs shining within the crook of his right arm.

The machine words fell: "Twenty-three distinct sources of pulsation are observable in the direction of Circinus."

Falkayn sat rigid. It leaped through him: *Nobody we know lives out that way. They must be headed here. We won't be sure of their course or distance unless we run off a base line and triangulate, or wait and see how they behave. But who can doubt they are the enemy?*

As if across an abyss he heard Chee Lan whisper, "Twenty...mortal...three of them. That's a task force! Unless— Can you make any estimates?"

"Signal-to-noise ratio suggests they are within one-half light-year," the computer said, with no more tone in its voice than ever before. "Its time rate of change indicates a higher pseudospeed than a Technic shipmaster would consider wise in approaching a star like Beta Crucis that is surrounded by an unusual density of gas and solid material. The ratio of the separate signal amplitudes would appear to fit the hypothesis of a fleet organized around one quite large vessel, approximately equivalent to a League battleship, three light cruisers or similar units, and nineteen smaller, faster craft. But of course these conclusions are tentative, predicated on assumptions such as that it is indeed an armed force and is actually bound our way. Even under that class of hypotheses, the probable error of the data is too large at present to allow reliable evaluations."

"If we wait for those," Chee growled, deep in her throat,

"we'll be reliably dead. I'll believe it's *not* a war fleet sent by our self-appointed enemies, with orders to swat anybody it finds, when the commander invites us to tea." She moved away from Falkayn, crouched before him on the blanket, tail bottled and eyes like jade lamps. "Now what's our next move?"

The man drew a breath. He felt the damp cold leave his palms, the heartbeat within him drop back to a steady slugging, a military officer take command of his soul. "We can't stay on Satan, or nearby," he declared. "They'd pick up our engines on neutrino detectors, if nothing else, and blast us. We could run away on ordinary gravitics, take an orbit closer to the sun, hope its emission would screen us till they go away. But that doesn't look any good either. They'll hardly leave before we'd've taken a lethal cumulative radiation dose . . . if they intend to leave at all. We might, alternatively, assume a very large orbit around Beta. Our minimal emission would be detectable against the low background; but we could pray that no one happens to point an instrument in our direction. I don't like that notion either. We'd be stuck for some indefinite time, with no way to get a message home."

"We'd send a report in a capsule, wouldn't we? There's a full stock of four aboard." Chee pondered. "No, effectively two, because we'd have to rob the others of their capacitors if those two are going to have the energy to reach Sol—or anyplace from which the word could go on to Sol, I'm afraid. Still, we do have a pair."

Falkayn shook his head. "Too slow. They'd be observed—"

"They don't emit much. It's not as if they had nuclear generators."

"A naval-type detector can nevertheless spot a capsule under hyperdrive at farther range than we've got available, Chee. And the thing's nothing more than a tube, for Judas's sake, with an elementary sort of engine, a robopilot barely able to steer where it's programmed for and holler, 'Here I am, come get me,' on its radio at journey's end. No, any pursuer can zero in, match-phase, and either blow the capsule up or take it aboard."

The Cynthian eased her thews somewhat. Having assimilated the fact of crisis, she was becoming as coldly rational as the Hermetian. "I gather you think we should run for home ourselves," she said. "Not a bad idea, if none of those units can outpace us."

"We're pretty fast," he said.

"Some kinds of combat ship are faster. They fill space with powerplant and oscillators that we reserve for cargo."

"I know. It's uncertain what the result of a race would be. Look, though." Falkayn leaned forward, fists clenched on knees. "Whether we have longer legs than they, or vice versa, a half light-year head start will scarcely make any difference across two hundred. We don't much increase the risk by going out to meet them. And we just might learn something, or be able to do something, or—I don't know. It's a hand we'll have to play as it is dealt. Mainly, however, think of this. If we go hyper with a powerful surge of 'wake,' we'll blanket the takeoff of a tiny message capsule. It'll be out of detection range before anybody can separate its emission from ours . . . especially if we're headed toward him. So whatever happens to us, we'll've got our information home. We'll've done the enemy that much damage, at least!"

Chee regarded him for a while that grew quite silent, until she murmured, "I suspect your emotions are speaking. But today they make sense."

"Start preparing for action," Falkayn rapped. He swung his feet to the deck and stood up. A wave of giddiness went through him. He rested against the bulkhead until it passed. Exhaustion was a luxury he couldn't afford. He'd take a stim pill and pay the metabolic price later, if he survived.

Chee's words lingered at the back of his mind. *No doubt she's right. I'm being fueled by anger at what they did to me. I want revenge on them.* A jag went along his nerves. He gasped. *Or is it fear . . . that they might do the thing to me again?*

I'll die before that happens. And I'll take some of them with me to—to Satan!

XIV

STARS glittered in their prismatic colors and multiple thousands, Beta Crucis little more than the brightest among them; the Milky Way spilled around crystal darkness; the far cold whirlpools of a few sister galaxies could be seen, when the League ship made contact with the strangers.

Falkayn sat in the bridge, surrounded by outside views and engine murmur. Chee Lan was aft, in the fire control center. Either one could have been anywhere aboard, to receive information from the computer and issue it orders. Their separation was no more than a precaution in case of attack, and no wider than a hull permeated by light-speed electronic webs. But loneliness pressed in on Falkayn. The uniform he wore beneath his space armor, in place of a long john, was less a diplomatic formality than a defiance.

He stared through his helmet, which was still open, first at the screens and then at the instruments. His merely flesh-and-blood organism could not apprehend and integrate the totality of data presented, as the computer could. But an experienced eye took in a general picture.

Muddlin' Through was plunging along a curve that would soon intercept one of the fleet's outriders. She must have been detected, from the moment she went on hyperdrive. But none of those vessels had altered course or reckless pseudospeed. Instead, they proceeded as before, in a tighter formation than any Technic admiral would have adopted.

It looked as if the alien commander wouldn't grant his subordinates the least freedom of action. His entire group moved in a unit, one hammer hurled at target.

Falkayn wet his lips. Sweat prickled along his ribs. "Damnation," he said, "don't they want to parley? To find out who we are, if nothing else?"

They didn't have to, of course. They could simply let *Muddlin' Through* pass between them. Or they might plan on a quick phase-match and assault, the moment she came in ready range—so quick that her chance of shifting the phase of her own quantum oscillations, thus becoming transparent to whatever they threw at her, would be slight.

"They may not recognize our signal for what it is," Chee Lan suggested. Her voice on the intercom made Falkayn visualize her, small, furry, and deadly . . . yes, she'd insist on operating one gun by hand, if battle broke—

"They know enough about us to establish spies in our home territory. So they know our standard codes," Falkayn snapped. "Give 'em another toot, Muddlehead."

Viewscreens flickered with the slight alterations in hypervelocity imposed by the outercom as it modulated drive vibrations to carry dots and dashes. That system was still new and crude (Falkayn could remember when, early in his career, he had been forced to turn his engines themselves on and off to transmit a message) but the call was simple. *Urgent. Assume normal state and prepare for radionic communication on standard band.*

"No response," the computer said after a minute.

"Cease transmission," Falkayn ordered. "Chee, can you think of any motive for their behavior?"

"I can imagine quite a number of different explanations," the Cynthian said. "That's precisely the trouble."

"Uh, yeh. Especially when none of 'em are apt to be right. One culture's rationality isn't quite the same as another's. Though I did think any civilization capable of space flight must necessarily— No matter. They obviously aren't going to detach a ship for talkie-talkie. So I don't propose to steer into a possible trap. Change course, Muddlehead. Run parallel to them."

Engines growled. Stars swung around the screens. The situation stabilized. Falkayn gazed toward the unseen strangers. They were crossing the clouded glory of

Sagittarius. . . . "We may learn a bit by analyzing their 'wake' patterns, now that we're close enough to get accurate readings," he said. "But we hardly dare follow them clear to Satan."

"I don't like accompanying them any distance," Chee said. "They travel too bloody-be-gibbeted fast for this kind of neighborhood."

Falkayn reached out an ungauntleted hand for the pipe he had laid on a table. It had gone cold. He made a production of rekindling it. The smoke gave tongue and nostrils a comforting love-bite. "We're safer than they are," he said. "We know more about the region, having been here a while. For instance, we've charted several asteroid orbits, remember?"

"You don't believe, then, they had a scout like ours, who paid a visit before we arrived?"

"No. That'd imply their home sun—or at least a large outpost of their domain—is nearby, as cosmic distances go. Now the Beta Crucis region isn't what you'd call thoroughly explored, but some expeditions have come through, like the one from Lemminkainen. And explorers always keep a weather eye out for signs of atomic-powered civilizations. I feel sure that somebody, sometime, would've identified the neutrino emission from any such planet within fifty light-years of here. True, conceivably those nuclear generators haven't arrived yet. But on the other hand, voyages have been made beyond this star. Altogether, every probability says these characters have come a considerable ways. The messenger ship from Luna must barely have had time to notify them about the existence of the rogue."

"And they committed a whole fleet immediately—with no preliminary investigation—and it's roaring down on goal as if this were clear one-hydrogen-atom-per-c.c. space—and not even trying to discover who we are? *Ki-yao!*"

Falkayn's grin was taut and brief. "If a Cynthian says an action is too impulsive, then by my battered halidom, it is."

"But these same beings . . . presumably the same . . . they organized Serendipity . . . one of the longest-range, most patience-demanding operations I've ever heard of."

"There are parallels in human history, if not in yours.

And, hm, humans—more or less humans—were involved in our case—"

The computer said, "Incoming hypercode." The display screen blinked with a series that Falkayn recognized: *Request for talk acknowledged. Will comply. Propose we rendezvous ten astronomical units hence, five hundred kilometers apart.*

He didn't stop to inform Chee—the ship would do that— nor shout his own astonishment, nor feel it except for an instant. Too much work was on hand. Orders rapped from him: Send agreement. Lay appropriate course. Keep alert for treachery, whether from the vessel that would stop and parley or from the rest of the fleet, which might double back under hyperdrive.

"The entire group remains together," Muddlehead interrupted. "Evidently they will meet us as one."

"What?" he choked. "But that's ridiculous."

"No." Chee's voice fell bleak. "If twenty-three of them fire on us simultaneously, we're dead."

"Perhaps not." Falkayn clamped the pipe more firmly between his jaws. "Or they may be honest. We'll know in another thirty seconds."

The ships cut off their quantum oscillators and flashed into the relativistic state of matter-energy. There followed the usual period of hastily calculated and applied thrust, until kinetic velocities were matched. Falkayn let Muddlehead take care of that and Chee stand by the defenses. He concentrated on observing what he might about the strangers.

It was little. A scanner could track a ship and magnify the image for him, but details got lost across those dimly lighted distances. And details were what mattered; the laws of nature do not allow fundamental differences between types of spacecraft.

He did find that the nineteen destroyers or escort pursuers, or whatever you wanted to call them, were streamlined for descent into atmosphere: but radically streamlined, thrice the length of his vessel without having appreciably more beam. They looked like stiffened conger eels. The cruisers bore more resemblance to sharks, with gaunt finlike structures that must be instrument or control turrets. The battleship was basically a huge spheroid, but this was obscured by the steel towers, pillboxes, derricks, and emplacements that covered her hull.

You might as well use naval words for yonder craft, even though none corresponded exactly to such classes in the League. They bristled with guns, missile launchers, energy projectors. Literally, they bristled. Falkayn had never before encountered vessels so heavily armed. With the machinery and magazines that entailed . . . where the devil was room left for a crew?

Instruments said that they employed force screens, radars, fusion power—the works. It was hardly a surprise. The unorthodox, tight formation was. If they expected trouble, why not disperse? One fifty-megaton warhead exploding in their midst would take out two or three of them directly, and fill the rest with radiation. Maybe that wouldn't disable their computers and other electronic apparatus—depended on whether they used things like transistors—but it would give a lethal dose to a lot of crewfolk, and put the rest in the hospital.

Unless the aliens didn't mind X-rays and neutrons. But then they couldn't be protoplasmic. With or without drugs, the organic molecule can only tolerate a certain bombardment before it shatters. Unless they'd developed some unheard-of-screen to deflect uncharged particles. Unless, unless, unless!

"Are you in communication with any of their mechanisms?" Falkayn asked.

"No," Muddlehead answered. "They are simply decelerating as they would have had to sooner or later if they wish to take orbit around Satan. The task of matching velocities is left to us."

"Arrogant bastards, aren't they?" Chee said.

"With an arsenal like theirs, arrogance comes easy." Falkayn settled into his chair. "We can play their game. Hold off on the masers. Let them call us." He wondered if his pipe looked silly, sticking out of an open space helmet. To hell with it. He wanted a smoke. A beer would have been still more welcome. The strain of wondering if their weapons were about to cut loose on him was turning his mouth dry.

An energy blast would smite before it could be detected. It might not penetrate the armor too fast for *Muddlin' Through* to go hyper and escape. That would be determined by various unpredictables, like its power and the exact place it happened to strike. *But if the aliens want to kill us, why bother to revert? They can overhaul us, maybe not their capital ships, but those destroyers must be faster. And we can't stay out of phase with nineteen different enemies, each trying to match us, for very long.*

Yet if they want to talk, why didn't they answer our call earlier?

As if she had read her companion's mind, Chee Lan said, "I have an idea that may account for parts of their behavior, Dave. Suppose they are wildly impulsive. Learning about Satan, they dispatch a task force to grab it. The grabbing may be away from members of their own race. We don't know how unified they are. And they can't have learned that Serendipity's cover is blown. Nor can they be sure that it isn't.

"Under those circumstances, most sophonts would be cautious. They'd send an advance party to investigate and report back, before committing themselves substantially. Not these creatures, though. These charge right ahead, ready to blast their way through any opposition or die in the attempt.

"And they do find someone waiting for them: us, one small ship, cheekily running out to make rendezvous. You or I would wonder if more vessels, bigger ones, aren't lying doggo near Satan. Our first thought would be to talk with the other. But they don't emote that way. They keep on going. Either we are alone and can safely be clobbered, or we have friends and there will be a battle. The possibility of retreat or negotiation isn't considered. Nor do they alter any vectors on our account. After all, we're headed straight for them. We'll bring ourselves in killing range.

"Well, we fool them, changing over to a parallel course. They decide they'd better hear us out; or, at least, that they might as well do so. Maybe it occurs to them that we could perhaps get away, bring word back to Earth, in spite of everything. You see, they'd have to detach one or more destroyers to chase us down. And their formation suggests that, for some reason, they're reluctant to do this.

"In short, another lightning decision has been made, regardless of what may be at hazard."

"It sounds altogether crazy," Falkayn objected.

"To you, not me. Cynthians are less stodgy than humans. I grant you, my people—my own society—is forethoughtful. But I know other cultures on my planet where berserk action is normal."

"But those're technologically primitive, Chee. Aren't they? Hang it, you can't operate an atomic-powered civilization that way. Things'd fall apart on you. Even Old Nick doesn't have absolute authority in his own outfit. He has to work with advisers, executives, people of every kind and rank. The normal distribution curve guarantees enough naturally cautious types to put the brakes on an occasional reckless—"

Falkayn broke off. The central receiver was flickering to life.

"They're calling us," he said. His belly muscles tightened. "Want an auxiliary screen to watch?"

"No," Chee Lan answered starkly. "I'll listen, but I want my main attention on our weapons and theirs."

The maser beams locked on. Falkayn heard the report, "Their transmission is from the battleship," with half an ear. The rest of him focused on the image that appeared before him.

A man! Falkayn almost lost his pipe. A man, lean, with gray-speckled hair, smoldering eyes, body clad in a drab coverall. . . . *I should've guessed. I should've been prepared.* Scant background was visible: an instrument console of obviously non-Technic manufacture, shining beneath a hard white light.

Falkayn swallowed. "Hello, Hugh Latimer," he said most softly.

"We have not met," the accented, unemotional Anglic replied.

"No. But who else might you be?"

"Who are you?"

Falkayn's mind scrambled. His name was a hole card in a wild game. He wasn't about to turn it up for the enemy to make deductions from. "Sebastian Tombs," he replied. The alias was unoriginal, but Latimer would scarcely have come upon the source. Mere chance had put those books in the library of Duke Robert for an inquisitive boy to find, and thus discover that ancient languages weren't all classics and compositions but were sometimes fun—"Master merchant and captain in the Polesotechnic League." Asserting his rank should do no harm, and possibly a little good. "Are you in command of your group?"

"No."

"Then I'd like to speak with whoever is in charge."

"You shall," Hugh Latimer told him. "He has ordered it."

Falkayn bridled. "Well, connect him."

"You do not understand," said the other. Still his voice had no inflection, and his eyes stared directly out of the hollow-cheeked, deeply tanned face. "Gahood wants you to come here."

The pipestem snapped between Falkayn's teeth. He cast it aside and exclaimed, "Are you living in the same universe as me? Do you expect I'd—" He curbed himself. "I have a few suggestions for your commander," he said, "but I'll reserve them, because his anatomy may not be adapted for such things. Just ask him if he considers it reasonable for me, for anyone in my crew, to put himself at your mercy that way."

Did the least hint of fear cross Latimer's rigid features? "My orders have been given me. What value for you if I went back, argued, and was punished?" He hesitated. "You have two choices, I think. You can refuse. In that case, I imagine Gahood will start firing. You may or may not escape; he does not seem to care greatly. On the other hand, you can come. He is intrigued at the thought of meeting a . . . wild human. You may accomplish something. I do not know. Perhaps you and I can work out conditions beforehand that will give you assurance of being able to return. But we mustn't take long, or he will grow impatient. Angry." His fear was now unmistakable. "And then anything might happen."

XV

THE danger in coming near the enemy was obvious. Not only an energy beam, but a material missile could hit before effective reaction was possible. However, the danger was mutual. *Muddlin' Through* might be a gnat compared to the battlewagon, but she was every bit as mean. Falkayn didn't fancy leaving five hundred kilometers between him and her. He was dismayed when Latimer insisted.

"Do not forget, my life's work was learning everything I could about Technic civilization," the gaunt man said. "I know the capabilities of a vessel like yours. Besides an assortment of small arms, and several light guns for dogfights, she mounts four heavy blast cannon and carries four nuclear torpedoes. At close range, such armament makes us too nearly equal. Let a dispute arise, and we could doubtless kill you, but ships of ours might also perish."

"If my crew are too far off to strike effectively, what'll stop you from taking me prisoner?" Falkayn protested.

"Nothing," Latimer said, "except lack of motive. I think Gahood merely wants to interrogate you, and perhaps give you a message to take back to your masters. If you delay, though, he'll lose patience and order you destroyed."

"All right!" Falkayn said harshly. "I'll come as fast as I can. If I don't report back within an hour of entering, my crew will assume treachery on your part and act accordingly. In that case, you might get a rude surprise." He broke the connection and sat for a moment, clenching the arms of his chair, trying not to shudder.

Chee Lan padded in, squatted at his feet and looked

upward. "You don't want to go," she said with uncommon gentleness. "You're afraid of being drugged again."

Falkayn nodded, a jerk of his head. "You can't imagine what it's like," he said through a tightened gullet.

"I can go."

"No. I am the skipper." Falkayn rose. "Let's get me ready."

"If nothing else," Chee said, "we can guarantee you won't be captured."

"What? How?"

"Of course, the price might be death. But that's one fear you've been trained to control."

"Oh-h-h," Falkayn breathed. "I see what you mean." He snapped his fingers. His eyes sparked. "Why didn't I think of it?"

And so presently he departed.

He wore an impeller on his space armor, but this was reserve. His actual transportation was a gravsled. He kept the canopy down, the cockpit filled with air, as another reserve; in case his helmet got cracked or something, he needn't spend time preparing this minimal, skeletal vehicle for departure. But atmosphere or no, he rode in ghostly silence, naught save a faint tug of acceleration making his broomstick flight feel real. The stars had dimmed and withdrawn in his vision. That was prosaically due to the panel lights, their greenish glow desensitizing his retinae. Nevertheless, he missed the stars. He grasped his controls more tightly than required and whistled up a tune for company.

> *Oh, a tinker came a-strollin',*
> *A-strollin' down the Strand—*

It didn't seem inappropriate for what might be the last melody ever to pass his lips. Solemnity had no appeal. His surroundings, that mountain of a ship bulking closer and closer before him, furnished as much seriousness as anybody could want.

Latimer's radio voice chopped off his bawdy little ballad. "You will be guided to an airlock by a beam at 158.6

megaherz. Park your sled in the chamber and wait for me."

"What?" Falkayn gibed. "You don't aim to pipe me aboard?"

"I do not understand."

"You wouldn't. Forget it. I'm not ambitious to become a haggis anyway." Falkayn tuned in the signal and set the sled to home on it. He got busy photographing the battleship as he neared, studying the fortress-like superstructures himself, stowing every possible datum in memory. But part of his mind freewheeled, wondering.

That Latimer is sure one overworked chap. He acts like a kind of executive officer for Gahood, whatever Gahood is. But he also acts like the communications officer, boatswain...everything!

Well, given sufficient automation, you don't need much crew. The all-around Renaissance man has come back these days, with a battery of computers to specialize for him. But some jobs remain that machines don't do well. They haven't the motivation, the initiative, the organismic character of true sophonts. We—each civilized species man's encountered—we've never succeeded in building a hundred percent robotic vessel for more than the elementary, cut-and-dried jobs. And when you're exploring, trading, conducting a war, anything that takes you into unpredictable situations, the size of crew you need goes up. Partly to meet psychological necessities, of course; but partly to fulfill the mission itself in all its changing complexity.

Look how handicapped Chee and I have been, in being just two. That was because of an emergency, which Gahood did not face. Why is Latimer the only creature I've spoken to in yonder armada?

His approach curve brought Falkayn near a cruiser. More than ever he was struck by the density of her armament. And those fin-shaped turrets were thinner than he had imagined. They were fine for instruments, with that much surface area, and indeed they appeared to be studded with apparatus. But it was hard to see how an animal of any plausible size and shape could move around inside them. Or, for that matter, inside the hull, considering how packed it must be.

The thought did not jolt Falkayn. It had grown in him for

a while and was quietly born. He plugged the jack on his helmet into the maser unit locked on *Muddlin' Through.* "You read me, Chee Lan?" he asked.

"Aye. What report?"

Falkayn switched to the Eriau they had learned on Merseia. Latimer would scarcely know it, if he had ways to monitor. The Hermetian described what he had seen. "I'm damn near convinced that everything except the battleship is strictly robot," he finished. "That'd account for a lot of things. Like their formation. Gahood has to keep closer tabs on them than he would on live captains. And he cares less about losses in battle. They're merely machines. Probably radiation-proof anyhow. And if he's got a single crewed ship, it'd be easy—even natural—for him to charge off the way he did. Of course, no matter how his race has organized its economy, a fleet like this is expensive. But it's more replaceable than several hundred or thousand highly skilled crewpeople. For a prize like Satan, one might well take the gamble."

"I-yirh, your idea sounds plausible, David. Especially if Gahood is something like a war lord, with a personal following ready to go anywhere at any moment. Then he might not have needed to consult others... I feel a touch more hope. The enemy isn't quite as formidable as he seemed."

"Formidable enough. If I don't report back to you in the hour, or if you have any other reason to suspect something's fused, don't you play Loyal Retainer. Get the devil out of here."

She started to object. He overrode her words with the reminder: "I'll be dead. Nothing you can do for me, except whatever revenge may come from getting our information home."

She paused. "Understood," she said finally.

"You have a fifty-fifty chance of eluding pursuit, I'd say, if there is any," he told her. "Nineteen destroyers can phase-match you by sheer random trying if nothing else. But if they're robots, you might outfox them first. Or at least send another message capsule off without their noticing.... Well, I'm closing in now. Will be out of touch. Good faring, Chee."

He could not follow her answer. It was in an archaic version of her native language. But he caught a few words, like "blessing," and her voice was not altogether steady.

The battleship loomed sheer before him. He cut off his autopilot and proceeded on manual. As he left the shadow of a turret, light spilled blindingly into his view. It came from a circle big as a cargo hatch, the airlock he must be supposed to use. He steered with care past the thick coaming and outer gate. The inner valve was shut. Ship's gravity caught at him, making it a little tricky to set down. Having done so, he cycled out through the cockpit minilock as fast as he was able.

Quickly, then, he unhooked the thing at his belt and made it ready. Held in his left hand, it gave him a frosty courage. Waiting for Latimer, he examined the sled's instrument panel through the canopy. Gravpull felt higher than Earth standard, and the scale confirmed this with a value of 1.07. Illumination was more than a third again what he was used to. Spectra distribution indicated an F-type home star, though you couldn't really tell from fluorescents. . . .

The inner valve opened. Little air whiffed through; the lock was compound, with another chamber behind the first. A spacesuited human figure trod in. Behind the faceplate, Latimer's austere features showed in highlights and darknesses. He carried a blaster. It was an ordinary pistol type, doubtless acquired on Luna. But at his back moved a metal shape, tall, complex, a multitude of specialized limbs sprouting from the cylindrical body to end in sensors and effectors: a robot.

"What a rude way to receive an ambassador," Falkayn said. He did not raise his hands.

Latimer didn't ask him to. "Precaution," he explained matter-of-factly. "You are not to enter armed. And first we check for bombs or other surprises you may have brought."

"Go ahead," Falkayn answered. "My vehicle's clean and, as agreed, I left my guns behind. I do have this, however," He elevated his left fist, showing the object it grasped.

Latimer recoiled. *"Jagnath hamman!* What is that?"

"Grenade. Not nuclear, only an infantry make. But the stuffing is tordenite, with colloidal phosphorus for seasoning. It could mess things up rather well within a meter or two radius right here. Much nastier in an oxygenous atmosphere, of course. I've pulled the pin, and counted almost the whole five seconds before driving the plunger back in. Nothing except my thumb keeps it from going off. Oh, yes, it spits a lot of shrapnel too."

"But—you—no!"

"Don't fret yourself, comrade. The spring isn't too strong for me to hold down for an hour. I don't want to be blown up. It's just that I want even less to be taken prisoner, or shot, or something like that. You abide by the diplomatic courtesies and we won't have any problems."

"I must report," Latimer said thickly. He plugged into what was evidently an intercom. Emotionless, the robot checked out the sled as it had been ordered, and waited.

Latimer said, "He will see you. Come." He led the way, his movements still jerky with outrage. The robot brought up the rear.

Falkayn felt walled between them. His grenade was no defense against anything except capture. If the others wished, they could maneuver him into destruction without suffering undue damage. Or their ship wouldn't be harmed in the least if they potted him on his return, after he was well clear.

Forget it. You came here to learn what you might. You're no hero. You'd one hell of a lot rather be quite far away, a drink in your grip and a wench on your knee, prevaricating about your exploits. But this could be a war brewing. Whole planets could get attacked. A little girl, as it might be your own kid niece, could lie in an atom-blasted house, her face a cinder and her eyeballs melted, screaming for her daddy who's been killed in a spaceship and her mother who's been smashed against the pavement. Maybe matters aren't really that bad. But maybe they are. How can you pass up a chance to do something? You've got to inhabit the same skin as yourself.

It itches. And I can't scratch. A grin bent one corner of Falkayn's mouth. The second lock chamber had been closed, pressure had been restored, the inner valve was opening. He stepped through.

There was not much to see. A corridor led off, bare metal, blazingly lit. Footfalls rang on its deck. Otherwise a quiver of engines, hoarse murmur of forced-draft ventilation, were the sole relief in its blankness. No doors gave on it, merely grilles, outlets, occasional enigmatic banks of instruments or controls. Another robot passed through a transverse hall several meters ahead: a different model, like a scuttling disc with tentacles and feelers, doubtless intended for some particular kind of maintenance work. But the bulk of the ship's functioning must be integrated, even more than on a human-built vessel; she was herself one vast machine.

Despite the desertion, Falkayn got a sense of raw, overwhelming vitality. Perhaps it came from the sheer scale of everything, or the ceaseless throbbing, or a more subtle clue like the proportions of that which he saw, the sense of masses huge and heavy but crouched to pounce.

"The atmosphere is breathable," Latimer's radio voice said. "Its density is slightly above Earth sea level." Falkayn imitated him with his free hand, opening the bleeder valve to let pressures equalize gradually before he slid back his faceplate and filled his lungs.

Except for the added information, he wished he hadn't. The air was desert hot, desert dry, with enough thunder-smelling ozone to sting. Other odors blew on those booming currents, pungencies like spice and leather and blood, strengthening as the party approached what must be living quarters. Latimer didn't seem to mind the climate or the glare. But he was used to them. Wasn't he?

"How big a crew do you have?" Falkayn asked.

"Gahood will put the questions." Latimer looked straight before him, one muscle twitching in his cheek. "I advise you in the strongest terms, give him full and courteous answers. What you did with that grenade is bad already. You are fortunate that his wish to meet you is high and his irritation at your insolence slight. Be very careful, or his punishment may reach beyond your own death."

"What a jolly boss you've got." Falkayn edged closer, to watch his guide's expression. "If I were you, I'd've quit long ago. Spectacularly."

"Would you quit your world—your race and everything it

means—because its service grew a little difficult?" Latimer retorted scornfully. His look changed, his voice dropped. "Hush! We are coming there."

The layout was not too strange for Falkayn to recognize a gravshaft rising vertically. Men and robot were conveyed up a good fifteen meters before they were deposited on the next deck.

Anteroom? Garden? Grotto? Falkayn looked around in bewilderment. An entire cabin, ballroom big, was filled with planters. The things grown in them ranged from tiny, sweet-scented quasi-flowers, through tall many-branched succulents, to whole trees with leaves that were spiky or fringed or intricately convoluted. The dominant hue was brownish gold, as green is dominant on Earth. Near the center splashed a fountain. Its stone basin must have stood outdoors for centuries, so weathered was it. Regardless of the wholly foreign artistic conventions, Falkayn could see that the shape and what remained of the carvings were exquisite. In startling contrast were the bulkheads. Enormous raw splashes of color decorated them, nerve-jarring, tasteless by almost any standards.

Latimer led the way to an arched door at the end. Beyond lay the first stateroom of a suite. It was furnished—overfurnished—with barbaric opulence. The deck was carpeted in pelt that might almost have belonged to angora tigers. One bulkhead was sheathed in roughly hammered gold plate, one was painted like the outer compartment, one was draped in scaly leather, and one was a screen whereon jagged abstract shapes flashed in a lightning dance to the crash of drums and bray of horns. The skull of a dinosaur-sized animal gaped above the entrance. From several four-legged stands wafted a bitter smoke. Two of the censers were old: time-worn, delicate, beautiful as the fountain. The rest were hardly more than iron lumps. Seating arrangements consisted of a pair of striped daises, each with space for three humans to lie on, and cushions scattered about the deck. A lot of other stuff lay carelessly heaped in odd places or on shelves. Falkayn didn't try to identify most of those objects. He thought some might be containers, musical instruments, and toys, but he'd need acquaintance with the owner before he could make anything except wild guesses.

And here we go!

A thick sheet of transparent material, possibly vitryl, had been leaned against the inner doorway. It would shield whoever stood behind, if the grenade went off. The someone would have been safer yet, talking to him via telecom. But no, Gahood didn't have that kind of mentality. He trod into view. Falkayn had seen more than his share of nonhumans, but he must suppress an oath. He confronted the Minotaur.

XVI

No... not that exactly... any more than Adezel was exactly a dragon. The impression was archetypical rather than literal. Yet as such it was overwhelming.

The creature was a biped, not unlike a man. Of course, every proportion was divergent, whether slightly, as in the comparative shortness of legs, or grotesquely, as in the comparative length of arms. Few if any humans had so stocky a build, and the muscles made different ripples across the limbs and bands across the abdomen. The feet were three-toed and padded, the hands four-fingered; and these digits were stubby, with greenish nails. The same tint was in the skin, which sprouted bronze hairs as thickly as the shaggiest of men though not enough to be called furred. Since the mouth, filled with flat yellow teeth, was flexible, but vestigial nipples were lacking, one couldn't tell offhand if the basic type was mammalian in a strict sense or not. However, the being was grossly male and surely warm-blooded.

The head— Comparisons between species from separate planets are nearly always poor. But that massive head, with its short broad snout, dewlapped throat, black-smoldering wide-set eyes under heavy brow ridges and almost no forehead, long mobile ears... was more tauroid than anthropoid, at least. Naturally, variances exceeded resemblances. There were no horns. A superb mane enclosed the face, swept backward, tumbled over the shoulders and halfway to the hips. Those hairs were white, but must have a microgroove structure, because rainbows of iridescence played across their waves.

Falkayn and Latimer were tall, but Gahood towered over them, an estimated 230 centimeters. Such height, together with the incongruous breadth and thickness and the hard muscularity, might well bring his mass to a couple of hundred kilos.

He wore nothing except a jeweled necklace, several rings and heavy gold bracelets, a belt supporting a pouch on one side and a knife, or small machete, on the other. His breathing was loud as the ventilators. A musky scent hung around him. When he spoke, it was like summer thunder.

Latimer brought his gun to his lips—a salute?—lowered it again and addressed Falkayn. "You meet Gahood of Neshketh." His vocal organs weren't quite right for pronouncing the names. "He will question you. I have already told him you are called Sebastian Tombs. Are you from Earth?"

Falkayn rallied his courage. The being behind the shield-screen was intimidating, yes: but hang it, mortal! "I'll be glad to swap information," he said, "on a two-way basis. Is Neshketh his planet, or what?"

Latimer looked agitated. "*Don't*," he muttered. "For your own sake, answer as you are instructed."

Falkayn skinned his teeth at them. "You poor scared mamzer," he said. "It could go hard with you, couldn't it? I haven't such a terrible lot to lose. You're the one who'd better cooperate with me."

A bluff, he thought inwardly, tensely. *I don't want to provoke an attack that'd end with me getting blown up. How very, very, very much I don't want to. And Gahood obviously has a hair-trigger temper. But if I can walk the tightrope from here to there . . .* An imp in him commented: *What a majestic lot of metaphors. You are playing poker while doing a high-wire act above a loaded revolver.*

"After all," he went on, into the dismayed face and the blaster muzzle, "sooner or later you'll deal with the League, if only in war. Why not start with me? I come cheaper than a battle fleet."

Gahood grunted something. Latimer replied. Sweat glistened on his countenance. The master clapped hand to knife hilt, snorted, and spoke a few syllables.

Latimer said, "You don't understand, Tombs. As far as Gahood is concerned, you are trespassing on his territory. He is showing rare restraint in not destroying you and your ship on the spot. You must believe me. Not many of his kind would be this tolerant. He will not be for long."

"His" territory? Falkayn thought. *He acts insane, I admit; but he can't be so heisenberg that he believes one flotilla can keep the Polesotechnic League off Satan. Quite possibly, getting here first gives him special claim under the law of his own people. But his group has got to be only the vanguard, the first hastily organized thing that could be sent. I imagine the woman—what's-her-name, Thea Beldaniel's sister— went on to notify others. Or maybe she's rejoined a different Minotaur. Latimer's attitude suggests Gahood is his personal owner. . . . I suspect I'm being counterbluffed. Gahood's natural impulse likely is to squash me: which makes Latimer nervous, considering he has no protection against what's in my fist. But Gahood's actually curbing his instinct, hoping to scare me too so I'll spill information.*

"Well," he said, "you being the interpreter, I don't see why you can't slip me a few answers. You aren't directly forbidden to, are you?"

"N-n-no. I—" Latimer drew a shaky breath. "I will tell you the, ah, place name mentioned refers to a . . . something like a domain." Gahood rumbled. "Now answer me! You came directly from Earth?"

"Yes. We were sent to investigate the rogue planet." A claim that *Muddlin' Through* had found it by accident was too implausible, and would not imply that the League stood ready to avenge her.

Gahood, through Latimer: "How did you learn of its existence?"

Falkayn, donning a leer: "Ah, that must have been a shock to you, finding us on tap when you arrived. You thought you'd have years to build impregnable defenses. Well, friends, I don't believe there is anything in the galaxy that we of the Polesotechnic League can't get pregnant.

What's the name of your home planet?"

Gahood: "Your response is evasive. How did you learn? How many of you are here? What further plans have you?"

Falkayn: A bland stare.

Latimer, swallowing: "Uh...I can't see any harm in— The planet is called Dathyna, the race itself the Shenna. In General Phonetic, D-A-Thorn-Y-N-A and Sha-E-N-N-A. The singular is 'Shenn.' The words mean, roughly, 'world' and 'people.'"

Falkayn: "Names like that do, as a rule."

He noted that the Shenna seemed confined to their home globe, or to a few colonies at most. No surprise. Clearly, they didn't live at such a distance that they could operate on a large scale without Technic explorers soon chancing on spoor of them and tracking them down.

It did not follow from this that they were not, possibly, mortally dangerous. The information Serendipity must have fed them over the years—not to mention the capability demonstrated by their creating such an outfit in the first place—suggested they were. A single planet, heavily armed and cunningly led, might best the entire League through its ability to inflict unacceptable damage. Or, if finally defeated, it might first destroy whole worlds, their civilizations and sentient species.

And if Gahood is typical, the Shenna might seriously plan on just that, Falkayn thought. His scalp crawled.

Too damned many mysteries and contradictions yet, though. Robotics won't explain every bit of the speed with which this group reacted to the news. And that, in turn, doesn't square with the far-reaching patience that built Serendipity—patience that suddenly vanished, that risked the whole operation (and, in the event, lost it) by kidnapping me.

"Speak!" Latimer cried. "Answer his questions."

"Eh? Oh. Those," Falkayn said slowly. "I'm afraid I can't. All I know is, our ships got orders to proceed here, check out the situation, and report back. We were warned someone else might show up with claim-jumping intentions. But no more was told us." He laid a finger alongside his nose and winked. "Why should the League's spies risk letting you find out how much they've found out about you...and where and how?"

Latimer gasped, whirled, and talked in fast, coughing gutturals. The suggestion that Dathynan society had itself been penetrated must be shocking even to Gahood. He wouldn't dare assume it was not true. Would he? But what he'd do was unpredictable. Falkayn balanced flex-kneed, every sense alert.

His training paid off. Gahood belched an order. The robot slipped unobtrusively to one side. Falkayn caught the movement in the corner of an eye. With his karate stance, he didn't need to jump. He relaxed the tension in one leg and was automatically elsewhere. Steel tendrils whipped where his left hand had been.

He bounded into the nearest corner. "Naughty!" he rapped. The machine whirred toward him. "Latimer, I can let go this switch before that thing can squeeze my fingers shut around it. Call off your iron dog or we're both dead."

The other man uttered something that halted the robot. Evidently Gahood endorsed the countermand, for at his word the machine withdrew until it no longer hemmed Falkayn in. Across the room he saw the Minotaur stamp, hungrily flex his hands, and blow through distended nostrils—furious behind his shield.

Latimer's blaster aimed at the Hermetian's midriff. It wavered, and the wielder looked ill. Though his life had been dedicated to the cause of Dathyna, or whatever the cause was, and though he was doubtless prepared to lay it down if need be, he must have felt a shock when his master so impulsively risked it. "Give up, Tombs," he well-nigh pleaded. "You cannot fight a ship."

"I'm not doing badly," Falkayn said. The effort was cruel to hold his own breathing steady, his voice level. "And I'm not alone, you know."

"One insignificant scoutcraft— No. You did mention others. How many? What kind? Where?"

"Do you seriously expect the details? Listen close, now, and translate with care. When we detected you, my ship went out to parley because the League doesn't like fights. They cut into profit. When fights become necessary, though, we make damn sure the opposition will never louse up our bookkeeping again. You spent enough time in the Commonwealth, Latimer, and maybe elsewhere in the territory covered by Technic civilization, to vouch for that. The message I have for you is this. Our higher-ups are willing to dicker with yours. Time and place can be arranged through any envoys you send to the League secretariat. But for the moment, I warn you away from Beta Crucis. We were here first, it's ours, and our fleet will destroy any intruders. I suggest you let me return to my ship, and go home yourselves and think it over."

Latimer looked yet more profoundly shaken. "I can't . . . address him . . . like that!"

"Then don't address him." Falkayn shrugged. Gahood lowered his ponderous head, stamped on the deck, and boomed. "But if you ask me, he's getting impatient."

Latimer began stumblingly to speak to the Dathynan.

I suspect he's shading his translation, Falkayn thought. *Poor devil. He acted boldly on Luna. But now he's back where he's property, physical, mental, spiritual property. Worse off than I was; he doesn't even need to be chained by drugs. I don't know when I've watched a ghastlier sight.* The thought was an overtone in a voiceless scream: *Will they play safe and release me? Or must I die?*

Gahood bellowed. It was no word, it was raw noise, hurting Falkayn's eardrums. Echoes flew. The creature hurled himself against the barricading slab. It weighed a ton or better in this gravity, but he tipped it forward. Leaning upon it, he boomed a command. Latimer sprang, clumsy in his spacesuit, toward him.

Falkayn understood: *He'll let his slave in, lean the shelter back, and when both of them are safe, he'll tell the robot to go after me. It's worth a robot and the treasures in this room, to kill me who insulted him—*

And Falkayn's body was already reacting. He was farther from the arch, and must sidestep the machine. But he was youthful, in hard condition, accustomed to wearing space armor . . . and driven by more love of life. He reached the slab simultaneously with Latimer, on the opposite side. It stood nearly vertical now, with a one-meter gap giving admittance to the room beyond. The ireful beast who upheld it did not at once notice what had happened. Falkayn got through along with the other man.

He skipped aside. Gahood let the slab crash into its tilted position again and whirled to grab him. "Oh, no!" he called. "Get him off me, Latimer, or he's the third chunk of hamburger here!"

Slave threw himself upon owner and tried to wrestle Gahood to a halt. The Dathynan tore him loose and pitched him to the deck. Space armor clanged where it struck. But then reason appeared to enter the maned head. Gahood stopped cold.

For a minute, tableau. Latimer sprawled, bloody-nosed and semiconscious, under the bent columns of Gahood's legs. The Minotaur stood with arms dangling, chest heaving, breath storming, and glared at Falkayn. The spaceman poised a few meters off, amidst another jumble of barbarous luxuries. Sweat plastered the yellow hair to his brow, but he grinned at his enemies and waved the grenade aloft.

"That's better," he said. "That's much better. Stand fast, you two. Latimer, I'll accept your gun."

In a dazed fashion, the slave reached for the blaster, which he had dropped nearby. Gahood put one broad foot on it and snorted a negative.

"Well . . . keep it, then," Falkayn conceded. The Dathynan was rash but no idiot. Had Falkayn gotten the weapon, he could have slain the others without dooming himself. As it was, there must be a compromise. "I want your escort, both of you, back to my sled. If you summon your robots, or your merry men, or anything that makes my capture seem feasible, this pineapple goes straight up."

Latimer rose, painfully. "Merry men—?" he puzzled. His gaze cleared. "Oh. The rest of our officers and crew. No, we will not call them." He translated.

Falkayn kept impassive. But a new excitement boiled within him. Latimer's initial reaction confirmed what had already begun to seem probable, after no one heard the racket here and came to investigate, or even made an intercom call.

Gahood and Latimer were alone. Not just the other craft,

the flagship too was automatic.

But that was impossible!

Maybe not. Suppose Dathyna—or Gahood's Neshketh barony, at least—suffered from an acute "manpower" shortage. Now the Shenna did not expect that anyone from the League would be at Beta Crucis. They had no reason to believe Serendipity had been exposed. Assuming a rival expedition did appear, it would be so small that robots could dispose of it. (Serendipity must have described this trait in Technic society, this unwillingness to make large commitments sight unseen. And, of course, it *was* the case. No League ship except *Muddlin' Through* was anywhere near the blue star.) Rather than go through the tedious business of recruiting a proper complement—only to tie it up needlessly, in all apparent likelihood—Gahood had taken what robots he commanded. He had gone off without other live companionship than the dog-man who brought him the word.

What kind of civilization was this, so poor in trained personnel, so careless about the requirements for scientific study of a new planet, and yet so rich and lavish in machines?

Gahood cast down the barrier. Probably robots had raised it for him; but none came in response to its earthquake fall, and the one in the cabin stood as if frozen. In the same eerie wordlessness, Falkayn trailed his prisoners: out the antechamber, down the gravshaft, through the corridor to the airlock.

There the others stopped and glowered defiance. The Hermetian had had time to make a plan. "Now," he said, "I'd like to take you both hostage, but my vehicle's too cramped and I won't risk the chances that Gahood's riding along might give him. You'll come, Latimer."

"No!" The man was appalled.

"Yes. I want some assurance of not being attacked en route to my fleet."

"Don't you understand? M-my information...what I know...you could learn.... He'll have to sacrifice me."

"I thought of that already. I don't reckon he's anxious to vaporize you. You're valuable to him, and not simply as an interpreter. Else you wouldn't be here." *You had the name in the Solar System of being an uncommonly good spaceman, Hugh Latimer. And at the moment, though I hope he doesn't know I know, you're half his party. Without you, never mind how good his robots are, he's got big problems. He could return home, all right; but would he dare do anything else, as long as the possibility exists I did not lie about having an armada at my back? Besides—who knows?—there may well be a kind of affection between you two.* "He won't attack a vessel with you aboard if he can avoid it. Correct? Well, you're already spacesuited. Ride with me as far as my ship. I'll let you off there. His radar can confirm that I do, and he can pick you up in space. If he does not spot you separating from my sled, shortly before it joins my ship, then he can open fire."

Latimer hesitated. "Quick!" Falkayn barked. "Translate and give me his decision. My thumb's getting tired."

The truth was, he aimed to keep them both off balance, not give them a chance to think. The exchange was brief, under his profane urging. "Very well." Latimer yielded sullenly. "But I keep my blaster."

"And I our mutual suicide pact. Fair enough. Cycle us through."

Latimer instructed the airlock by voice. Falkayn's last glimpse of Gahood, as the inmost valve closed again, was of the huge form charging up and down the corridor, pounding the bulkheads with fists until they clamored, and bellowing.

The sled waited. Falkayn sent Latimer first through its minilock in order that he, entering afterward, would present the full menace of the grenade. It was awkward, squeezing one spacesuit past another in the tiny cockpit, and guiding the sled by one hand was worse. He made a disgraceful liftoff. Once in motion, he let the vehicle do as it would while he broadcast a call.

"Dave!" Chee Lan's voice shuddered in his earplugs. "You're free— *Yan-tai-i-lirh-ju*."

"We may have to run hard, you and I," he said in Anglic, for Latimer's benefit. "Give my autopilot a beam. Stand by to reel me in and accelerate the moment I'm in tractor range. But, uh, don't pay attention when I first discharge a passenger."

"Hostage, eh? I understand. Muddlehead, get off your fat electronic duff and lock onto him!"

A minute later, Falkayn could let go the main stick. The sled flew steadily, the ominous shape of the battleship dwindled aft. He glanced at Latimer, crowded more or less beside him. In the dim glow of stars and instrument panel, he saw a shadow bulk and a gleam off the faceplate. The blaster muzzle was poked almost in his belly.

"I don't imagine Gahood will shoot at us," he said low.

"I think not, now." Latimer's reply sounded equally exhausted.

"Whoo-oo. How about relaxing? We've a tedious ride ahead of us."

"How can you relax, with that thing in your hand?"

"Sure, sure. We keep our personal deterrents. But can't we take it easy otherwise? Open our helmets, light each other's cigarettes."

"I do not smoke," Latimer said. "However—" He undogged and slid back his faceplate concurrently with Falkayn. A sigh gusted from him. "Yes. It is good to...to uncramp."

"I don't bear you any ill will, you know," Falkayn said, not quite truthfully. "I'd like to see this dispute settled without a fight."

"Me, too. I must admire your courage. It's almost like a Shenn's."

"If you could give me some idea what the quarrel is about—"

"No." Latimer sighed, "I'd better not say anything. Except...how are they, back on Luna? My friends of Serendipity?"

"Well, now—"

Latimer shifted position and Falkayn saw his chance. He had been prepared to wait for it as long as need be, and do nothing if it didn't happen to materialize. But the sled had already gotten so far away from the battleship that no scanner could give a clue as to what went on in this cockpit. There was no contact in either direction, apart from Muddlehead's beam and Gahood's tracking radar. In the low weight of acceleration, Latimer's tired body had settled into his seat harness. The blaster rested laxly on one knee and the face lolled in its frame of helmet near Falkayn's right shoulder.

"—it's like this," the Hermetian continued. *Here goes—for broke!* His left fist, with the grenade to lend mass, swept about, battered the gun barrel aside and pinned it against the cockpit wall. His right hand darted through the faceplate opening and closed on Latimer's throat.

XVII

THE blaster flared once, while the man tried to struggle. Then both were still.

Panting, Falkayn released the judo strangle. "Got to work fast," he muttered aloud, as if to offset the hiss of escaping air. But that hole was sealing itself while the reserve tanks brought pressure back up. He stuffed the blaster into his tool belt and strained his eyes aft. Nothing stirred in the Shenn fleet. Well, it had always been unlikely that one little flash and brief puff of water mist would be seen.

Getting rid of the grenade was more tricky. Falkayn cut the main drive and swiveled the sled transversely to its path, so that the minilock faced away from the battleship. On this model, the valves had been simplified to a series of sphinctered diaphragms on either side of a rigid cylinder. It meant some continuous gas leakage, and comparatively high loss whenever you went in or out. But it compensated with speed and flexibility of use; and the sled wasn't intended for long hops through space anyway. Helmet reclosed, Falkayn braced feet against the opposite side of the cockpit and pushed head and shoulders out into the void. He tossed the grenade, flat and hard. It exploded at a reasonably safe distance. A few shrapnel chunks ricocheted off the vehicle, but no serious damage was done.

"Wowsers!" His left hand ached. He flexed the fingers, trying to work some tension out, as he withdrew to the interior. Latimer was regaining consciousness. With a bit of reluctance—rough way to treat a man—Falkayn choked him again. Thus the Hermetian won the extra few seconds he needed, undisturbed, to put his sled back on acceleration before Gahood should notice anything and grow suspicious.

He placed himself with care vis-à-vis Latimer, leveled the blaster, opened his helmet, and waited. The captive stirred, looked around him, shuddered, and gathered himself for a leap. "Don't," Falkayn advised, "or you're dead. Unharness; back off to the rear; get out of your suit."

"What? *Logra doadam!* You swine—"

"Oink," Falkayn said. "Listen, I don't want to shoot you. Quite apart from morals and such, you've got a lot of hostage value. But you're most certainly not returning to help Gahood. I have my whole people to worry about. If you cause me any trouble, I'll kill you and sleep quite well, thank you. Get moving."

Still dazed, by his stunning reversal as well as physically, the other man obeyed. Falkayn made him close up the spacesuit. "We'll eject it at the right moment and your boss will think it's you," he explained. "His time loss collecting it is my gain."

A growl and glare through the shadows: "It is true what I was told about your sort, what I observed for myself. Evil, treacherous—"

"Desiccate it, Latimer. I signed no contract, swore no oath. Earlier, you types weren't exactly following the usual rules of parley. I didn't enjoy the hospitality I received in your Lunar castle, either."

Latimer jerked backward. "Falkayn?" he whispered.

"Right. Captain David Falkayn, M.M.P.L., with a hydrocyanic personal grudge and every reason to believe your gang is out for blood. Can you prove this is a pillow fight we're in? If it is, then you've put bricks in your pillow. Which led me to put nails in mine. Be quiet, now, before I get so mad I fry you!"

The last sentence was roared. Latimer crouched rather than cowered, but he was certainly daunted. Falkayn himself was astounded. *I really pushed that out, didn't I? The idea was to keep him stampeded, so he won't think past the moment, guess my real intentions, and become desperate. But Judas, the fury I feel!* He trembled with it.

Time passed. The enemy receded farther, *Muddlin'*

Through came nearer. When they were quite close, Falkayn ordered Latimer to shove the empty spacesuit through the minilock: an awkward job, eardrum-popping if one had no armor, but performed in tight-lipped silence.

"Haul us in, Chee," Falkayn said.

A tractor beam clamped on. The drive was shut off. A cargo hatch stood open to one of the after holds. No sooner was the sled inboard, protected by the ship's gee-field from acceleration pressures, then Chee started off under full drive. The hum and bone-deep vibration could be felt.

She scurried below to meet the humans. They had just emerged, and stood glaring at each other in the coldly lit cavern. Chee hefted the stun pistol she carried. "Ah, s-s-so," she murmured. Her tail waved. "I rather expected you'd do that, Dave. Where shall we lock this klong up?"

"Sick bay," Falkayn told her. "The sooner we begin on him, the better. We may be hounded down, you see, but if we can launch our other capsule with something in it—"

He should not have spoken Anglic. Latimer divined his intention, screamed, and hurled himself straight at the blaster. Hampered by his spacesuit, Falkayn could not evade the charge; and he did not share the prisoner's desire that he shoot. They went to the deck, rolling over and over in their struggle. Chee Lan eeled between them and gave Latimer a judicious jolt.

He sprawled limp. Falkayn rose, breathing hard, shaking. "How long'll he be out?"

"Hour; maybe two," the Cynthian answered. "But I'll need a while to prepare anyway." She paused. "I'm not a psychotechnician, you realize, and we don't have a full battery of drugs, electroencephalic inducers, all that junk they use. I don't know how much I can wring out of him."

"You can get him to babble something, I'm sure," Falkayn said. "What with the stuff left over from curing me, and the experience you got then. Just the coordinates of Dathyna—of the enemy's home system—would be invaluable."

"Haul him topside and secure him for me. After which, if you aren't too shredded in the nerves, you'd better take the bridge."

Falkayn nodded. Weariness, reaction, had indeed begun to invade him. Latimer's body was a monstrous weight over his shoulders. The thin face looked tormented even in slumber. And what waited was a will-less half-consciousness.... *Tough*, Falkayn thought sarcastically.

Coffee, a sandwich, a quick shower, grabbed while he related via intercom what had happened, made him feel better. He entered the bridge with his pipe at a jaunty angle. "What's the situation, Muddlehead?" he asked.

"As respects ourselves, we are bound back toward the rogue planet at maximum thrust," said the computer. It was the only way to continue the bluff of armed support. "Our systems check satisfactory, although a fluctuation in line voltage on circuit 47 is symptomatic of malfunction in a regulator that should be replaced next we make port."

"Repaired," Falkayn corrected automatically.

"Replaced," Muddlehead maintained. "While data do indicate that Freeman van Rijn is describable, in terms of the vocabulary you instructed me to use, as a cheapskate bastard, it is illogical that my operations should be distracted, however slightly, by—"

"Great Willy! We may be radioactive gas inside an hour, and you indent for a new voltage regulator! Would you like it goldplated?"

"I had not considered the possibility. Obviously, only the casing could be. It would lead to a pleasing appearance, provided of course that every similar unit is similarly finished."

"Up your rectifier," Falkayn said. His teeth clamped hard on the pipe bit. "What readings on the enemy?"

"A destroyer has put a tractor beam on the suit and is bringing it near the battleship."

"Which'll take it aboard," Falkayn predicted without difficulty. Things were going as he'd anticipated ... thus far. The Dathynan ships were delayed in their recovery operation by the need to get detailed instructions from Gahood.

They had electronic speed and precision, yes, but not full decision-making capacity. No robot built in any known civilization does. This is not for lack of mystic vital forces. Rather, the biological creature has available to him so much more physical organization. Besides sensor-computer-effector systems comparable to those of the machine, he has feed-in from glands, fluids, chemistry reaching down to the molecular level—the integrated ultracomplexity, the entire battery of *instincts*—that a billion-odd years of ruthlessly selective evolution have brought forth. He perceives and thinks with a wholeness transcending any possible symbolism; his purposes arise from within, and therefore are infinitely flexible. The robot can only do what it was designed to do. Self-programming has extended these limits, to the point where actual consciousness may occur if desired. But they remain narrower than the limits of those who made the machines.

To be sure, given an unequivocal assignment of the type for which it is built, the robot is superior to the organism. Let Gahood order his fleet to annihilate *Muddlin' Through*, and the contest became strictly one between ships, weapons, and computers.

Didn't it?

Falkayn sat down, drummed fingers on his chair arm, blew acrid clouds at the star images that enclosed him.

Chee's voice pulled him from his brown study: "I've got your boy nicely laid out, intravenous insertions made, brain and vagus nerve monitored, life-support apparatus on standby, everything I can do with what's available. Should I jolt him awake with a stim shot?"

"M-m-m, no, wait a while, It'd be hard on his body. We don't want to damage him if we can possibly help it."

"Why not?"

Falkayn sighed. "I'll explain some other time. But practically speaking, we can pump him drier if we treat him carefully."

"They can do still better in a properly equipped lab."

"Yeah, but that's illegal. So illegal that it's a toss-up whether anyone would do the job for us on the q.t. Let's get what we can, ourselves. We're also violating law, but that can be winked at if we're well beyond civilization. . . . Of course, we can't predict whether Gahood will give us the days you need for a thorough and considerate job of quizzing."

"You met him. What do you think?"

"I didn't get exactly intimate with him. And even if I knew his inner psychology, which I don't except for his tendency to make all-out attacks at the first sign of opposition—even then, I wouldn't know what pragmatic considerations he might have to take into account. On the one hand, we have his trusty man for a hostage, and he has at least some reason to believe we may have husky friends waiting at Satan. He should cut his losses, return, and report. On the other hand, he may be so bold, or so angry, or so afraid Latimer will reveal something vital to us, that he'll strike."

"Supposing he does?"

"We run like hell, I guess. A stern chase is a long chase. We may throw him off the scent, like in Pryor's Nebula. Or we may outrun his heavy ships altogether, and he recall his destroyers rather than— Whoops! Hang on!"

Muddlehead spoke what flickered on the 'scope faces: "They are starting after us."

"Rendezvous point?" Chee demanded.

"Data cannot yet be evaluated with precision, considering especially the velocity we have already gained. But." For an instant, it hummed. "Yes, the destroyers are lining out on courses effectively parallel to ours, with somewhat greater acceleration. Under such conditions, they will overhaul us in slightly less than one astronomical unit."

"Their shooting can overhaul us sooner than that," Chee stated. "I'm going ahead on Latimer."

"I suppose you must," Falkayn said reluctantly, half wishing he had not captured the man.

"Commence hyperdrive," Chee ordered from sick bay.

"No," Falkayn said. "Not right now."

"*Chi'in-pao?*"

"We're safe for a little while. Keep driving toward Satan, Muddlehead. They might just be testing our bluff."

"Do you really believe that?" the Cynthian asked.

"No." Falkayn said. "But what can we lose?"

Not much, he answered himself. *I knew the chances of our coming out of this web alive aren't good. But as of this moment, I can't do anything but sit and feel the fact.*

Physical courage was schooled into him, but the sense of life's sweetness was born in. He spent a time cataloguing a few of the myriad awarenesses that made up his conscious being. The stars burned splendid across night. The ship enclosed him in a lesser world, one of power-thrum, ventilator breath, clean chemical odors, music if he wanted it, the battered treasures he had gathered in his wanderings. Smoke made a small autumn across his tongue. Air blew into his nostrils, down into the lungs, as his chest expanded. The chair pressed back against the weight of his body; and it had texture; and seated, he nevertheless operated an interplay of muscles, an unending dance with the universe for his lady. A sleeve of the clean coverall he had donned felt crisp, and tickled the hair on one arm. His heart beat faster than usual, but steadily, and that pleased him.

He summoned memories from the deeps: mother, father, sisters, brothers, retainers, old weather-beaten soldiers and landsmen, in the windy halls of the castle on Hermes. Hikes through the woods; swims in the surf; horses, boats, aircraft, spaceships. Gourmet dinners. A slab of black bread and cheese, a bottle of cheap wine, shared one night with the dearest little tart.... Had there actually been so many women? Yes. How delightful. Though of late he had begun to grow wistful about finding some one girl who—well, had the same quality of friendship that Chee or Adzel did—who would be more than a partner in a romp—but hadn't he and his comrades enjoyed their own romps, on world after wild world? Including this latest, perhaps last mission to Satan. If the rogue was to be taken away, he hoped the conquerors would at least get pleasure from it.

How can they tell if they will? None of them have been there yet. In a way, you can't blame Gahood for charging in. He must be eager too, I think, to see what the place is like. The fact that I know, that I've landed there already, must hone the edge of his impatience....

Wait! Drag that thought by slowly. You'd started playing with it before, when Chee interrupted—

Falkayn sat rigid, oblivious, until the Cynthian grew nervous and shouted into the intercom, "What ails you?"

"Oh." The man shook himself. "Yes. That. How're we doing?"

"Latimer is responding to me, but deliriously. He's in worse shape than I realized."

"Psychic stress," Falkayn diagnosed without paying close attention. "He's being forced to betray his master—his owner, maybe his god—against a lifetime's conditioning."

"I think I can haul him back into orbit long enough at a time to put a question or two. What about the enemy, Muddlehead?"

"The destroyers are closing the gap," reported the ship. "How soon they will be prepared to fire on us depends on their armament, but I would expect it to be soon."

"Try to raise the battleship by radio," Falkayn ordered. "Maybe they—he—will talk. Meanwhile, prepare to go hyper at the first sign of hostile action. Toward Satan."

Chee had evidently not heard him, or was too intent to comment. The mutter of her voice, Latimer's incoherence, the medical machines, drifted unpleasantly over the intercom. "Shall I revert to normal when we reach the planet?" Muddlehead inquired.

"Yes. Starting at once, change our acceleration. I want nearly zero kinetic velocity with respect to goal," Falkayn said.

"That, in effect, involves deceleration," Muddlehead warned. "The enemy will come in effective firing range correspondingly faster."

"Never mind. Do you think you can find a landing spot, once we're there?"

"It is uncertain. Meterological violence, and diastrophism, appeared to be increasing almost exponentially when we left."

"Still, you've got a whole world to pick and choose from. And you know something about it. I can't guess how many billion bits of information regarding Satan you've got stashed away. Prepare to devote most of your computer capacity to them, as well to observation on the spot. I'll give you generalized instructions—make the basic decisions for you—as we proceed. Clear?"

"I presume you wish to know whether your program has been unambiguously comprehended. Yes."

"Good." Falkayn patted the nearest console and smiled through his gathering, half-gleeful tension. "We come through this, and you can have your gold-plated regulators. If need be, I'll pay for them out of my own account."

There was no perceptible change of forces within the ship, nor in the configuration of light-years-remote stars or the luridness of Beta Crucis. But meters said the ship was slowing down. Magnifying viewscreens showed the glints that were Gahood's vessels growing into slivers, into toys, into warcraft.

"I've got it!" ripped from Chee.

"Huh?" Falkayn said.

"The coordinates. In standard values. But he's spinning off into shock. I'd better concentrate on keeping him alive."

"Do. And, uh, don safety harness. We may dive right into Satan's atmosphere. The compensators may get overloaded."

Chee was quiet a moment before she said, "I see your plan. It is not a bad one."

Falkayn gnawed on his pipe. This was the worst part, now, this waiting. Gahood must have detected the change of vector, must see what was like an attempt to rendezvous, must know about at least one of the communication beams on different bands that probed toward his flagship. But his fleet plunged on, and nothing spoke to Falkayn save a dry cosmic hiss.

If he'll try to talk... if he'll show any sign of goodwill... Judas, we don't want a battle—

Whiteness flared in the screens, momentarily drowning the constellations. Alarm bells rang. "We were struck by an energy bolt," Muddlehead announced. "Dispersion was sufficient at this range that damage was minimal. I am taking evasive action. A number of missiles are being released from the fleet. They behave like target-seekers."

Doubts, terrors, angers departed from Falkayn. He became entirely a war animal. "Go hyper to Satan as instructed," he said without tone. "One-tenth drive."

The wavering sky, the keening noises, the shifting forces:

then steadiness again, a low throb, Beta Crucis swelling perceptibly as the ship ran toward it faster than light.

"So slow?" Chee Lan's voice asked.

"For the nonce," Falkayn said. "I want to keep a close watch on what they do."

Only instruments could tell, the fleet being already lost in millions of kilometers. "They aren't going hyper immediately," Falkayn said. "I expect they're matching our kinetic velocity first, more or less. Which suggests they intend to start shooting again at their earliest opportunity."

"Whether or not we have reinforcements at Satan?"

"Whether or not. I imagine the battleship will bring up the rear, though, at a goodly distance, and wait to see how things develop before making any commitment." Falkayn laid his pipe aside. "No matter how hot-tempered he is, I doubt if Gahood will rush into an unknown danger right along with his robots. They're more expendable than him. Under present conditions, this fact works in our favor."

"Hyperdrive pulses detected," the computer said a few minutes later.

Falkayn whistled. "Can they normal-decelerate that fast? Very well, open up, flat out. We don't want them to overtake us and maybe phase-match before we reach Satan."

The engine pulse became a drumbeat, a current, a cataract. The flames of Beta Crucis seemed to stretch and seethe outward. The computer said, "All but one unit, presumably the largest, are in pursuit. The cruisers are lagging behind us but the destroyers are gaining. However, we will reach goal several minutes in advance of them."

"How much time do you want for scanning the planet and picking us a course down?"

Click. Click-click. "A hundred seconds should suffice."

"Reduce speed so we'll arrive, let's see, three minutes before the leading destroyer. Commence descent one hundred seconds after we're back to normal state. Make it as quick as possible."

The power-song dropped a touch lower. "Are you in your own harness, Dave?" Chee asked.

"Uh . . . why, no," Falkayn suddenly realized.

"Well, get into it! Do you think I want to scrub the deck

clean of that clabbered oatmeal you call brains? Take care of yourself!"

Falkayn smiled for half a second. "Same to you, fluffykins."

"*Fluffykins —!*" Oaths and obscenities spattered the air. Falkayn sat down and webbed in. Chee needed something to take her mind off the fact that in this hour she could do nothing about her own fate. It was a condition harder for a Cynthian to endure than a human.

Then they were upon the rogue. Then they flashed into relativistic state. Then engines roared, hull structure groaned and shuddered, while the last adjustments in velocity were made, within seconds.

They were not far out, just enough so that most of the daylit hemisphere could be observed. Satan loomed frightful, filling the screens, stormclouds, lightnings, winds gone crazy, volcanoes, avalanches, floods, mountainous waves raised on the oceans and torn into shreds of spume, air nearly solid with rain and hail and flung stones, one immense convulsion beneath the demon disc of the star. Momentarily Falkayn did not believe there was any spot anywhere on the globe where a ship might descend, and he readied himself for death.

But the League vessel sprang ahead. On a comet-like trajectory, she arced toward the north pole. Before reaching it, she was in the upper atmosphere. Thin it might be, but it smote her so the hull rang.

Darkness, lit with explosions of lightning, rolled beneath. Falkayn glanced aft. Did the screens truly reveal to him the shark-shape destroyers of Gahood? Or was that an illusion? Torn clouds whipped across sun and stars. Thunder and shrieking and the cry of metal filled his ship, his skull, his being. The interior field regulators could not handle every shock, as *Muddlin' Through* staggered downward. The deck pitched, yawed, swayed, fell away, rose savagely again. Something crashed off something else and broke. Lights flickered.

He tried to understand the instruments. Nuclear sources, behind, coming nearer . . . yes, the whole nineteen, stooping on their quarry!

They were meant for aerodynamic work. They had orders to catch and kill a certain vessel. They were robots.

They did not have sophontic judgment, nor any data to let them estimate how appalling these totally unprecedented conditions were, for any mandate to wait for further instructions if matters looked doubtful. Besides, they observed a smaller and less powerful craft maneuvering in the air.

They entered at their top atmospheric speed.

Muddlehead had identified a hurricane and plotted its extent and course. It was merely a hurricane—winds of two or three hundred kilometers per hour—a kind of back eddy or dead spot in the storm that drove across this continent with such might that half an ocean was carried before it. No matter how thoroughly self-programmed, on the basis of how much patiently collected data, no vessel could hope to stay in the comparatively safe region long.

The destroyers blundered into the main blast. It caught them as a November gale catches dead leaves in the northlands of Earth. Some it bounced playfully between cloud-floor and wind-roof, for whole minutes, before it cast them aside. Some it peeled open, or broke apart with the meteoroidal chunks of solid matter it bore along, or drowned in the spume-filled air farther down. Most it tossed at once against mountainsides. The pieces were strewn, blown away, buried, reduced in a few weeks to dust, mud, atoms locked into newly forming rock strata. No trace of the nineteen warships would ever be found.

"Back aloft!" Falkayn had already cried. "Locate those cruisers. Use cloud cover. With this kind of electric noise background, they aren't likely to detect us fast."

A roll and lurch rattled his teeth together. Slowly, fighting for every centimeter, *Muddlin' Through* rose. She found a stratospheric current she could ride for a while, above the worst weather though beneath a layer where boiled-off vapors were recondensing in vast turbulent masses that, from below, turned heaven Stygian. Her radars could penetrate this, her detectors pick up indications that came to her. The three cruisers were not supposed to make planetfall. Obviously, they were to provide cover against possible space attack. Their attention must be almost wholly directed outward. They orbited incautiously close, in inadvisably tight formation. But they were also robots, whose builders had more faith in strength than in strategy.

Falkayn sent off three of his nuclear torpedoes. Two connected. The third was intercepted in time by a countermissile. Reluctantly, he ordered the fourth and last shot. It seemed to achieve a near miss and must have inflicted heavy damage, judging by what the meters recorded.

And . . . the cruiser was limping off. The battleship, whose mass made ominous blips on half a dozen different kinds of screen, was joining her. They were both on hyperdrive— retreating—dwindling toward the Circinus region whence they came.

Falkayn whooped.

After a while, he recovered his wits sufficiently to order, "Get us into clear space again, Muddlehead. Barely outside the atmosphere. Take orbit, with systems throttled down to minimum. We don't want to remind Gahood of us. He could change his mind and return before he's too far off ever to catch us."

"What does he believe happened?" Chee asked, so weakly she could barely be heard.

"I don't know. How does his psyche work? Maybe he thinks we have a secret weapon. Or maybe he thinks we lured his destroyers down by a suicide dive, and we've got friends who fired those torps. Or maybe he's guessed the truth, but figures that with his fleet essentially gone, and the possibility that a League force might soon arrive, he'd better go home and report."

"Lest we outfox him again, eh?" Exhausted and battered though she was, Chee began to have a note of exultation in her voice.

Likewise Falkayn. "What do you mean, 'we,' white puss?" he teased.

"I obtained those coordinates for you, didn't I? Bloodiest important thing we've accomplished this whole trip."

"You're right," Falkayn said, "and I apoligize. How's Latimer?"

"Dead."

Falkayn sat straight. "What? How?"

"The life-support apparatus got knocked out of kilter, that battering we took. And in his weakened condition, with his whole organism fighting itself— Too long a time has passed now for resuscitation to mean anything." Falkayn could imagine Chee Lan's indifferent gesture, her probable thoughts. *Pity for us. Oh, well, we got something out of him; and we're alive.*

His went, surprisingly to himself: *Poor, damned devil. I have my revenge, I've been purged of my shame; and I find it didn't really matter that much.*

Quietness grew around the ship, the stars trod forth, and she reentered open space. Falkayn could not stay sorry. He felt he ought to, but the knowledge of deliverance was too strong. They'd give their foeman an honorable burial, an orbit straight into yonder terrible, glorious sun. And they'd steer for Earth.

No. The realization struck like a fist. *Not that. We can't go home yet.*

The work of survival had barely been started.

XVIII

WELL-ESTABLISHED laws of nature are seldom overthrown by new scientific discovery. Instead, they turn out to be approximations, or special cases, or in need of rephrasing. Thus—while a broader knowledge of physics permits us to do things he would have considered impossible, like traversing a light-year in less than two hours—Einstein's restrictions on the concept of simultaneity remain essentially valid. For no matter how high a pseudo-velocity we reach, it is still finite.

So did Adzel argue. "You may not correctly ask what our friends are doing 'now', when interstellar distances separate us from them. True, after they have rejoined us, we can compare their clocks with ours, and find the same time lapse recorded. But to identify any moment of our measured interval with any moment of theirs is to go beyond the evidence, and indeed to perpetrate a meaningless statement."

"Hokay!" Nicholas van Rijn bawled. He windmilled his arms in the air. "Hokay! Then give me a meaningless answer! Four weeks, close as damn, since they left. Couldn't need much more than two for getting at Beta Crosseyes, ha? They maybe finding thawed-out glaciers of beer and akvavit, we haven't heard diddly-dong from them yet?"

"I understand your concern," Adzel said quietly. "Perhaps I feel a little more of it than you do. But the fact is that a message capsule is slower than a ship like *Muddlin' Through*. Had they dispatched one immediately upon arrival, it would barely have gotten to the Solar System by today. And they would not logically do so. For surely David, after he recovered, credited you with the ability to pry as much out of the SI computer as it gave him. Why, then, should he waste a capsule to confirm the mere fact of the rogue's existence? No, he and Chee Lan will first have gathered ample data. With luck, they need not have taken the trouble and risk of interception involved in sending any written report. They ought to be returning home . . . quite soon . . . if at all."

His huge scaly form got off the deck where he rested. His neck must bend under the overhead, his tail curl past a corner. Hoofs rattled on steel. He took several turns around the command bridge before he stopped and gazed into the simulacrum of the sky that made a black, bejeweled belt for this compartment.

The ship was on gravdrive, accelerating outward. Earth and Luna had shrunk to a double star, blue and gold, and Sol had visibly dwindled. Ahead glistened the southern stars. An X etched into the bow section of the continuous screen centered on a region near the constellation Circinus. But Adzel's gaze kept straying to another point of brilliance, second brightest in the Cross.

"We could return and wait," he suggested. "Maybe Freelady Beldaniel can nonetheless be induced to withdraw her threat to cancel the meeting. Or maybe the threat was always an empty one."

"No," said van Rijn from the chair he overflowed, "I think not. She is tough, I found out while we haggled. *Ja*, I bet she puts spaghetti sauce on barbed wire. And best we believe her when she says her bosses is not terrible anxious to talk with us anyways, and she can't guarantee they will come to the rendezvous, and if we do anything they don't like—or she don't like so she is not enthusiastic about telling them they should negotiate—why, then they go home in a huff-puff."

He drew on his churchwarden, adding more blue reek to that which already filled the air. "We know practicalistically nothings about them, they know lots about us," he went on. "Ergo, where it comes to meetings and idea exchanges, we is buyers in a seller's market and can't do a lot else than ask very polite if they mind using not quite so big a reamer on us. Q.," he finished gloomily, "E. D."

"If you worry about David and Chee," Adzel said, "you might get on the radio before we go hyper, and dispatch another ship or two for reinforcement to them."

"No pointing in that unless we get a holler for help from them, or a long time has gone by with no word. They are good experienced pioneers what should could handle any planet by their own selfs. Or if they got hurt, too late now, I am afraid."

"I was thinking of assistance against hostile action. They may encounter armed forces, alerted by the first two Serendipity partners who left several weeks ago."

"To fight, how much power we need send? No telling, except got to be plenty." Van Rijn shook his head. "They don't give out second prizes for combat, dragon boy. We send less fighting power than the enemy, we don't likely get none back. And we can't spare enough warcraft for making sure of victories over these unknown villains trying to horn us out of our hardbegotten profit."

"Profit!" Adzel's tailtip struck the deck with a thud and a dry rattle. Unwonted indignation roughened his basso. "We'd have plenty of available power if you'd notify the Commonwealth, so regular naval forces could be mobilized. The more I think about your silence, the more I realize with horror that you are deliberately letting whole planets, a whole civilization, billions upon billions of sentient beings, lie unsuspecting and unprepared... lest you miss your chance at a monopoly!"

"Whoa, whoa, horsey." Van Rijn lifted one palm. "Is not that bad. Look here, I don't make no money if my whole society goes down guggle-guggle to the bottom. Do I? And besides, I got a conscience. I got to answer to God my own poor self, someday." He pointed to the little Martian sandroot statuette of St. Dismas that usually traveled with him. It stood on a shelf; candles had been overlooked in the haste of departure, but numerous IOU's for them were tucked under its base. He crossed himself.

"No," he said, "I got to decide what gives everybody his best chance. Not his certainty—is no such thing—but his best chance. With this tired old brain, all soggy and hard to light, I got to decide our action. Even if I decide to let you do the deciding, that is a deciding of mine and I got to answer for it. Also, I don't think you would want that responsibility."

"Well, no," Adzel admitted. "It is frightful. But you show dangerous pride in assuming it unilaterally."

"Who else is better? You is too naïve, too trusting, for one exemplar. Most others is stupids, or hysterics, or toot some political theory they chop up the universe to fit, or is greedy or cruel or— Well, me, I can ask my friend yonder to make interceding in Heaven for me. And I make connections in this life too, you understand. I am not playing every card alone; no, no, I got plenty good people up my sleeve, who is being told as much as they need to know."

Van Rijn leaned back. "Adzel," he said, "down the corridor you find a cooler with beer. You bring me one like a good fellow and I review this whole affair with you what has mostly waited patient and not sat in on the talks I had. You will see what a bucket of worms I must balance on each other—"

Those who are not afraid of death, even at their own hands, may get power beyond their real strength. For then their cooperation has to be bargained for.

The partners in Serendipity had not suffered total defeat. They held several counters. For one, there was the apparatus they had built up, the organization, the computers and memory banks. It would be difficult, perhaps impossible, to keep them from destroying this before its sale went through, if they chose. And more was involved here than someone's money. Too many key enterprises were already too dependent on the service; many others were potentially so; though the loss would be primarily economic, it would give a severe shock to the League, the Commonwealth, and allied peoples. In effect, while untold man-years would not be lost as lives, their productivity would be.

Of course, the system contained no information about its ultimate masters. A few deductions might perhaps be made, e.g., by studying the circuits, but these would be tentative and, if correct, not very important. However, perusal of the accumulated data would have some value as an indicator of the minimum amount of knowledge that those masters had about Technic civilization.

Hence the partners could exact a price for sparing their machines. The price included their own free departure, with no one trailing them: a fact they could verify for themselves.

Van Rijn, in his turn, could demand some compensation for helping to arrange this departure. He was naturally anxious to learn something, anything concerning the Shenna (as he soon did worm out that they were called in at least one of their languages). He wanted a meeting between their people and his. Before Kim Yoon-Kun, Anastasia Herrera, and Eve Latimer left the Solar System, he got their promise to urge their lords to send a delegation. Where it would be sent they did not specify. Thea Beldaniel, who stayed behind, was to reveal this at the appropriate time if she saw fit.

Another mutual interest lay in preserving discretion. Neither Serendipity nor van Rijn wanted Technic governments directly involved . . . as yet, anyhow. But if either got disgusted with these private chafferings, that party could stop them by making a public statement of the facts. Since van Rijn probably had less to lose from any such outcome, this was a more powerful chess piece in his hand than in Thea's. Or so he apparently convinced her. She bought his silence initially by helping him get the information from the computers, about Beta Crucis and the rogue, that Falkayn had gotten earlier.

Nevertheless, negotiations between him and her dragged on. This was partly because of the legal formalities involved in the sale of the company, and tussles with news agencies that wanted to know more. Partly, too, it was due to his own stalling. He needed time. Time for *Muddlin' Through* to report back. Time to decide what word should be quietly passed to whom, and what should then be done in preparation against an ill-defined danger. Time to begin those preparations, but keep them undercover, yet not too well hidden. . . .

In contrast, Thea's advantage—or that of her masters— lay in making an early start for the rendezvous. This should not be too soon for the Shenna to have received ample warning from Kim's party. But neither should it give van Rijn more time to organize his forces than was unavoidable.

She told him that the Shenna had no overwhelming reason to dicker with anybody. Their spy system being wrecked, they might wish to meet with someone well informed like van Rijn, feel out the changed situation, conceivably work toward an agreement about spheres of influence. But then again, they might not. Powerful as they were, why should they make concessions to inferior races like man? She proposed that the merchant go unaccompanied to the rendezvous, in a spaceship chosen by her, viewports blanked. He refused.

Abruptly she broke off the talks and insisted on leaving in less than a week. Van Rijn howled to no avail. This was the deadline she and her partners had agreed on, when they also set the meeting place they would suggest to their lords. If he did not accept it, he would simply not be guided.

He threatened not to accept. He had other ways to trace down the Shenna, he said. The haggling went back and forth. Thea did have some reason for wanting the expedition to go. She believed it would serve the ends of her masters; at a minimum, it ought to give them an extra option. And, a minor but real enough consideration, it would carry her home, when otherwise she was doomed to suicide or lifelong exile. She gave in on some points.

The agreement reached at last was for her to travel alone, van Rijn with none but Adzel. (He got a partner in exchange for the fact that his absence would, he claimed, badly handicap the League.) They were to leave at the time she wanted. However, they would not travel blind. Once they went hyper, she would instruct the robopilot, and he might as well listen to her as she specified the coordinates. The goal wasn't a Shen planet anyway.

But she would not risk some booby trap, tracing device, clandestine message ejector, or whatever else he might put into a ship he had readied beforehand. Nor did he care to take corresponding chances. They settled on jointly ordering a new-built vessel from a nonhuman yard—there happened to be one that had just completed her shakedown cruise and was advertising for buyers—with an entire supply stock. They boarded immediately upon Solar System delivery, each having inspected the other's hand baggage, and started the moment that clearance was granted.

This much Adzel knew. He had not been party to van Rijn's other activities. It came as no surprise to him that confidential couriers had been dispatched from end to end of the Solar Spice & Liquors trading territory, carrying orders for its most reliable factors, district chiefs, "police" captains, and more obscure employees. But he had not realized the degree to which other merchant princes of the League were alerted. True, they were not told everything. But the reason for that was less to keep secret the existence of the rogue than it was to head off shortsighted avarice and officiousness that must surely hamper a defense effort. The magnates were warned of a powerful, probably hostile civilization beyond the rim of the known. Some of them were told in more detail about the role Serendipity had played. They must gather what force they had.

And this was sufficient to bring in governments! A movement of Polesotechnic fighting units could not escape notice. Inquiries would be rebuffed, more or less politely. But with something clearly in the wind, official military-naval services would be put on the qui vive. The fact that League ships were concentrating near the important planets would cause those charged with defense to apportion their own strength accordingly.

Given out-and-out war, this would not serve. The merchant lords must work as closely as might be with the lords spiritual and temporal that legal theory (the different, often wildly different legal theories of the various races and cultures) said were set over them in any of the innumerable separate jurisdictions. But in the immediate situation, where virtually everything was unknown—where the very existence of a dangerous enemy remained unproven—such an alliance was impossible. The rivalries involved were too strong. Van Rijn could get more action faster by complicated flimflammery than by any appeal to idealism or common sense.

At that, the action was far too slow. Under perfect conditions, with everyone concerned a militant angel, it would still be too slow. The distances involved were so immense, lines of communication so thin, planets so scattered and diverse. No one had ever tried to rally all of those worlds at once. Not only had it never been necessary, it did not look feasible.

"I done what I could," van Rijn said, "not even knowing what I should. Maybe in three-four months—or three-four years, I don't know—the snowball I started rolling will bear fruit. Maybe then everybody is ready to ride out whatever blow will go bang on them. Or maybe not.

"I left what information I didn't give out in a safe place. It will be publicated after a while if I don't come back. After that, hoo-hoo, me I can't forespeak what happens! Many players then come in the game, you see, where now is only a few. It got demonstrated centuries back, in early days of theory, the more players, the less of a stable is the game.

"We go off right now, you and me, and try what we can do. If we don't do nothing except crash, well, we begun about as much battering down of hatches as I think could have been. Maybe enough. Maybe not. *Vervloekt,* how hard I wish that Beldaniel witch did not make us go away so soon like this!"

XIX

THE ship went under hyperdrive and raced through night. She would take about three weeks to reach her destination.

In the beginning Thea held aloof, stayed mainly in her cabin, said little beyond the formulas of courtesy at mealtimes and chance encounters. Van Rijn did not press her. But he talked at the table, first over the food and afterward over large bottles of wine and brandy. It sounded like idle talk, reminiscence, free association, genial for the most part though occasionally serious. Remarks of Adzel's often prompted these monologues; nonetheless, van Rijn seemed to take for granted that he was addressing the thin, jittery, never-smiling woman as well as the mild-mannered draco-centauroid.

She excused herself immediately after the first few meals. But soon she stayed, listening till all hours. There was really nothing else to do; and a multiple billion light-years of loneliness enclosed this thrumming metal shell; and van Rijn's tongue rambled through much that had never been public knowledge, the stuff of both science and saga.

"—we could not come near that white dwarf star, so bad did it radiate...*ja,* hard X-ray quanta jumping off it like fleas abandoning a sinking dog... only somehow we had got to recover the derelict or our poor little new company would be bankrupted. Well, I thought, fate had harpooned me in the end. But by damn, the notion about a harpoon made me think maybe we could—"

What she did not know was that Adzel received his

instructions prior to each such occasion. What he was to say, ask, object to, and confirm was listed for him. Thus van Rijn had a series of precisely planned conversations to try on Thea Beldaniel.

He soon developed a pretty good general idea of what subjects interested and pleased her, what bored or repelled. No doubt she was storing away in memory everything that might possibly be useful to the Shenna. But she must recognize that usefulness was marginal, especially when she had no way of telling how much truth lay in any given anecdote. It followed that her reaction to whatever he told her came chiefly from her own personality, her own emotions. Even more self-revealing were her reactions to the various styles he used. A story might be related in a cold, impersonal, calculating manner; or with barbaric glee; or humorously; or philosophically; or tenderly; or poetically, when he put words in the mouth of someone else; or in any number of other ways. Of course, he did not spring from one method straight to another. He tried different proportions.

The voyage was not half over when he had learned what face to adopt for her. Thereafter he concentrated on it. Adzel was no longer needed. She responded directly, eagerly to the man.

They were enemies yet. But he had become a respected opponent—or more than respected—and the hope was pathetic to see growing in her, that peace might be made between him and her lords.

"Natural, I want peace myself," he boomed benevolently. "What we got to fight for? Two or three hundred billion stars in our galaxy. Plenty room, *nie?*" He gestured at Adzel, who, well rehearsed, trotted off to fetch more cognac. When it arrived, he made a fuss—"Wa-a-agh! Not fit for pouring in burned-out chemosensors, this, let alone our lady friend what don't drink a lot and keeps a fine palate. Take it back and bring me another what better be decent! No, don't toss it out neither! You got scales on your brain like on your carcass? We take this home and show it to the dealer and make him consume it in a most unlikely way!"—although it was a perfectly good bottle which he and the Wodenite would later share in private. The act was part of the effect he was creating. Jove must loose occasional thunders and lightnings.

"Why is your Shenna scared of us?" he asked another time.

Thea bristled. "They are not! Nothing frightens them!" (Yes, they must be Jove and she their worshiper. At least to a first approximation. There were hints that the relationship was actually more subtle, and involved a master-figure which was actually primitive.) "They were being careful...discreet...wise...to study you b-b-beforehand."

"So, so, so. Don't get angry, please. How can I say right things about them when you won't tell me none?"

"I can't." She gulped. Her hands twisted together. "I mustn't." She fled to her cabin.

Presently van Rijn followed. He could drift along like smoke when he chose. Her door was shut and massive; but he had worn a button in his ear, hidden by the ringlets, when he embarked. It was a transistorized sound amplifier, patterned after hearing aids from the period before regenerative techniques were developed. He listened to her sobs for a while, neither bashfully nor gloatingly. They confirmed that he had her in psychological retreat. She would not surrender, not in the mere days of travel which remained. But she would give ground, if he advanced with care.

He jollied her, the next watch they met. And at the following supper, he proceeded to get her a little drunk over dessert. Adzel left quietly and spent half an hour at the main control board, adjusting the color and intensity of the saloon lights. They became a romantic glow too gradually for Thea to notice. Van Rijn had openly brought a player and installed it that they might enjoy dinner music. "Tonight's" program ran through a calculated gamut of pieces like *The Last Spring, Là, Ci Darem La Mano, Isoldes Liebestod, Londonderry Air, Evenstar Blues.* He did not identify them for her. Poor creature, she was too alienated from her own people for the names to mean anything. But they should have their influence.

He had no physical designs on her. (Not that he would have minded. She was, if not beautiful, if far less well filled out than he liked, rather attractive—despite her severe white suit—now that she had relaxed. Interest turned her finely boned features vivid and kindled those really beautiful green eyes. When she spoke with a smile, and with no purpose except the pleasure of speaking to a fellow human, her voice grew husky.) Any such attempt would have triggered her defenses. He was trying for a more rarefied, and vital, kind of seduction.

"—they raised us," she said dreamily. "Oh, I know the Earthside jargon. I know it gave us deviant personalities. But what is the norm, honestly, Nicholas? We're different from other humans, true. But human nature is plastic. I don't believe you can call us warped, any more than you yourself are because you were brought up in a particular tradition. We are healthy and happy."

Van Rijn raised one eyebrow.

"We are!" she said louder, sitting erect again. "We're glad and proud to serve our . . . our saviors."

"'The lady doth protest too much, methinks,'" he murmured.

"What?"

"A line in Old Anglic. You would not recognize. Pronunciation has changed. It means I am very interested. You never told nobody about your background before, the shipwreck and all."

"Well, I did tell Davy Falkayn . . . when he was with us—" Tears gleamed suddenly on her lashes. She squeezed the lids together, shook her head, and drained her glass. Van Rijn refilled it.

"He's a sweet young man," she said fast. "I never wanted to harm him. None of us did. Not our fault he was, was, was sent off to danger. By you! I do hope he'll be lucky."

Van Rijn did not pursue the point she had inadvertently verified: that Latimer and her sister had carried word to the Shenna, who would promptly have organized a Beta Crucis expedition of their own. It was a rather obvious point. Instead, the merchant drawled:

"If he was a friend like you say, you must have hurt when you lied to him."

"I don't know what you mean." She looked shocked.

"You spun him one synthetic yarn, you." Van Rijn's mild

165

tone took the edge off his words. "That radiation accident, and you getting found later, is too big, spiky a coincidence for me to swallow. Also, if the Shenna only wanted to return you home, with a stake, they would not set you up for spies. Also, you is too well trained, too loyal, for being raised by utter aliens from adolescence. You might have been grateful to them for their help, but you would not be their agents against your own race what never harmed you—not unless you was raised from pups. No, they got you sooner in life than you tell. *Nie?*"

"Well—"

"Don't get mad." Van Rijn raised his own glass and contemplated the colors within. "I am simple-minded, good-hearted trying to come at some understandings, so I can figure how we settle this trouble and not have any fights. I don't ask you should pass out no real secrets from the Shenna. But things like, oh, what they call their home planet—"

"Dathyna," she whispered.

"Ah. See? That did not hurt you nor them for saying, did it? And makes our talking a lot handier, we don't need circumlocomotions. Hokay, you was raised from babies, for a purpose, as might be because the Shenna wanted special ambassadors. Why not admit it? How you was raised, what the environment was like, every little friendly datum helps me understand you and your people, Thea."

"I can't tell you anything important."

"I know. Like the kind of sun Dathyna got is maybe too good a clue. But how about the kind of living? Was your childhood happy?"

"Yes. Yes. My earliest memory is . . . Isthayan, one of my master's sons, took me exploring . . . he wanted someone to carry his weapons, even their toddlers have weapons. . . . We went out of the household, into the ruined part of the huge old, old building . . . we found some machinery in a high tower room, it hadn't rusted much, the sunlight struck through a hole in the roof like white fire, off metal, and I laughed to see it shine. . . . We could look out, across the desert, like forever—" Her eyes widened. She laid a hand across her lips. "No, I'm talking far too freely. I'd better say goodnight."

"Verweile doch, du bist so schön," van Rijn said, "what is another old Earth quotation and means stay a while and have some Madeira, my dear. We discuss safe things. For instance, if you babies didn't come off no colonizer ship, then where?"

The color left her cheeks. "Goodnight!" she gasped, and once again she ran. By now he could have shouted an order to stay and she would have heeded; for the reflex of obedience to that kind of stimulus had become plain to see in her. He refrained, though. Interrogation would only produce hysteria.

Instead, when he and Adzel were alone in the Wodenite's stateroom—which had been prepared by ripping out the bulkhead between two adjoining ones—he rumbled around a nightcap:

"I got a few information bits from her. Clues to what kind of world and culture we is colliding with. More about the psychologics than the outside facts. But that could be helpful too." His mustaches rose with the violence of his grimace. "Because what we face is not just troublesome, it is nasty. Horrible."

"What have you learned, then?" the other asked calmly.

"Obvious, the Shenna made slaves—no, dogs—out of humans on purpose that they got from babies. Maybe other sophonts too, but anyways humans."

"Where did they obtain the infants?"

"I got no proof, but here is a better guess than Beldaniel and her partners maybe thought I could make. Look, we can assume pretty safe the rendezvous planet we is bound for is fairly near Dathyna so they got the advantage of short communications while we is far from home and our nice friends with guns. Right?"

Adzel rubbed his head, a bony sound. "'Near' is a relative term. Within a sphere of fifty or a hundred light-years' radius there are so many stars that we have no reasonable chance of locating the centrum of our opponents before they have mounted whatever operation they intend."

"*Ja, ja, ja*. What I mean is, though, somewhere around where we aim at is territory where Shenna been active for a longish while. Hokay? Well, happens I remember, about fifty years back was an attempt for planting a human colony out this way. A little utopian group like was common in those days. Late type G star, but had one not bad planet what they called, uh, *ja,* Leandra. They wanted to get away from anybody interrupting their paradise. And they was successful. No profit for traveling that far to trade. They had one ship for their own would visit Ifri or Llynathawr maybe once a year and buy things they found they needed, for money they had along. Finally was a long time with no ship. Somebody got worried and went to see. Leandra stood abandoned. The single village was pretty burned—had been a forest fire over everywhere for kilometers around—but the ship was gone. Made a big mystery for a while. I heard about it because happened I was traveling by Ifri some years afterward. Of course, it made no splash on Earth or any other important planet."

"Did no one think of piracy?" Adzel asked.

"Oh, probable. But why should pirates sack a tiny place like that? Besides, had been no later attacks. Whoever heard of one-shot pirates? Logical theory was, fire wiped out croplands, warehouses, everything that Leandrans needed to live. They went after help, all in their ship, had troubles in space and never made port. The matter is pretty well forgot now. I don't believe nobody has bothered with Leandra since. Too many better places closer to home." Van Rijn scowled at his glass as if it were another enemy. "Tonight I guess different. Could be Shenna work. They could of first landed, like friendly explorers from a world what lately begun space travel. They could learn details and figure what to do. Then they could kidnap everybody and set fire for covering the evidence."

"I believe I see the further implications," Adzel said softly. "Some attempt, perhaps, to domesticate the older captive humans. Presumably a failure, terminated by their murder, because the youngest ones don't remember natural parents. No doubt many infants died too, or were killed as being unpromising material. Quite possibly the half-dozen of

Serendipity are the sole survivors. It makes me doubt that any nonhumans were similarly victimized. Leandra must have represented a unique opportunity."

"What it proves is bad enough," van Rijn said. "I can't push Beldaniel about her parents. She must feel suspicions, at least, but not dare let herself think about them. Because her whole soul is founded on being a creature of the Shenna. In fact, I got the impression of she being the special property of one among them—like a dog."

His hand closed around the tumbler with force that would have broken anything less strong than vitryl. "They want to make us the same, maybe?" he snarled. "No, by eternal damn! *Liever dood dan slaaf!*" He drained the last whisky. "What means, I'll see them in Hell first...if I got to drag them down behind me!" The tumbler crashed warheadlike on the deck.

XX

THE rendezvous site was listed in Technic catalogues. Scanning its standard memory units, the ship's computer informed van Rijn that this system had been visited once, about a century ago. A perfunctory survey revealed nothing of interest, and no one was recorded as having gone back. (Nothing except seven planets, seven worlds, with their moons and mysteries, life upon three of them, and one species that had begun to chip a few stones into handier shapes, look up at the night sky and gropingly wonder.) There were so uncountably many systems.

"I could have told you that," Thea said.

"Ha?" Van Rijn turned, planet-ponderous himself, as she entered the command bridge.

Her smile was shy, her attempt at friendliness awkward from lack of practice. "Obviously we couldn't give you a hint at anything you didn't already know. We picked a sun arbitrarily, out of deserted ones within what we guessed is a convenient volume of space for the Shenna."

"Hm-hm." Van Rijn tugged his goatee. "I wouldn't be an ungentleman, but wasn't you never scared I might grab you and pump you, I mean for where Dathyna sits?"

"No. The information has been withheld from me. Only the men, Latimer and Kim, were ever told, and they received deep conditioning against revealing it." Her gaze traveled around the stars which, in this craft built by nonhumans, showed as a strip engirdling the compartment. "I can tell you what you must have guessed, that some of the constellations are starting to look familiar to me." Her voice dropped. She reached her arms forth, an unconscious gesture of yearning. "They, the Shenna, will take me home. Moath himself may be waiting. *Eyar wathiya grazzan tolya....*"

Van Rijn said quietly, into her growing rapture, "Suppose they do not come? You said they might not. What do you do?"

She drew a quick breath, clenched her fists, stood for a moment as the loneliest figure he remembered seeing, before she turned to him. Her hands closed around his, cold and quick. "Then will you help me?" she begged. Fire mounted in her countenance. She withdrew. "But Moath will not abandon me!" She turned on her heel and walked out fast.

Van Rijn glowered at the star that waxed dead ahead, and took out his snuffbox for what consolation was in it.

But his hunch was right, that Thea had no real reason for worry. Sweeping inward, the ship detected emanations from a sizable flotilla, at an initial distance indicating those vessels had arrived two or three days ago. (Which meant they had departed from a point not much over a hundred light-years hence—unless Shenna craft could travel a great deal faster than Technic ones—and this was unlikely, because if the Shenna were not relative newcomers to space, they would surely have been encountered already by explorers—not to mention the fact that today's hyperdrive oscillator frequencies were crowding the maximum which quantum theory allowed—) They accelerated almost at the instant van Rijn came within detection range. Some fanned out, doubtless to make sure he didn't have followers. The rest converged on him. A code signal, which the Shenna must have learned from human slaves, flashed. Van Rijn obeyed, dropped into normal state, assumed orbit around the sun, and let the aliens position themselves however they chose.

Gathered again in the bridge before the main outercom, all three waited. Thea shivered, her face now red and now white, staring and staring at the ships which drew closer. Van Rijn turned his back on her. "I don't know why," he muttered to Adzel in one of the languages they were sure she did not have in common with them, "but I get some feeling I can't name from the sight of her like that."

"Embarrassment, probably," the Wodenite suggested.

"Oh, is that how it feels?"

"She is unlike me, of course, in her deepest instincts as well as her upbringing," Adzel said. "Regardless, I do not find it decent either to observe a being stripped so naked."

He concentrated his attention on the nearest Shenn craft. Its gaunt high-finned shape was partly silhouetted black upon the Milky Way, partly asheen by the distant orange sun. "A curious design," he said. "It does not look very functional."

Van Rijn switched to Anglic. "Could be hokay for machines, that layout," he remarked. "And why this many of them—fifteen, right?—big and hedgehoggy with weapons and would need hundreds in the crews—to meet one little unarmed speedster like us, unless they is mostly robots? I think they is real whizzards at robotics, those Shenna. Way beyond us. The SI computer system points likewise."

Thea reacted in her joy as he had hoped. She could not keep from boasting, rhapsodizing, about the powerful and complex automatons whose multitudes were skeleton and muscle of the whole Dathynan civilization. Probably no more than three or four living Masters were in this group, she said. No more were needed.

"Not even for making dicker with us?" van Rijn asked.

"They speak for themselves alone," Thea said. "You don't have plenipotentiary powers either, you know. But they will confer with their colleagues after you have been interviewed." Her tone grew more and more absent-minded while she spoke, until it faded into a kind of crooning in the guttural Shenn tongue. She had never ceased staring outward.

"'They will confer with their colleagues,'" Adzel quoted slowly, in the private language. "Her phrase suggests that decision-making authority rests with an exceedingly small group. Yet it does not follow that the culture is an extreme oligarchy. Oligarchs would prefer live crews for most tasks, like us, and for the same reasons. No matter how effective a robot one builds, it remains a machine—essentially, an auxiliary to a live brain—because if it were developed so highly as to be equivalent to a biological organism, there would be no point in building it."

"*Ja,* I know that line of argument," van Rijn said. "Nature has already provided us means for making new biological organisms, a lot cheaper and more fun than producing robots. Still, how about the computer that has been speculated about, fully motivated but superior in every way to any being born from flesh?"

"A purely theoretical possibility in any civilization we have come upon thus far; and frankly, I am skeptical of the theory. But supposing it did exist, such a robot would rule, not serve. And the Shenna are obviously not subordinates. Therefore they have—well, on the whole, perhaps somewhat better robots than we do, perhaps not; certainly more per capita; nevertheless, only robots, with the usual inherent limitations. They employ them lavishly in order to compensate as best they can for those limitations. But why?"

"Little population? That would explain why they do not have many decision makers, if they do not."

"*Zanh-h-h* . . . maybe. Although I cannot offhand see how a society few in numbers could build—could even design— the vast, sophisticated production plant that Dathyna evidently possesses."

They had been talking largely to relieve their tension, quite well aware of how uncertain their logic was. When the ship said, "Incoming signal received," they both started. Thea choked a shriek. "Put them on, whoever they is," van Rijn ordered. He wiped sweat off his jowls with the soiled lace of one cuff.

The visiscreen flickered. An image sprang forth. It was half manlike; but swelling muscles, great bull head, iridescent mane, thunder that spoke from the open mouth: were such embodied volcano power that Adzel stepped backward hissing.

"Moath!" Thea cried. She fell to her knees, hands outstretched toward the Shenn. Tears whipped down her face.

Life is an ill-arranged affair, where troubles and triumphs both come in lots too big to cope with, and in between lie arid stretches of routine and marking time. Van Rijn often spoke sharply to St. Dismas about this. He never got a satisfactory reply.

His present mission followed the pattern. After Thea said Moath her lord commanded her presence aboard the vessel where he was—largest of the flotilla, a dreadnought in size, fantastically beweaponed—and entered a flitter dispatched for her, nothing happened for forty-seven hours and twenty-nine minutes by the clock. The Shenna sent no further word nor heeded any calls addressed to them. Van Rijn groaned, cursed, whined, stamped up and down the passages, ate six full meals a day, cheated at solitaire, overloaded the air purifiers with smoke and the trash disposal with empty bottles, and would not even be soothed by his Mozart symphonies. At last he exhausted Adzel's tolerance. The Wodenite locked himself in his own room with food and good books, and did not emerge until his companion yelled at the door that the damned female icicle with the melted brain was ready to interpret and maybe now something could be done to reward him, Nicholas van Rijn, for his Griselda-like patience.

Nonetheless, the merchant was showing her image a certain avuncular courtliness when Adzel galloped in. "—wondered why you left us be when everybody traveled this far for meeting."

Seated before a transmitter pickup on the battleship, she was changed. Her garb was a loose white robe and burnoose and her eyes bore dark contact lenses, protection from the harsh light in that cabin. She was altogether self-possessed again, her emotional needs fulfilled. Her answer came crisp: "My lords the Shenna questioned me in detail, in preparation for our discussions. No one else from Serendipity was brought along, you see."

Below the viewfield of his own sender, van Rijn kept a scrib on his lap. Like fast hairy sausages, his fingers moved across the noiseless console. Adzel read an unrolling tape: *That was foolish. How could they be sure nothing would have happened to her, their link with us? More proof they rush into things, not stopping for thought.*

Thea was continuing. "Furthermore, before I could talk rationally, I must get the *haaderu*. I had been so long away from my lord Moath. You would not understand *haaderu*."

She blushed the faintest bit, but her voice might have described some adjustment to a machine. "Consider it a ceremony in which he acknowledges my loyalty to him. It requires time. Meanwhile, the scoutships verified no one else had treacherously accompanied us at a distance."

Van Rijn wrote: *Not Jove. The Minotaur. Raw power and maleness.*

"I do not identify the reference," Adzel breathed in his ear.

What the Shenn beast really is to her. She is only somewhat a slave. I have known many women like her in offices, spinsters fanatically devoted to a male boss. No wonder the SI gang were four women, two men. Men seldom think quite that way. Unless first they are conditioned, broken. I doubt if those people have had any sex relationship. The Latimer marriage was to prevent gossip. Their sexuality has been directed into the channel of serving the Shenna. Of course, they don't realize that.

"My lords will now hear you," Thea Beldaniel said. For an instant, humanness broke through. She leaned forward and said, low and urgent, "Nicholas, be careful. I know your ways, and I'll translate what you mean, not what you say. But be careful what you mean, too. I won't lie to them. And they are more easily angered than you might think. I—" She paused a second. "I want you to go home unhurt. You are the, the only man who was ever kind to me."

Bah, he wrote, *I played Minotaur myself, once I saw she wished for something like that, though I supposed at the time that it was Jove. She responded, not conscious of what moved her. Not but what she doesn't deserve to be led back into her own species. That is a filthy thing they have done to her.*

Thea gestured. A robot responded. The view panned back, revealing a great conference chamber where four Shenna sat on cushions. Van Rijn winced and mumbled an oath when he saw the décor. "No taste, not by our standards nowhere in the universe or Hell! They skipped right past civilization, them, gone straight from barbarism to decadence." It was Adzel who, as the conference progressed and the focus of view shifted about, remarked on a few ancient-looking objects in that overcrowded room which were lovely.

A voice rolled from one shaggy deep chest. Dwarfed and lost-looking, but her glance forever straying back to adore the Shenn called Moath, Thea interpreted: "You have come to speak of terms between your people and mine. What is the dispute?"

"Why, nothings, really," van Rijn said, "except could be a few pieces of dirt we divvy up like friends instead of blowing our profit on squabbles. And maybe we got things we could trade, or teach each other, like how about one of us has a fine new vice?"

Thea's translation was interrupted halfway through. A Shenn asked something at some length which she rendered as: "What is your alleged complaint against us?"

She must have shaded her interpretation from that side also, but van Rijn and Adzel were both too taken aback to care. "Complaint?" the Wodenite nearly bleated. "Why, one scarcely knows where to begin."

"I do, by damn," van Rijn said, and commenced.

The argument erupted. Thea was soon white and shaking with nerves. Sweat plastered her hair to her brow. It would be useless to detail the wranglings. They were as confused and pointless as the worst in human history. But piece by piece, through sheer stubbornness and refusal to be outshouted, van Rijn assembled a pattern.

Item: Serendipity had been organized to spy upon the Polesotechnic League and the whole Technic civilization.

Answer: The Shenna had provided the League with a service it was too stupid to invent for itself. The forced sale of Serendipity was a bandit act for which the Shenna demanded compensation.

Item: David Falkayn had been kidnapped and drugged by Shenn agents.

Answer: One inferior organism was not worth discussing.

Item: Humans had been enslaved, and probably other humans had been massacred, by Shenna.

Answer: The humans were given a nobler life in service to a higher cause than could ever have been theirs otherwise.

Ask them if this was not true.

Item: The Shenna had tried to keep knowledge of a new planet from those who were entitled to it.

Answer: The ones entitled were the Shenna. Let trespassers beware.

Item: Despite their espionage, the Shenna did not seem to appreciate the strength of the Technic worlds and especially the League, which was not in the habit of tolerating menaces.

Answer: Neither were the Shenna.

—About that time, Thea collapsed. The being called Moath left his place and went to stoop over her. He looked, briefly, into the screen. His nostrils were dilated and his mane stood erect. He snorted a command. Transmission ended.

It was probably just as well.

Van Rijn woke so fast that he heard his own final snore. He sat up in bed. His stateroom was dark, murmurous with ventilation, a slight sugary odor in the air because no one had adjusted the chemosystem. The mechanical voice repeated, "Incoming signal received."

"Pestilence and pustules! I heard you, I heard you, let me haul my poor tired old body aloft, by damn." The uncarpeted deck was cold under his feet. From a glowing clock face he saw he had been asleep for not quite six hours. Which made over twenty hours since the conference broke off. If you could dignify that slanging match by that name. What ailed those shooterbulls, anyhow? A high technological culture such as was needed to build robots and spaceships ought to imply certain qualities—a minimum level of diplomacy and caution and enlightened self-interest—because otherwise you would have wrecked yourself before you progressed that far.... Well, maybe communications had stayed off until now because the Shenna were collecting their tempers.... Van Rijn hurried down the corridor. His nightgown flapped around his ankles.

The bridge was another humming emptiness. Taking its orders literally, the computer had stopped annunciating when it got a response. Adzel, his ears accustomed to denser air, was not roused in that short time. The machine continued as programmed by reporting, "Two hours ago, another spacecraft was detected in approach from the Circinus region. It is still assuming orbit but is evidently in contact with those already present—"

"Shut up and put me on," van Rijn said. His gaze probed the stars. An eel-like destroyer, a more distant cruiser, a point of light that could be the Shenn flagship, drifted across his view. No visible sign of the newcomer. But he did not doubt that was what had caused this summons.

The viewscreen came on. Thea Beldaniel stood alone in the harsh-lit, machine-murmurous cavern of the conference chamber. He had never seen her so frantic. Her eyes were white-rimmed, her mouth was stretched out of shape.

"Go!" Nor was her voice recognizable. "Escape! They're talking with Gahood. They haven't thought of ordering the robots to watch you. You can leave quietly—maybe—get a head start, or lose them in space—but they'll kill you if you stay!"

He stood altogether unmoving. His deepened tone rolled around her. "Please to explain me more."

"Gahood. He came...alone...Hugh Latimer's dead or—I sleep in my lord Moath's cabin by the door. An intercom call. Thellam asked him to come to the bridge, him and everyone. He said Gahood was back from Dathyna, Gahood who went to the giant star where the rogue is, and something happened so Gahood lost Latimer. They should meet, hear his full story, decide—" Her fingers made claws in the air. "I don't know any more, Nicholas. Moath gave me no command. I w-w-would not betray him ...them...never...but what harm if you stay alive? I could hear the fury gather, *feel* it; I know them; whatever this is, they'll be enraged. They'll have the guns fire on you. Get away!"

Still van Rijn had not stirred. He was quiet until some measure of control returned to her. She shuddered, her breath was uneven, but she regarded him half sanely. Then he asked, "Would they for sure kill Adzel and me? Hokay, they are mad and don't feel like more jaw-jaw right now. But would not sense be for them, they take us home? We got information. We got hostage value."

178

"You don't understand. You'd never be freed. You might be tortured for your knowledge, you'd surely be drugged. And I would have to help them. And in the end, when you're no further use—"

"They knock me on the head. *Ja, ja,* is clear. But I got a hard old noggle." Van Rijn leaned forward, resting his fingertips lightly on a chairback and his weight on them, catching her look and not letting go. "Thea, if we run, maybe we get away, maybe we don't. I think chances is not awesome good. Those destroyers at least, I bet can outrun me, what is fat in the shanks. But if we go to Dathyna, well, maybe we can talk after your bosses cool down again. Maybe we strike a bargain yet. What they got to lose, anyhows, taking us along? Can you get them not to kill us, only capture us?"

"I . . . well, I—"

"Was good of you to warn me, Thea. I know what it cost you, I think. But you shouldn't get in trouble, neither, like you might if they find we skedoodled and guessed it was your fault. Why don't you go argue at your Moath? You remind him here we is and he better train guns on us and you better tell us we is prisoners and got to come to Dathyna. Think he does?"

She could not speak further. She managed a spastic nod.

"Hokay, run along." He blew her a kiss. The effect would have been more graceful if less noisy. The screen blanked. He stumped off to find a bottle and Adzel, in that order. But first he spent a few minutes with St. Dismas. If rage overrode prudence among the Shenna, despite the woman's pleas and arguments, he would not be long alive.

XXI

At full pseudospeed, from the nameless star to the sun of Dathyna took a bit under a week. The prisoner ship must strain to keep pace with the warcraft that surrounded her. But she succeeded, which told Earthman and Wodenite something about Shenn space capabilities.

They gathered quite a few other facts en route. This did not include the contents of Gahood's message, nor the reason why it sent the team plunging immediately homeward. But their captors questioned them at irregular intervals, by hypercom. The interrogation was unsystematic and repetitive, seemingly carried out whenever some individual Shenn got the impulse, soon degenerating into boasts and threats. Van Rijn gave many truthful answers, because the aliens could generally have obtained them directly from Thea—population, productivity, etc., of the major Technic worlds; nature and activities of the Polesotechnic League; picturesque details about this or that life form, this or that culture— She was plainly distressed at the behavior of her lords, and tried to recast their words into something better organized. By playing along with her, van Rijn was able to draw her out. For example:

"Lord Nimran wants to hear more about the early history of Earth," she told the merchant. Computers on either vessel converted between dot-dash transmission and voice. "He is especially interested in cases where one civilization inherited from another."

"Like Greeks taking over from Minoans, or Western Christendom from Roman Empire, or Turks from Byzantines?" van Rijn asked. "Cases are not comparable. And was long ago. Why should he care?"

He could imagine how she flushed. "It suffices that he does care."

"Oh, I don't mind making lectures at him. Got nothings else to do except pour me another beer. Speaking about which—" Van Rijn leaned over and fumbled in the cooler that Adzel had carried to the bridge for him. "Ah, there you are, fishie."

The computer turned this into hyperimpulses. The receiving computer was not equipped to translate, but its memory bank now included an Anglic vocabulary. Thea must have told Nimran that he had not properly replied. Did the Minotaur growl and drop hand to gun? Her plea was strained through the toneless artificial voice: "Do not provoke him. They are terrible when they grow angry."

Van Rijn opened the bottle and poured into a tankard. "*Ja,* sure, sure. I only try for being helpful. But tell him I got to know where he wants his knowledge deepened before I can drill in the shaft. And why. I feel the impression that Shenn culture does not produce scientists what wants to know things from pure curiosity."

"Humans overrate curiosity. A monkey trait."

"Uh-huh, uh-huh. Every species got its own instincts, sometimes similar at some other race's but not necessary so. I try now to get the basic instinct pattern for your . . . owners . . . because elsewise what I tell them might not be what they want, might not make any sense to them whatsomever. Hokay, you tell me there is no real seience on Dathyna. No interest in what isn't practical or edible or drinkable *(Aaahhh!)* or salable or useful in other ways I should not mention to a lady."

"You oversimplify."

"I know. Can't describe one single individual being in a few words, let alone a whole intelligent race. Sure. But speaking rough, have I right? Would you say this society is not one for abstracted science and odd little facts what aren't relevancy right away?"

"Very well, agreed." There came a pause, during which Thea was probably calming Nimran down again.

Von Rijn wiped foam off his nose and said, "I collect from this, is only one Shenn civilization?"

"Yes, yes. I must finish talking to him." After a couple of minutes: "If you do not start answering, the consequences may be grave."

"But I told you, sweetling, I'm not clear what is his question. He has not got a scientific curiosity, so he asks about successions of culture on Earth because might be is something useful to his own recent case on Dathyna. True?"

After hesitation: "Yes."

"All right, let us find out what kind of succession he is interested in. Does he mean how does a supplanter like Hindu appear, or a hybrid like Technic or Arabic, or a segue of one culture into another like Classical into Byzantine, or what?"

No doubt forlornness crossed her eyes. "I don't know anything myself about Earth's history."

"Ask him. Or better I should ask him through you."

In this manner, von Rijn got confirmation of what he suspected. The Shenna had not created the magnificent cybernetic structure they used. They took it over from an earlier race, along with much else. Still more appeared to have been lost, for the Shenna were conquerors, exterminators, savages squatting in a house erected by civilized beings whom they had murdered. (How was this possible?)

They were not less dangerous on that account, or because they were herbivorous. (What kind of evolution could produce warlike herbivores?)

They had the wit to heed the recommendation of the Serendipity computer as regards the planet at Beta Crucis. They could see its industrial potential. But they were more concerned with denying this to others than with making intensive use of it themselves. For they were not traders or manufacturers on any significant scale. Their robots produced for them the basic goods and services they required, including construction and maintenance of the machinery itself. They had no desire for commercial or intellectual relations with Technic societies. Rather, they believed that coexistence was impossible. (Why?)

The Serendipity operation typefied them. When they first

happened upon other races that traveled and colonized through space, out on the fringe of the existing Technic sphere, they proceeded to study these. Their methods were unspecified, and doubtless varied from place to place and time to time, but need not always have been violent. A Shenn could be cunning. Since no one can remember all the planets whose natives may go aroving, he need not admit he came from Outside, and he could ask many natural-sounding questions.

Nevertheless, they could not secretly get the detailed information they wanted by such hit-and-run means. One brilliant male among them conceived the idea of establishing spies in the heart of the other territory: spies who could expect the eager cooperation of their victims. His fellows agreed to help start the enterprise. No Shenn had the patience to run that shop in Lunograd. But computers and dog-humans did.

Even so, the basic program for the machines and doctrine for the people were drawn up by Shenna. And here the nature of the beast again revealed itself. *When something important and urgent comes up, react aggressively—fast!* Most species would have given an agency more caution, more flexibility. The Shenna could not endure to. Their instinct was such that to them, in any crisis, action was always preferable to wait-and-see. The pieces could be picked up later.

The Shenna did have a rationale for their distrust of other spacegoing races. (Which distrust automatically produced murderous hatred in them.) They themselves were not many. Their outplanet colonies were few, small, and none too successful. Four-fifths of their adults must be counted out as significant help—because the females outnumbered the polygynous males by that fraction, and were dull-brained subservient creatures. Their political structure was so crude as to be ridiculous. Baronial patriarchs, operating huge estates like independent kingdoms, might confer or cooperate at need, on a strictly voluntary basis; and this constituted the state. Their economics was equally primitive. (How had a race like this gone beyond the Paleolithic, let alone destroyed another people who had covered the planet

183

with machines and were reaching for the stars?)

The companies of the League could buy and sell them for peanuts. The outward wave of Technic settlement would not necessarily sweep over them when it got that far—why bother?—but would certainly engulf every other desirable world around Dathyna. At best, with enormous effort, the Shenna might convert themselves into one more breed of spacefarers among hundreds. To natures like theirs, that prospect was intolerable.

However their society was describable, they were not ridiculous themselves. On the contrary, they were as ominous as the plague bacillus when first it struck Europe. Or perhaps more so; Europe did survive.

XXII

THE sun of Dathyna looked familiar to Adzel—
middle F-type, 5.4 times as luminous as Sol, white more than
gold—until he studied it with what instruments he had
available. Astonished, he repeated his work, and got the
same results. "That is not a normal star," he said.

"About to go nova?" van Rijn asked hopefully.

"No, not that deviant." Adzel magnified the view,
stepping down the brilliance, until the screen showed a disc.
The corona gleamed immense, a beautiful serene nacre; but
it was background for the seething of flares and prominences, the dense mottling of spots. "Observe the level of
output. Observe likewise the intricate patterns. They show a
powerful but inconstant magnetic field. . . . Ah." A pinpoint
of eye-hurting light flashed and died on the surface. "A
nuclear explosion, taking place within the photosphere.
Imagine what convection currents and plasma effects were
required. Spectroscopy is consistent with visual data, as is
radiation metering. Even at our present distance, the solar
wind is powerful; and its pattern as we move inward is highly
changeable." He regarded the scene with his rubbery lips
pulled into a disconcerting smile. "I had heard of cases like
this, but they are rare and I never thought I would have the
good fortune to see one."

"I'm glad you get fun out of now," van Rijn grumbled.
"Next funeral I attend, I want you along for doing a buck
and wing while you sing Hey nonny nonny. So what we got
here?"

"A sun not only massive, but of unusual composition,
extremely rich in metals. Probably it condensed in the
neighborhood of a recent supernova. Besides the normal

main-sequence evolution, a number of other fusion chains, some of which terminate in fission, go on during its life. This naturally influences interior phenomena, which in turn determine the output. Consider it an irregularly variable star. It isn't really, but the pattern is so complex that it does not repeat within epochs. If I interpret my findings correctly, it is at present receding from a high peak which occurred— *zanh-h-h,* several thousand years ago, I would guess."

"But did not wipe out life on Dathyna?"

"Obviously not. The luminosity will never become that great, until the sun leaves the main sequence altogether. Nevertheless, there must have been considerable biological effect, especially since the charged-particle emission did reach an extreme."

Van Rijn grunted, settled deeper in his chair, and reached for his churchwarden. He usually smoked it when he wanted to think hard.

The flotilla approached Dathyna. The computer of the captive ship kept all sensors open as instructed, and reported much activity in surrounding space—ships in orbit, ships coming and going, ships under construction. Adzel took readings on the globe itself.

It was the fourth one out from its sun, completing a period of 2.14 standard years at a mean distance of two a.u. In mass it likewise resembled Mars: 0.433 Terrestrial, the diameter only 7950 kilometers at the equator. Despite this, and a third again the heat and light which Earth receives, Dathyna had an extensive oxynitrogen atmosphere. Pressure dropped off rapidly with altitude, but at sea level was slightly greater than Terrestrial. Such an amount of gas was surely due to the planetary composition, an abundance of heavy elements conferring an overall specific gravity of 9.4 and thus a surface acceleration of 1057 cm/sec^2. The metal-rich core must have produced enormous outgassing through vulcanism in the world's youth. Today, in combination with the fairly rapid spin—once around in seventeen and a quarter hours—it generated a strong magnetic field which screened off most of the solar particles that might otherwise have kicked air molecules free. The fact was also helpful that Dathyna had no moons.

Visually, swelling upon blackness and stars, the planet

was equally strange. It had far less hydrosphere than Earth; quanta from the ultraviolet-spendthrift sun had split many a water molecule. But because mountains and continental masses were less well defined, the surface flatter on the average, water covered about half. Shallow, virtually tideless, those seas were blanketed with alga-like organisms, a red-brown-yellow mat that was sometimes ripped apart to show waves, sometimes clotted into floating islands.

With slight axial tilt and comparatively small edge effect, the polar regions did not differ spectacularly from the equatorial. But with a steep air pressure gradient, the uplands were altogether unlike the valleys beneath—were glacier and naked rock. Some lowlands, especially along the oceans, appeared to be fertile. The brownish-gold native vegetation colored them; forests, meadows, croplands showed in the magniscreen. But enormous regions lay desert, where dust storms scoured red rock. And their barrenness was geologically new—probably not historically too old— because one could identify the towers and half-buried walls of many great dead cities, the grid of highways and power pylons that a large population once required.

"Did the sun burn the lands up when it peaked?" For once, van Rijn almost whispered a question.

"No," Adzel said. "Nothing that simple, I think."

"Why not?"

"Well, increased temperature would cause more evaporation, more clouds, higher albedo, and thus tend to control itself. Furthermore, while it might damage some zones, it would benefit others. Life should migrate poleward and upward. But you can see that the high latitudes and high altitudes have suffered as badly as anyplace. . . . Then too, a prosperous, energetic machine culture ought to have found ways of dealing with a mere change in climate—a change which did not come about overnight, remember."

"Maybe they held a war what got rough?"

"I see no signs of large-scale misuse of nuclear energies. And would any plausible biological or chemical agents wreck the entire ecology of an entire planet, right down to the humble equivalents of grass? I think," said Adzel grimly, "that the catastrophe had a much larger cause and much deeper effects."

He got no chance to elaborate then, for the ship was ordered into atmosphere. A pair of destroyers accompanied. Moath and Thea directed the robots from a tender. The group landed near the Shenn's ancestral castle. An armed swarm ran forth to meet them.

In the next three days, van Rijn and Adzel were given a look around. Thea guided them. "My lord permits this on my recommendation, while he is away at the Grand Council that's been called," she said. "By giving you a better comprehension of our society, we make you better able to help us with information." Pleadingly, not meeting their eyes: "You will help, won't you? You can't do anything else, except die. My lord will treat you well if you serve him well."

"So let's see what it's like where we got to pass our lives," van Rijn said.

The party was heavily guarded, by young males—the sons, nephews, and retainers who comprised Moath's fighting cadre—and robot blastguns that floated along on gravity platforms. Adzel's size inspired caution, though he acted meek enough. Youngsters and idle servants trailed after. Females and workers goggled as the outworlders passed by. The Shenn race was not absolutely devoid of curiosity; no vertebrate is, on any known planet. They simply lacked the intensity of it that characterizes species like Homo or Dracocentaurus sapiens. They were quite analogous in their love of novelty.

"Castle" was a misleading word for the establishment. Once there had been an interlinked set of buildings, an enormous block, five or six kilometers on a side, a full tenth as high—yet for all that mass, graceful, many-colored, with columns of crystal that were nonfunctional but a joy to the eye, with towers that soared so far above the walls that their petal-shaped spires nearly vanished in heaven. It had been a place where millions lived and worked, a community which was an engineered unit, automated, nuclear-powered, integrated through traffic and communication with the whole planet.

Now half of it was a ruin. Pillars were fallen, roofs gaped to the sky, machines had corroded away, creatures like birds nested in the turrets and creatures like rats scuttered through the apartments. Though destruction had passed the rest by, and the patient self-maintaining robots kept it in repair, the echoing hollowness of too many corridors, the plundered bareness of too many rooms and plazas and terraces, were more oppressive than the broken sections.

Thea refused to say what had happened, centuries past. "Are you forbidden to tell us?" Adzel asked.

She bit her lip. "No," she said in a sad little voice, "not exactly. But I don't want to." After a moment: "You wouldn't understand. You'd get the wrong idea. Later, when you know our lords the Shenna better—"

About half of the functional half of the complex was occupied today. The dwellers were not haunted by the past. They seemed to regard its overwhelming shell as part of their landscape. The ruins were quarried—that was one reason they were in poor condition—and the remainder would be taken over as population grew. A busy, lusty, brawling life surged between the walls and across the countryside. While robots did most of the essential work, Moath's folk had plenty of tasks left to do, from technical supervision to their crude arts and crafts, from agriculture and forestry to prospecting and hunting, from education for one's state in a hierarchical society to training for war. Aircraft bore passengers and cargo from other domains. Gravships shuttled between the planets of this system; hyperships trafficked with colonies newly planted among the nearer stars, or prowled farther in exploration and imperialism. Even the peaceful routines of Dathyna had that thunderous vigor which is the Minotaur's.

Nonetheless, here was a life-impoverished world—metal-rich but life-impoverished. The crops grew thin in dusty fields. A perpetual faint stench hung in the air, blown from the nearby ocean, where the vast sea-plant blanket was dying and rotting faster than it replenished itself. The eastern hills were wooded, but with scrubby trees growing among the traces of fallen giants. At night, a hunter's trumpet sounded from them lonelier than would have been the howl of the last wolf alive.

Adzel was astounded to learn that the Shenna hunted and, in fact, kept meat animals. "But you said they are herbivorous," he protested.

"Yes, they are," Thea replied. "This sunlight causes plants to form high-energy compounds which will support a more active, hence intelligent, animal than on the world of a Sol-type star."

"I know," Adzel said. "I am native to an F_5 system myself—though on Zatlakh, Woden, animals generally spend the extra energy on growing large, and we sophonts are omnivorous. I suppose the Shenna must process meat before they can digest it?"

"Correct. Of course, I am sure you know better than I how vague the line is between 'carnivore' and 'herbivore.' I have read, for instance, that on Earth, ungulates habitually eat their own placentas after bringing forth young, whereas cats and dogs often eat grass. Here on Dathyna, a further possibility exists. Certain fruit juices make meat nourishing for any normally vegetarian creature, through enzyme action. The treatment process is simple. It was discovered in—in early times, by the primitive ancestors of today's Shenna. Or perhaps even earlier."

"And on a planet which has suffered ecological disaster like this one, every food source must be utilized. I see." Adzel was satisfied.

Until van Rijn said, "But the Shenna goes hunting, tally-hoo, for fun. I'm sure they does. I watched that young buck ride home yesterday wearing the horns off his kill. He'd used a bow, too, when he got a perfect good gun. That was sport."

Thea arched her brow. "And why not?" she challenged. "I'm told most intelligent species enjoy hunting. And combat. Including your own."

"Ja, ja. I don't say is bad, unless they start chasing me. But where do we get the instinct that makes us feel good when we catch and kill? Maybe just catch a photograph...though very few people what would never kill a deer do not get happy to swat a fly. How come?" Van Rijn wagged a finger. "I tell you. You and me is descended from hunters. Preman in Africa was a killer ape. Those what was not naturalborn killers, they did not live to pass on their squeamery. But ancestors of Shenna was browsers and grazers! Maybe they had fights at mating season, but they did not hunt down other animals. Yet Shenna now, they do. How come *that?*"

Thea changed the subject. It was easy to do, with so much

to talk about, the infinite facets of a planet and a civilization. One must admit that Shenna were civilized in the technical sense of the word. They had machines, literacy, a worldwide culture which was becoming more than worldwide. To be sure, they were inheritors of what the earlier society had created. But they had made a comeback from its destruction, restored part of what it had been, added a few innovations.

And their patriarchs aimed to go farther. Elsewhere on Dathyna, they met in stormy debate to decide—what? Van Rijn shivered in a gathering dusk. The nights of this semi-desert were cold. It would be good to enter the warmth and soft light of his ship.

He had won that concession after the first night, which he and Adzel spent locked in a room of the castle. The next morning he had been at the top of his form, cursing, coughing, wheezing, weeping, swearing by every human and nonhuman saint in or out of the catalogue that one more bedtime without respite from the temperatures, the radiation, the dust, the pollen, the heavy metals whose omnipresence not only forced outworlders to take chelating pills lest they be poisoned but made the very air taste bad, the noises, the stinks, the everything of this planet whose existence was a potent argument for the Manichaean heresy because he could not imagine why a benevolent God would wish it on the universe: another night must surely stretch his poor old corpse out stiff and pitiful— Finally Thea grew alarmed and took it upon herself to change their quarters. A couple of engineer officers with robot assistance disconnected the drive units of the League vessel. It was a thorough job. Without parts and tools, the captives had no possibility of lifting that hull again. They might as well sleep aboard. A guard or two with a blastcannon could watch outside.

Late on the third day, Moath returned.

Van Rijn and Adzel observed the uproar from a distance, as his folk boiled around the overlord. He addressed them from an upper airlock chamber in his personal spaceflitter. His voice rolled like surf and earthquake. Hurricane answered from the ground. The young Shenna roared, capered, danced in rings, hammered on the boat's side till it rang, lifted archaic swords and fired today's energy weapons into the air. From the highest remaining tower, a banner was raised, the color of new blood.

"What's he say?" van Rijn asked. Thea stood moveless, eyes unfocused, stunned as if by a blow to the head. He seized her arm and shook her. "Tell me what he said!" A guard tried to intervene. Adzel put his bulk between long enough for van Rijn to trumpet loud as Moath himself, "Tell me what is happening! I order you!"

Automatically in her shock, she obeyed the Minotaur.

Soon afterward, the prisoners were herded into their ship. The lock valves hissed shut behind them. Viewscreens showed frosty stars above a land turned gray and shadowful, the castle ablaze with light and immense bonfires leaping outside. Sound pickups brought the distant wail of wind, the nearby bawling, bugling, clangor, and drum-thud of the Shenna.

Van Rijn said to Adzel, "You do what you like for an hour. I will be with St. Dismas. Got to confess to somebody." He could not refrain from adding, "Ho, ho, I bet he never heard a hotter confession that he's going to!"

"I shall relive certain memories and meditate upon certain principles," Adzel said, "and in one hour I will join you in the command bridge."

That was where van Rijn had explained why he surrendered to the enemy, back in the system of the nameless sun.

"But we could perhaps give them the slip," Adzel had protested. "Granted, the chance of our success is not good. At worst, though, they will overtake and destroy us. A quick, clean death, in freedom, almost an enviable death. Do you really prefer to become a slave on Dathyna?"

"Look," van Rijn answered with rare seriousness, "is necessary, absolute necessary our people learn what these characters is up to, and as much as possible about what they is like. I got a hunch what smells like condemned Limburger, they may decide on war. Maybe they win, maybe they lose. But even one surprise attack on a heavy-populated planet, with nuclear weapons—millions dead? Billions? And burned, blind, crippled, mutated. . . . I am a sinful man, but not that sinful I wouldn't do what I could for trying to stop the thing."

"Of course, of course," Adzel said; and he was

unwontedly impatient. "But if we escape, we can convey an added warning, to emphasize what will be read when your papers are released on Earth. If we go to Dathyna, though—oh, granted, we probably will gather extremely valuable information. But what good will it do our people? We will surely not have access to spacecraft. The great problem of military intelligence has always been less its collection than its transmission home. This is a classic example."

"Ah," said van Rijn. "You would ordinary be right. But you see, we will probable not be alone there."

"*Yarru!*" Adzel said. That relieved him sufficiently that he sat down, curled his tail around his haunches, and waited for an explanation.

"See you," van Rijn said around a glass of gin and a cigar, "this Gahood fellow was Hugh Latimer's owner. We know that from Thea. We know too Latimer's lost to him. And we know he brought news what has got eggbeaters going in everybody's guts here. That is all we know for sure. But we can deduce a snorky lot from it, I tell you.

"Like from the timing. Dathyna got to be about one week from this star. We can assume a straight line Sol-here-there, and not be too far off. Beta Crucis is like two weeks from Sol. Do a little trigonometrizing, angle between Southern Cross and Compass—is very rough approximations, natural, but timing works out so close it makes sense, like follows.

"Latimer would report straight to his boss, Gahood, on Dathyna. Gahood would go straight to Beta Crucis for a look—we seen how these Shenna is bulls in a china shop, and life is the china shop—and Latimer would go along. Takes them maybe two and a half weeks. So they arrive when Davy Falkayn and Chee Lan is still there. Our friends could not get decent data on the rogue in less time, two of them in one ship. Right away, though, Gahood returns to Dathyna. When he comes there, he learns about this meeting with you and me. He runs here and tells his chumsers about something. The timing is right for that kind of Gahood-trek, and it fits the pattern for everything else."

"Yes-s-s," Adzel breathed. His tailtip stirred. "Gahood arrives in great agitation, and without Latimer, who is gone."

"Gone—where else but at Beta Crucis?" van Rijn said. "If

he was lost anyplace else, nobody would care except maybe Gahood. Looks like Gahood tangled with our friends yonder. And he was the one got knotted. Because if he had won over them, he would hardly come out here to brag about it...and for sure the other Shenna would not react with anger and pre-turbation.

"Also: it would not matter if Latimer got killed in a fight. Only another slave, *nie?* But if he got captured, now—ho-ho! That changes a whole picture. From him can be squeezed many kinds fine information, starting with where is Dathyna. No wondering that Gahood galloped straight out here! These Shenna got to be warned about a changed situation before they maybe make a deal with us. Not so?" Van Rijn swigged deep.

"It appears plausible, then, that *Muddlin' Through* is bound home with her gains." Adzel nodded. "Do you think, therefore, we may be liberated by friendly forces?"

"I would not count on it," van Rijn said, "especial not when we is held by people like these, what would likely take out their irritations at being defeated on us. Besides, we don't know for sure a war is fermenting. And we want to prevent one if we can. I don't think, though, neither, that *Muddlin' Through* is homeheaded. I just hope the Shenna assume so, like you."

"What else?" Adzel asked, puzzled again.

"You is not human, and you don't always follow human mental processing. Likewise Shenna. Has you forgot, Falkayn can send a message capsule back with his data? Meanwhile, he sees Gahood going off. He knows Gahood will alert Dathyna. Will soon be very hard to scout that planet. But if he goes there direct, fast, to a world what has relied on its whereabouts not being known to us and therefore probably has not got a lot in the way of pickets—he should could sneak in."

"And be there yet?"

"I am guessing it. Takes time to study a world. He'll have a way planned for outsneaking too, of course." Van Rijn lifted his head, straightened his back, squared his shoulders, and protruded his belly. "Maybe he can get us away. Maybe he can't. But *Deo volente*, he might be able to carry home extra information, or urgent information, we slip to him. There is lots of ugly little ifs in my logic, I know. The odds is not good. But I don't think we got any choice except taking the bet."

"No," said Adzel slowly, "we do not."

The celebration was fading at the castle when Wodenite met human in the bridge. As the fires burned low, the stars shone forth more coldly bright.

"We are fortunate that they did not dismantle our communicators," Adzel said. There was no reason to speak otherwise than impersonally. What they were about to do might bring immediate death upon them. But they considered themselves doomed already, they had made their separate peaces, and neither was given to sentimentalism. When van Rijn sat down, though, the dragon laid one great scaly hand on his shoulder; and the man patted it briefly.

"No reason they should," van Rijn said. "They don't think Davy and Chee might be doing a skulkabout somewhere near. Besides, I told Beldaniel it would help me understand the Shenna if I could tune in their programs." He spat. "Their programs is terrible."

"What waveband will you use?"

"Technic Standard Number Three, I guess. I been monitoring, and don't seem like the Shenna use it often. *Muddlin' Through* will have one receiver tuned in on it automatic."

"If *Muddlin' Through* is, indeed, free, functional, and in range. And if our transmission does not happen to be intercepted."

"Got to assume somethings, boy. Anyhow, a Shenn radio operator what chances to hear us making our code might well assume it is ordinary QRN. It was made up with that in mind. Open me a beer, will you, and fill my pipe yonder? I should start sending."

His hand moved deftly across the keyboard.

Nicholas van Rijn, Master Merchant of the Polesotechnic League, calling . . . .

The following has been learned about Dathyna and its inhabitants. . . .

Now stand by for my primary message.

Realizing that the location of their planet is, with fair

probability, no longer a secret, the Shenna have not reacted as most sophonts would, by strengthening defenses while searching for ways and means of accommodation with us. Instead, their Grand Council has decided to hazard all on an offensive launched before the sprawling, ill-organized Technic sphere can gather itself.

From what little we have learned of it, the idea is militarily not unsound. Though inefficient, Shenn warships are numerous, and each has more firepower than any of ours in the corresponding class. From the Serendipity operation, their naval intelligence has an enormous amount of precise information about those races and societies we lump together as "Technic." Among other things, the Shenna know the Commonwealth is the heart of that complex, and that the Commonwealth has long been at peace and does not dream any outsiders would dare attack. Hostile fleets could pass through its territory unbeknownst; when they did come in detection range, it would be too late for a world that was not heavily defended.

The Shenn scheme is for a series of massive raids upon the key planets of the Commonwealth, and certain others. This will create general chaos, out of which Dathyna may hope to emerge dominant if not absolutely supreme. Whether the Shenna succeed or not, obviously whole civilizations will be wiped out, perhaps whole intelligent species, surely untold billions of sophonts.

It will doubtless take the enemy some time to marshal his full strength, plan the operation, and organize its logistics. The time will be increased above a minimum by the arrogance of the Shenn lords and the half-anarchic character of their society. On the other hand, their built-in aggressiveness will make them cut corners and accept deficiencies for the sake of getting on with the assault.

The League should be able to take appropriate countermeasures, without calling upon governmental assistance, if it is warned soon enough. That warning must be delivered at once. To David Falkayn, Chee Lan, and/or any other entities who may be present: Do not spend a minute on anything else. Go home immediately and inform the leadership of the League.

XXIII

NIGHT was younger where the Cynthian lurked. But the desert was fast radiating the day's heat outward to the stars. Their swarms, and the shimmer of a great aurora, were sufficiently bright for crags and dunes to stand ghost-gray, for the walls she gazed upon to cast shadows. She fluffed her fur in the chill. For minutes after landing she waited behind the thorny bush she had chosen from aloft. No scent came to her but its own acridity, no sound but a wind-whimper, no sight but a veil of blowing dust.

Her caution was only partly because animals laired in abandoned places. The guns she wore—blaster, slugthrower, needler, and stunner—could handle any beast of prey; against the possibility of venomous creatures she put her senses and reflexes. But most of the ruins she had seen thus far were inhabited by Dathynans, and correspondingly dangerous. While those little groups appeared to be semibarbatic hunters and herders—she and Falkayn were still too ignorant about conditions to try spying on the larger and more advanced communities—they owned firearms. Worse, Muddlehead reported detecting electronic transceivers in their huddling places, doubtless supplied by traders from the "baronies."

It had not been difficult for the ship to descend secretly, or to flit around after dark and hole up in the wastelands by day. The lords of this world had not expected its location to become known and had thus not done much about posting sentinels in orbit. Nor had they installed anything like an atmospheric traffic monitor. Let some sheik relate an encounter with an alien, though, and matters would change in a hurry.

Falkayn dared not visit any settlement. He was too big and awkward. Chee Lan could fly close with a gravity impeller, then work her little self into a position from which she observed what went on.

The present location, however, was empty. She had rather expected that. The interwoven buildings stood in the middle of a region which erosion had scoured until it could probably support none except a few nomads. She saw signs of them, cairns, charcoal, scattered trash. But nothing was recent. The tribe—no, patriarchal clan was probably more accurate—must be elsewhere on its annual round. Good; Falkayn could bring the ship here and work. This site looked richer than the one he was currently studying. More and more, it seemed that the key to Dathyna's present and future lay in its near past, in the downfall of a mighty civilization.

Of an entire species. Chee was becoming convinced of that.

She left her concealment and approached the ruins. Shards of masonry, broken columns, rust-eaten machines thrust from the sand like tombstones. Walls loomed high above her; but they were worn, battered, smashed open in places, their windows blind and their doors agape. Few if any Dathynan communities had simply been left when their hinterlands failed them. No, they were burst into, plundered and vandalized. Their people were massacred.

Something stirred in the shadows. Chee arched her back, bottled her tail, dropped hand to gun belt. But it was only a beast with several pairs of legs, which ran from her.

The entry, lobby, whatever you wanted to call the section behind the main gate, had been superb, a vista of pillars and fountains and sculpture, exquisitely veined marble and malachite that soared a hundred meters aloft. Now it was an echoing black cave. Sand and nomad rubbish covered the floor; the stonework was chipped, the grand mosaics hidden under soot from centuries of campfires. But when Chee sent a beam upward from her lamp, color glowed back. She activated her impeller and rose for a closer look. Winged things fled, thinly chittering.

The walls were inlaid to the very ceiling. No matter how strange the artistic conventions, Chee could not but respond to an intrinsic nobility. The hues were at once rich and restrained, the images at once heroic and gentle. She did not know what facts or myths or allegories were portrayed; she knew she never would, and that knowledge was an odd small pain. Partly for anodyne, she bent her whole attention to the factual content.

Excitement sprang to life in her. This was the clearest portrayal she had ever found of the Old Dathynans. Falkayn was digging up their bones where the ship rested, noting crushed skulls and arrowheads lodged in rib cages. But here, by the lamp's single shaft of light, surrounded by limitless night and cold and wind and beating wings and death, here they themselves looked forth. And a tingle went along Chee Lan's nerves.

The builders were not unlike Shenna. Falkayn could not prove from his relics that they were not as close as Mongoloid is to Negroid on Earth. In their wordless language, these pictures said otherwise.

It was not mere typological difference. You could get a scale from objects that were shown, like still-extant plants and animals. They indicated the ancients were smaller than today's race, none over 180 centimeters tall, more slender, more hairy, though lacking the male mane. Within those limits, however, many variants appeared. In fact, the section that Chee was looking at seemed to make a point of depicting every kind of autochthon, each wearing native costume and holding something that was most likely emblematic of his or her land. Here came a burly golden-furred long-headed male with a sickle in one hand and an uprooted sapling in the other; there stood a tiny dark female in an embroidered robe, a distinct epicanthic fold in her eyelids, playing a harp; yonder a kilted baldpate with a large and curved muzzle raised his staff, as if in protection, over a bearer of ripe fruits whose face was almost solar in its roundness. The loving spirit and the expert hand which put together this scene had been guided by a scientifically trained eye.

Today one solitary race existed. That was so unusual—so disturbing—that Chee and Falkayn had made it their special business to verify the fact as they slunk about the planet.

And yet the Shenna, altogether distinct in appearance and culture, were shown nowhere on a mosaic which had tried to represent everybody. Nowhere!

A taboo, a dislike, a persecution? Chee spat in contempt of the thought. Every sign pointed to the lost civilization as having been unified and rationalistic. A particular series of pictures on this wall doubtless symbolized progress up from savagery. A nude male was vividly shown defending his female against a large predatory beast—with a broken branch. Later on, edged metal implements appeared: but always tools, never weapons. Masses of Dathynans were seen working together: never fighting. But this could not be because the topic excluded strife. Two scenes of individual combat did appear; they must be key incidents in a history or legendry forever vanished. The earliest had one male wielding a kind of brush knife, the other an unmistakable wood ax. The second armed the enemies with primitive matchlock guns which were surely intended for help against dangerous animals ... seeing that the background depicted steam vehicles and electric power lines.

Occupations through the ages were likewise re-created here. Some were recognizable, like agriculture and carpentry. Others could only be guessed at. (Ceremonial? Scientific? The dead cannot tell us.) But hunting was not among them, nor herding except for a species that obviously provided wool, nor trapping, nor fishing, nor butchering.

Everything fitted together with the most basic clue of all: diet. Intelligence on Dathyna had evolved among herbivores. Though not common, this occurs often enough for certain general principles to be known. The vegetarian sophonts do not have purer souls than omnivores and carnivores. But their sins are different. Among other things, while they may sometimes institutionalize the duello or accept a high rate of crimes of passion, they do not independently invent war, and they find the whole concept of the chase repugnant. As a rule they are gregarious and their social units—families, clans, tribes, nations, or less nameable groups—merge easily into larger ones as communication and transportation improve.

The Shenna violated every such rule. They killed for sport, they divided their planet into patriarchies, they built weapons and warships, they menaced a neighbor civilization which had never given them offense.... *In short,* thought Chee Lan, *they act like humans. If we can understand what brought them forth, out of this once promising world, maybe we'll understand what to do about them.*

Or, at least, what they want to do about us.

Her communicator interrupted. It was a bone-conduction device, so as not to be overheard; the code clicks felt unnaturally loud in her skull. "Return without delay." Neither she nor Falkayn would have transmitted except in emergency. Chee switched her impeller to lift-and-thrust, and streaked out the doorway.

The stars glittered frigid, the aurora danced in strange figures, the desert rolled stark beneath her. With no hostiles around, and no warning about them near the ship, she lowered her facemask and flew at top speed. Wind hooted and cut at her. That was a long hundred kilometers.

Muddlin' Through lay in the bottom of a dry, brush-grown canyon, hidden from above. Chee slanted past the snags of that minor community on its edge which Falkayn was excavating. Descending into shadow, she switched both her lamp and her goggles to infrared use. There was still no observable reason for caution, but to a carnivore like her it was instinctive. Twigs clawed at her, leaves rustled, she parted the branches and hovered before an airlock. Muddlehead's sensors identified her and the valves opened. She darted inside.

"Dave!" she yelled. "What in Tsucha's flaming name's the matter?"

"Plenty." His intercom voice had never been bleaker. "I'm in the bridge."

She could have flitted along the hall and companionway, but it was almost as quick and more satisfying to use her muscles. Quadrupedal again, tail erect, fangs agleam, eyes a green blaze, she sped through the ship and soared into her chair. "*Niaor!*" she cried.

Falkayn regarded her. Since he didn't sleep while she was out, he wore the dusty coveralls of his day's work, which had begrimed his nails and leathered his skin. A sun-bleached lock of hair hung past one temple. "Word received," he told her.

"What?" She tensed till she quivered. "From who?"

"Old Nick in person. He's on this planet . . . with Adzel." Falkayn turned his face to the main control board, as if the ship herself lived there. "Read back the massage in clear," he ordered.

The phrases fell curt and flat.

They were followed by a silence which went on and on.

At last Chee stirred. "What do you propose to do?" she asked quietly.

"Obey, of course," Falkayn said. His tone was as bare as the computer's. "We can't get the message home too soon. But we'd better discuss first how to leave. Muddlehead keeps getting indications of more and more ships on picket. I suppose the Shenna are finally worried about spies like us. Question is, should we creep out, everything throttled down to minimum, and hope we won't be noticed? Or should we go at full power and rely on surprise and a head start and possible evasive action in deep space?"

"The latter," Chee said. "Our rescue operation will already have alerted the enemy. If we time it right, we can jump between their patrollers and—"

"Huh?" Falkayn sat straight. "What rescue operation?"

"Adzel," Chee said. Her manner was forbearing but her whiskers vibrated. "And van Rijn, no doubt. We have to pick up Adzel, you know."

"No, I do not know! Listen, you spinheaded catamonkey—"

"We have squabbled, he and I," Chee said, "but he remains my shipmate and yours." She cocked her head and considered the man. "I always took you for a moral person, Dave."

"Well, but—but I am, God damn it!" Falkayn yelled. "Didn't you listen? Our orders are to start directly for home!"

"What has that got to do with the price of eggs? Don't you want to rescue Adzel?"

"Certainly I do! If it cost me my own life, I'd want to. But—"

"Will you let a few words from that potgutted van Rijn stop you?"

Falkayn drew a shaken breath. "Listen, Chee," he said. "I'll explain slowly. Van Rijn wants us to abandon him too. He hasn't even told us where he's at. Since he necessarily used a waveband that would bounce around the planet, he could be anywhere on it."

"Muddlehead," asked Chee, "can you work out the source of his transmission?"

"By the pattern of reflections off the ionosphere, yes, to a fair approximation," answered the computer. "It corresponds to one of the larger communities, not extremely far from here, which we identified as such during our atmospheric entry."

Chee turned back to Falkayn. "You see?" she said.

"You're the one that doesn't see!" he protested. "Adzel and van Rijn aren't important compared to what's at stake. Neither are you and me. It merely happens they can't warn the League but we can."

"As we shall, after we fetch Adzel."

"And risk getting shot down, or caught ourselves, or—" Falkayn paused. "I know you, Chee. You're descended from beasts of prey that operated alone, or in minimum-size groups. You get your instincts from that. Your world never knew any such thing as a nation. The idea of universal altruism is unreal to you. Your sense of duty is as strong as mine, maybe stronger, but it stops with your kinfolk and friends. All right. I realize that. Now suppose you exercise your imagination and realize what I'm getting at. Hell's balls, just use arithmetic! One life is not equal to a billion lives!"

"Certainly not," Chee said. "However, that doesn't excuse us from our obligation."

"I tell you—"

Falkayn got no farther. She had drawn her stun pistol and aimed it between his eyes. He might have attempted to swat it from her, had she been human, but he knew she was too fast for him. He sat frozenly and heard her say:

"I'd rather not knock you out and tie you up. Lacking your help, I may well fail to get our people out. I'll try anyhow, though. And really, Dave, be honest. Admit we have a reasonable chance of pulling the job off. If we didn't, against these Shenn yokels, we ought to turn ourselves in at the nearest home for the feeble-minded."

"What do you want of me?" he whispered.

"Your promise that we'll try our best to take Adzel with us."

"Can you trust me?"

"If not, one of us shall have to kill the other." Her gun remained steady, but her head drooped. "I would hate that, Dave."

He sat a whole minute, unmoving. Then his fist smote the chair arm and his laughter stormed forth. "All right, you little devil! You win. It's pure blackmail . . . but Judas, I'm glad of it!"

Her pistol snicked back into its holster. She sprang to his lap. He rubbed her back and tickled her beneath the jaws. Her tail caressed his cheek. Meanwhile she said, "We need their help too, starting with a full description of the layout where they are. I expect they'll refuse at first. Point out to them in your message that they have no choice but to cooperate with us. If we don't go home together, none of us will."

XXIV

AGAIN Chee Lan worked alone. *Muddlin' Through* had come down below the horizon. Other spacecraft stood ahead, a pair of destroyers, a flitter, the disabled vessel where the prisoners were kept. Hulls glimmered hoarfrosted in the dying night. Behind them, Moath's stronghold lifted like a mountain. It was very quiet now.

Ghosting from rock to bush to hillock, Chee neared. The guards were said to be a pair. She could make out one, a shaggy-maned shadow, restlessly apace near the barrel of a mobile cannon. His breath smoked, his metal jingled. She strained her eyes, tasted the predawn wind, listened, felt with every hair and whisker. Nothing came to her. Either van Rijn and Adzel had been mistaken in what they related, or the guard's mate had gone off duty without a replacement—or, in an environment for which she was not evolved, she missed the crucial sensory cues.

No more time! They'll be astir in that castle before long. Ay-ah, let's go.

She launched herself across the final sandy stretch. It would have been better to strike from above. But her impeller, like close-range radio conversation with those in the ship, might trip some damned detector. No matter. The sentry was not aware of the white shape that flowed toward him. The instant she came in range, she flattened to earth, drew her stunner and fired. She would rather have killed, but that might be noisy. The supersonic bolt spun the Shenn around on his heel. He toppled with a doomsday racket. Or did he? Sounded like that, anyhow. Chee flashed her light at the ship, blink-blink-blink. They'd better be watching their screens, those two!

They were. An airlock slid open, a gangway protruded. Adzel came out, himself huge and steel-gray by starlight. On his back, where a dorsal plate had been removed for riders, sat Nicholas van Rijn. Chee bounded to meet them. Hope fluttered in her. If they could really make this break unnoticed—

A roar blasted from the darkness near the warships. A moment later, there sizzled an energy beam. "Get going... yonder way!" Chee yelled. Her flashbeam pointed toward unseen Falkayn. Whizzing upward on antigrav, she activated her communicator. "We've been seen, Dave. Muck-begotten guard must've strolled off to take a leak." She curved down again, to meet the shooter.

"Shall I come get you?" Falkayn's voice sounded.

"Hold back for a minute. Maybe—" A firebeam stabbed at her. She had been noticed too. She dodged, feeling its heat, smelling its ozone and ions, half dazzled by its brightness. The Shenn could have taken cover and tried to pick her off, but that was not his nature. He dashed forth. Chee dove at full power, pulled out of her screaming arc a few centimeters above his head, gave him a jolt as she did. He collapsed. She barely avoided smashing into the ship before her.

Alarms gonged through the castle. Its black mass woke with a hundred lights. Shenna streamed from the gate. Most were armed; they must sleep with their cursed weapons. Four of them were donning flit-harness. Chee headed after Adzel's galloping form. He couldn't outrun such pursuers. She'd provide air cover.... "What's wrong?" Falkayn barked. "Shouldn't I come?"

"No, not yet. We'll keep you for a surprise." Chee unholstered her own blaster. Enough of these la-de-da stun pistols. The enemy were aloft, lining out after Wodenite and human. They hadn't noticed her. She got altitude on them, aimed, and fired twice. One crashed, in a cloud of dust. The other flew on, but did not stir any longer save as the wind flapped his limbs.

The third angled after her. He was good. They started a

dogfight. She could do nothing about the fourth, who stooped upon the escapers.

Adzel slammed to a halt, so fast that van Rijn fell off and rolled yammering through the thornbushes. The Wodenite picked up a rock and threw. It struck with a clang. Impeller disabled, the Shenn fluttered to the ground.

His mates, incredibly swift on their feet, were not far behind. They opened fire. Adzel charged them, bounding from side to side, taking an occasional bolt or bullet in his scales but suffering no serious wound. He was mortal, of course. A shot sufficiently powerful or sufficiently well placed would kill him. But he got in among the Shenna first. Hoofs, hands, tail, fangs ripped into action.

The downed flier was not badly hurt either. He saw his gun lying where he had dropped it and ran to retrieve the weapon. Van Rijn intercepted him. "Oh, no, you don't, buddy-chum," the merchant panted. "I take that thing home and see if you got new ideas in it I can patent." Taller, broader, muscles like cables, the Minotaur sprang at the fat old man. Van Rijn wasn't there any more. Somehow he had flicked aside. He delivered a karate kick. The Shenn yelled. "Ha, is a tender spot for you too?" van Rijn said.

The Dathynan circled away from him. They eyed each other, and the blaster that sheened on the sand between them. The Shenn lowered his head and charged. Knowing he faced an opponent with some skill, he kept his hands in a guarding position. But no Earthling would survive on whom they closed. Van Rijn sped to meet him. At the last breath before collision, he sidestepped again, twirled, and was at the back of the onrushing giant warrior. "God send the right!" bawled van Rijn, reached into his tunic, drew forth St. Dismas, and sapped his foe. The Shenn went down.

"Whoo-hoo," van Rijn said, blowing out his cheeks above the dazed colossus. "I'm not so young like I used to be." He returned the statuette to its nesting place, collected the gun, studied it until he had figured out its operation, and looked around for targets.

There were none immediately on hand. Chee Lan had overcome her adversary. Adzel trotted back. The Shenn mob was scattered, fleeing toward the castle. "I hoped for

207

that result," the Wodenite remarked. "It accords with their psychology. The instinct to assail rashly should, by and large, be coupled with an equal tendency to stampede. Otherwise the ancestral species could not long have survived."

Chee descended. "Let's travel before they gather their wits," she said.

"*Ja*, they isn't really stupids, them, I am afraid," van Rijn said. "When they tell their robots to stop loafing—"

A deep hum cut through the night. One of the destroyers trembled on her landing jacks. "They just did," Chee said. Into her communicator: "Come and eat them, friends."

Muddlin' Through soared above the horizon. "Down!" Adzel called. He sheltered the other two with his body, which could better stand heat and radiation.

Beams flashed. Had either warcraft gotten off the ground, Falkayn and Muddlehead would have been in trouble. Their magazines were depleted after the battle of Satan. But they were forewarned, warmed up, ready and ruthless to exploit the advantage of surprise. The first destroyer loosed no more than a single ill-aimed shot before she was undercut. She fell, struck her neighbor, both toppled with an earthshaking metal roar. The League vessel disabled Moath's flitter— three bolts were needed, and the sand ran molten beneath— and landed.

"*Donder op!*" van Rijn cried. Adzel tucked him under one arm. "*Wat drommel?*" he protested. The Wodenite grabbed Chee by the tail and pounded toward the airlock.

He must squint into lightning dazzle, stagger from thunders, gasp in smoke and vapor, as the ship bombarded the castle. In the bridge, Falkayn protested, "We don't want to hurt non-combatants." Muddlehead replied, "In conformity with your general directive, I am taking the precaution of demolishing installations whose radio resonances suggest that they are heavy guns and missile racks."

"Can you get me through to somebody inside?" Falkayn asked.

"I shall tune in what we have noted as the usual Dathynan communication bands. . . . Yes. An attempt is being made to call us."

The screen flickered. Streaked, distorted, static-crazed, the image of Thea Beldaniel appeared. Her face was a mask of horror. Behind her, the room where she sat trembled and cracked under the ship's blows. By now, Falkayn could no longer see the castle façade. Nothing showed but dust, pierced through and through by the nuclear flames and the bursting shells. His skull shivered; he was himself half deafened by the violence he unleashed. Faintly he heard her: "Davy, Davy, are you doing this to us?"

He gripped the arms of his chair and said through clenched jaws, "I didn't want to. You force me. Listen, though. This is a taste of war for you and yours. The tiniest, gentlest, most carefully administered dose of the poison we can give. We're bound away soon. I'd hoped to be far off before you realized what'd happened. But maybe this is best. Because I don't think you can summon help from elsewhere in time to catch us. And you know what to expect."

"Davy...my lord Moath...is dead...I saw a bolt hit him, he went up in a spurt of fire—" She could not go on.

"You're better off without a lord," Falkayn said. "Every human being is. But tell the others. Tell them the Polesotechnic League bears no grudge and wants no fight. However, if we must, we will do the job once for all. Your Shenna won't be exterminated; we have more mercy than they showed the Old Dathynans. But let them try resisting us, and we'll strip the machinery from them and turn them into desert herders. I suggest you urge them to consider what terms they might make instead. Show them what happened here and tell them they were fools to get in the way of freemen!"

She gave him a shattered look. Pity tugged at him, and he might have said more. But Adzel, Chee Lan, Nicholas van Rijn were aboard. The stronghold was reduced: with few casualties, he hoped, nevertheless a terrible object lesson. He cut his transmission. "Cease barrage," he ordered. "Lift and make for Earth."

XXV

"THERE has been no trace of any hyperdrive except our own for a continuous twenty-four hours," Muddlehead reported.

Falkayn gusted a sigh. His long body eased into a more comfortable position, seated half on the spine, feet on the saloon table. "I reckon that settles it." He smiled. "We're home safe."

For in the illimitable loneliness that reaches between the stars, how shall a single mote be found, once it has lost itself and the lives it carries? Dathyna's sun was no more than the brightest glitter in those hordes that filled the cabin viewscreens. The engines murmured, the ventilators blew odors suggesting flowery meadows, tobacco was fragrant, one could look for peace throughout the month of flight that lay ahead.

And Judas, but they needed a rest!

A point of anxiety must first be blunted. "You're sure you didn't take undue radiation exposure while you were outside?" Falkayn asked.

"I tell you, I have checked each of us down to the chromosomes," Chee snapped. "I *am* a xenobiologist, you know—you do know, don't you?—and this vessel is well equipped for that kind of studies. Adzel got the largest dose, because he shielded us, but even in his case, no damage was done that available pharmaceuticals will not repair." She turned from her curled-up placement on a bench, jerked her cigarette holder at the Wodenite where he sprawled on the deck, and added, "Of course, I shall have to give you your treatments en route, when I might be painting or sculpting or— You big slobbersoul, why didn't you bring a chunk of lead to lie under?"

Adzel leered. "You had all the lead in your own possession," he said. "Guess where."

Chee sputtered. Van Rijn slapped the table—his beer glass leaped—and guffawed: "*Touché!* I did not think you was a wit."

"That's wit?" the Cynthian grumbled. "Well, I suppose for him it is."

"Oh, he needs to learn," van Rijn conceded, "but what makes matter is, he has begun. We will have him play at drawing room comedies yet. How about in *The Importance of Being Earnest?* Haw!"

The merchant's classical reference went by the others. "I'd suggest a party to celebrate," Falkayn said. "Unfortunately—"

"Right," van Rijn said. "Business before pleasure, if not too bloomering long before. We should assemble our various informations while they is fresh in our minds, because if we let them begin to rot and stink in our minds, we could lose parts of what they imply."

"Huh?" Falkayn blinked. "What do you mean, sir?"

Van Rijn leaned forward, cradling his chins in one great paw. "We need keys to the Shenn character so we know how to handle them."

"But isn't that a job for professionals?" inquired Adzel. "After the League had been alerted to the existence of a real threat, it will find ways to carry out a detailed scientific study of Dathyna and draw conclusions much more certain and complete than we possibly could on the basis of our inadequate data."

"*Ja, ja, ja,*" van Rijn said, irritated, "but our time is shortening. We don't know for sure what the Shenna do next. Could be they decide they will attack fast as they possible can, try and beat us to the rum punch, in spite of what you taught them, Muddlehead."

"I was not programmed to deliver formal instruction," the computer admitted.

Van Rijn ignored it. "Maybe they don't be that suicidal," he went on. "Anyhowever, we got to have some theory about them to start on. Maybe it is wrong, but even then it is better than nothing, because it will set xenological teams looking for something definite. When we know what the Shenna want in their bottom, then we can talk meaningful to them and maybe make peace."

"It is not for me to correct a Terrestrial's use of Terrestrial idiom," Adzel said, "but don't you wish to discuss what they *basically* want?"

Van Rijn turned red. "Hokay, hokay, you damn pedagoggle! What is the base desires of the Shenna? What drives them, really? We get insight—oh, not scientific, Chee Lan, not in formulas—but we get a feel for them, a poet's empathizing, and they is no longer senseless monsters to us but beings we can reason with. The specialists from the League can make their specials later. Time is so precious, though. We can save a lot of it, and so maybe save a lot of lives, if we bring back with us at Earth a tantivvy...a tentacle... *dood ook ondergang,* this Anglic!...a tentative program for research and even for action."

He drained his beer. Soothed thereby, he lit his pipe, settled back, and rumbled, "We got our experience and information. Also we got analogues for help. I don't think any sophonts could be total unique, in this big universe. So we can draw on our understanding about other races.

"Like you, Chee Lan, for instance: we know you is a carnivore—but a small one—and this means you got instincts for being tough and aggressive within reason. You, Adzel, is a big omnivore, so big your ancestors didn't never need to carry chips on their shoulders, nor fish either; your breed tends more to be peaceful, but hellish independent too, in a quiet way; somebody tries for dictating your life, you don't kill him like Chee would, no, you plain don't listen at him. And we humans, we is omnivores too, but our primate ancestors went hunting in packs, and they got built in a year-round sex drive; from these two roots springs everything what makes a man a human being. Hokay? I admit this is too generalistic, but still, if we could fit what we know about the Shenna in one broad pattern—"

Actually, the same idea had been germinating in each of

them. Talking, they developed several facets of it. These being mutually consistent, they came to believe their end result, however sketchy, was in essence true. Later xenological studies confirmed it.

Even a world like Earth, blessed with a constant sun, has known periods of massive extinction. Conditions changed in a geological overnight, and organisms that had flourished for megayears vanished. Thus, at the end of the Cretaceous, ammonites and dinosaurs alike closed their long careers. At the end of the Pliocene, most of the large mammals—those whose names, as bestowed afterward, usually terminate in *-therium*—stopped bumbling across the landscape. The reasons are obscure to this day. The raw fact remains: existence is precarious.

On Dathyna, the predicament was worse. The solar bombardment was always greater than Earth receives. At the irregular peaks of activity, it was very much greater. Magnetic field and atmosphere could not ward off everything. Belike, mutations which occurred during an earlier maximum led to the improbable result of talking, dreaming, tool-making herbivores. If so, a cruel natural selection was likewise involved: for the history of such a planet must needs be one of ecological catastrophes.

The next radiation blizzard held off long enough for the race to attain full intelligence; to develop its technology; to discover the scientific method; to create a worldwide society which was about to embark for the stars, had perhaps already done it a time or two. Then the sun burned high again.

Snows melted, oceans rose, coasts and low valleys were inundated. The tropics were scorched to savanna or desert. All that could be survived. Indeed, quite probably its harsh stimulus was what produced the last technological creativity, the planetary union, the reaching into space.

But again the assault intensified. This second phase was less an increase of electromagnetic energy, heat and light, than it was a whole new set of processes, triggered when a certain threshold was passed within the waxing star. Protons were hurled forth; electrons; mesons; X-ray quanta. The magnetosphere glowed with synchrotron radiation, the upper atmosphere with secondaries. Many life forms must have died within a year or two. Others, interdependent, followed them. The ecological, pyramid crumbled. Mutation went over the world like a scythe, and everything collapsed.

No matter how far it had progressed, civilization was not autonomous. It could not synthesize all its necessities. Croplands became dustbowls, orchards stood leafless, sea plants decayed into scum, forests parched and burned, new diseases arose. Step by step, population shrank, enterprises were abandoned for lack of personnel and resources, knowledge was forgotten, the area of the possible shrank. A species more fierce by nature might have made a stronger effort to surmount its troubles—or might not—but in any event, the Dathynans were not equal to the task. More and more of those who remained sank gradually into barbarism.

And then, among the barbarians, appeared a new mutation.

A favorable mutation.

Herbivores cannot soon become carnivores, not even when they can process meat to make it edible. But they can shed the instincts which make them herd together in groups too large for a devastated country to support. They can acquire an instinct to hunt the animals that supplement their diet—to defend, with absolute fantaticism, a territory that will keep them and theirs alive—to move if that region is no longer habitable, and seize the next piece of land—to perfect the weapons, organization, institutions, myths, religions, and symbols necessary—

—to become killer herbivores.

And they will go farther along that line than the carnivora, whose fang-and-claw ancestors evolved limits on aggressiveness lest the species dangerously deplete itself. They might even go farther than the omnivora, who, while not so formidable in body and hence with less original reason to restrain their pugnacity, have borne arms of some kind since the first proto-intelligence developed in them, and may thus have weeded the worst berserker tendencies out of their own stock.

Granted, this is a very rough rule-of-thumb statement

with many an exception. But the idea will perhaps be clarified if we compare the peaceful lion with the wild boar who may or may not go looking for a battle and him in turn with the rhinoceros or Cape buffalo.

The parent stock on Dathyna had no chance. It could fight bravely, but not collectively to much effect. If victorious in a given clash, it rarely thought about pursuing; if defeated, it scattered. Its civilization was tottering already, its people demoralized, its politico-economic structure reduced to a kind of feudalism. If any groups escaped to space, they never came back looking for revenge.

A gang of Shenna would invade an area, seize the buildings, kill and eat those Old Dathynans whom they did not castrate and enslave. No doubt the conquerors afterward made treaties with surrounding domains, who were pathetically eager to believe the aliens were now satisfied. Not many years passed, however, before a new land-hungry generation of Shenna quarreled with their fathers and left to seek their fortunes.

The conquest was no result of an overall plan. Rather, the Shenna took Dathyna in the course of several centuries because they were better fitted. In an economy of scarcity, where an individual needed hectares to support himself, aggressiveness paid off; it was how you acquired those hectares in the first place and retained them later. No doubt the sexual difference, unusual among sophonts, was another mutation which, being useful too, became linked. Given a high casualty rate among the Shenn males, the warriors, reproduction was maximized by providing each with several females. Hunting and fighting were the principal jobs; females, who must conserve the young, could not take part in this; accordingly, they lost a certain amount of intelligence and initiative. (Remember that the original Shenn population was very small, and did not increase fast for quite a while. Thus genetic drift operated powerfully. Some fairly irrelevant characteristics like the male mane became established in that way—plus some other traits that might actually be disadvantageous, though not crippling.)

At length the parricidal race had overrun the planet. Conditions began to improve as radiation slacked off, new

215

life forms developed, old ones returned from enclaves of survival. It would be long before Dathyna had her original fertility back. But she could again bear a machine culture. From relics, from books, from traditions, conceivably from a few last slaves of the first species, the Shenna began rebuilding what they had helped destroy.

But here the peculiar set of drives which had served them well during the evil millennia played them false. How shall there be community, as is required for a high technology, if each male is to live alone with his harem, challenging any other who dares enter his realm?

The answer is that the facts were never that simple. There was as much variation from Shenn to Shenn as there is from man to man. The less successful had always tended to attach themselves to the great, rather than go into exile. From this developed the extended household—a number of polygynous families in strict hierarchy under a patriarch with absolute authority—that was the "fundamental" unit of Shenn society, as the tribe is of human, the matrilineal clan of Cynthian, or the migratory band of Wodenite society.

The creation of larger groups out of the basic one is difficult on any planet. The results are all too likely to be pathological organizations, preserved more and more as time goes on by nothing except naked force, until finally they disintegrate. Consider, for example, nations, empires, and world associations on Earth. But it need not always be thus.

The Shenna were reasoning creatures. They could grasp the necessity for cooperation intellectually, as most species can. If they were not emotionally capable of a planet-wide government, they were of an interbaronial confederacy.

Especially when they saw their way clear to an attack—the Minotaur's charge—upon the stars!

"Ja," nodded van Rijn, "if they are like that, we can handle them hokay."

"By kicking them back into the Stone Age and sitting on them," Chee Lan growled.

Adzel raised his head. "What obscenity did you speak? I won't have it!"

"You'd rather let them run loose, with nuclear weapons?" she retorted.

"Now, now," said van Rijn. "Now, now, now. Don't let's say bad things about a whole race. I am sure they can do much good if they is approached right." He beamed and rubbed his hands together. "Sure, much fine money to make off them Shenna." His grin grew broader and smugger. "Well, friends, I think we finished our duty for today. We has clubbed our brains and come up with understandings and we deserve a little celebration. Davy, lad, suppose you start by bringing in a bottle Genever and a few cases beer—"

Falkayn braced himself, "I tried to tell you earlier, sir," he said. "That brew you drank was the end of our supply."

Van Rijn's prawnlike eyes threatened to leap from their sockets.

"This ship left Luna without taking on extra provisions," Falkayn said. "Nothing aboard except the standard rations. Including some beverages, of course... but, well, how was I to know you'd join us and—" His voice trailed off. The hurricane was rising.

"Wha-a-a-at?" Echoes flew around van Rijn's scream. "You mean...you mean...a month in space...and nothings for drinking except— *Not even any beer?*"

The next half-hour was indescribable.

XXVI

BUT half an Earth year after that—

Chandra Mahasvany, Assistant Minister of Foreign Relations of the Terrestrial Commonwealth, looked out at the ocher-and-gold globe which the battleship was orbiting, and back again, and said indignantly, "You cannot do it! You, a mere mutual-benefit alliance of . . . of capitalists . . . enslaving a species, a world!"

Fleet Admiral Wiaho of the Polesotechnic League gave him a chill stare. "What do you think the Shenna were planning to do to us?" He was born on Ferra; saber tusks handicapped him in speaking human languages. But his scorn was plain to hear.

"You hadn't even the decency to notify us. If Freeman Garver's investigations had not uncovered evidence strong enough to bring me here in person—"

"Why should the League consult the Commonwealth, or any government?" Wiaho jerked a claw at Dathyna, where it spun in the viewscreen. "We are quite beyond their jurisdictions. Let them be glad that we are dealing with a menace and not charging them for the service."

"Dealing?" Mahasvany protested. "Bringing an overwhelming armada here . . . with no overt provocation . . . forcing those poor, ah, Shenna to surrender everything they worked so hard to build, their space fleet, their key factories . . . tampering with their sovereignty . . . reducing them to economic servitude—do you call that dealing with the situation? Oh, no, sir. I assure you otherwise. It is nothing but the creation of a hatred which will soon explode in greater conflict. The Commonwealth government must insist on a policy of conciliation. Do not forget, any future war will involve us too."

"Won't be any," Wiaho said. "We're seeing to that. Not by

'enslavement,' either. I give you, *zuga-ya,* we have taken the warmaking capability out of their hands, we supervise their industry, we weave their economy together with ours till it cannot function independently. But the precise reason for this is to keep revanchism from having any chance of success. Not that we expect it to arise. The Shenna don't deeply resent being ordered about—by someone who's proven to them he's stronger."

A human female passed by the open door, memotape in one hand. Wiaho hailed her. "Would you come in for a minute, pray?... Freelady Beldaniel, Freeman Mahasvany from Earth.... Freelady Beldaniel is our most valuable liaison with the Shenna. She was raised by them, have you heard? Don't you agree, what the League is doing is best for their entire race?"

The thin, middle-aged woman frowned, not in anger but in concentration. "I don't know about that, sir," she answered frankly. "But I don't know what better can be done, either, than turn them into another member of Technic civilization. The alternative would be to destroy them." She chuckled. On the whole, she must enjoy her job. "Seeing that the rest of you insist on surviving too."

"But what about the economics?" Mahasvány protested.

"Well, naturally we cannot operate for nothing," Wiaho said. "But we are not pirates. We make investments, we expect a return on them. Remember, though, business is not a zero-sum game. By improving this world, we benefit its dwellers."

Mahasvany flushed. "Do you mean... your damned League, sir, has the eternal gall to arrogate to itself the functions of a government?"

"Not exactly," Wiaho purred. "Government couldn't accomplish this much." He uncoiled his length from the settee he occupied. "Now, if you will excuse Freelady Beldaniel and myself, we have work to do."

On Earth, in a garden, palm trees overhead, blue water and white surf below, girls fetching him drink and tobacco, Nicholas van Rijn turned from the screen on which was projected a view brought home by the latest expedition to

Satan. The great star had dwindled; highlands were beginning to stand calm above the storms that yet harried oceans and plains. He smiled unctuously at a boardful of lesser screens, wherein showed human and nonhuman faces, the mightiest industrialists in the known galaxy.

"Hokay, friends," he said, "you seen what I got a full clear claim on, namely you by the short hairs. However, I is a tired old man what mainly wants only sitting in the sun scratching his memories and having maybe just one more Singapore sling before evening—hurry it up, will you, my dear?—and anyhows is a dealer in sugar and spice and everything nice, not in dark Satanic mills. I don't want no managing for myself, on this fine planet where is money to make by the shipload every second. No, I will be happy with selling franchises... naturally, we make a little profit-sharing arrangement too, nothing fancy, a token like maybe thirty or forty percent of net... I is very reasonable. You want to start bidding?"

Beyond the Moon, *Muddlin' Through* accelerated outward. Falkayn looked long in the after screen. "What a girl she was," he murmured.

"Who, Veronica?" Chee asked.

"Well, yes. Among others." Falkayn lit his pipe. "I don't know why we're starting out again, when we're rich for life. I honestly don't."

"I know why you are," Chee said. "Any more of the kind of existence you've been leading, and you'd implode." Her tail switched. "And me, I grew bored. It'll be good to get out under fresh skies again."

"And find new enlightenments," Adzel said.

"Yes, of course," Falkayn said. "I was joking. It sounded too pretentious, though, to declaim that the frontier is where we belong."

Muddlehead slapped down a pack of cards and a rack of poker chips onto the table, with the mechanical arms which had been installed for such purposes. "In that event, Captain," it said, "and pursuant to the program you outlined for us to follow during the next several hours, it is suggested that you shut up and deal."